A Killing
Season

Books by Priscilla Royal

Wine of Violence
Tyrant of the Mind
Sorrow Without End
Justice for the Damned
Forsaken Soul
Chambers of Death
Valley of Dry Bones
A Killing Season

A Killing
Season

A Medieval Mystery

Priscilla Royal

Poisoned Pen Press

Copyright © 2011 by Priscilla Royal

First Edition 2011

10 9 8 7 6 5 4 3 2 1

Library of Congress Catalog Card Number: 2011926969

ISBN: 9781590589472   Hardcover
      9781590589496   Trade Paperback

Poisoned Pen Press
6962 E. First Ave., Ste. 103
Scottsdale, AZ 85251
www.poisonedpenpress.com
info@poisonedpenpress.com

Printed in the United States of America

To Marianne Silva and Sharon Silva
for all your support and the pleasure of your friendship.

Acknowledgments

Christine and Peter Goodhugh, Ed Kaufman of M is for Mystery Bookstore (San Mateo CA), Henie Lentz, Dianne Levy, Doug Lyle MD, Sharon Kay Penman, Barbara Peters of Poisoned Pen Bookstore (Scottsdale AZ), Diana and Bruce Reed, Robert Rosenwald and all the staff of Poisoned Pen Press, Marianne and Sharon Silva, Lyn and Michael Speakman, the staff at University Press Bookstore (Berkeley CA).

To every *thing there* is a season, and a time to every purpose under the heaven:

A time to be born, and a time to die; a time to plant, and a time to pluck up *that which is* planted;

A time to kill, and a time to heal…

—Ecclesiastes 3:1-3 (King James Version)

Chapter One

The travelers and their armed escort halted near the cliff's edge. Far below them, the moss-green sea lashed the black rocks and roared with the fury of a creature enraged beyond all reason.

Brother Thomas grimaced, his face stinging from the wind as if the air had been filled with ice shards. Even his thick woolen cloak did not protect him from the chill, and his horse shook, eager to be away from this inhospitable place. Whispering promises of imminent relief in a warm stable with dry straw, the monk stroked her bristled neck and silently prayed that his confidence would not prove false.

Out of the corner of his eye, Thomas glimpsed a well-bundled, square-shaped rider edging closer to him on an equally thickset horse. It was Master Gamel, the physician.

"What has caused this delay?" the man shouted. The screaming wind and thundering surf muted his words.

The monk pointed toward the front of the huddled company.

A single horseman separated himself from the others and rode slowly into the swirling grey mist. Within moments he had faded from sight.

"Sir Hugh just left to announce our arrival," Thomas yelled back to the physician. "The fortress is on an island, and we cannot enter until the soldiers lower the drawbridge over the chasm."

Squinting, Gamel peered ahead. "I see no island. Neither can I see Sir Hugh." Nervously, he laughed. "Were I not in the safe company of Prioress Eleanor, Sister Anne and you, I might conclude that we had arrived at the mouth of Hell. This thunderous noise must be little different from the howling of damned souls."

After Father Eliduc's visit to Tyndal last summer, Thomas was not as inclined to believe that those vowed to God's service offered protection from evil, but the physician knew nothing of those events. The monk replied with a comforting smile.

Master Gamel's horse inched nearer to Thomas' mount, seeking a fellow creature's warmth. The physician took advantage of this to incline his head and say, in a tone as discreet as the crashing sea would permit, "I would not have troubled you with my questioning had my true concern not been for the welfare of Sister Anne."

Alarmed, the monk straightened and looked over the physician's shoulder.

Seated on a docile mare just a few feet away, the sub-infirmarian of Tyndal Priory bent almost double against the wind's assault. Although her face was obscured by the hood of a cloak, her posture expressed great suffering from the bitter cold.

"A man must endure these circumstances," Gamel continued. "Women are tender creatures. As a physician, I am obliged to warn you that she might suffer a deadly chill if she remains here much longer." Suddenly his cheeks flushed, perhaps more than the wind had provoked. "I offered my extra blanket, and she refused." His fingers twitched as they played with the loose ends of the reins. "I swear I meant no offence to her virtue. The blanket may have warmed me often enough, but surely the intended charity washed the wool clean of my touch, sinful mortal that I am."

"God knows when a man's heart is pure," Thomas replied as he noticed the physician's reddened face. His acquaintance with this Master Gamel had been short, but he had no cause to conclude he was anything except the worthy man his reputation suggested.

Without doubt he was a physician who took his oaths seriously. Why else would he have left his warm hearth in London, at Sir Hugh's request, and journeyed to this storm-blasted, decidedly eerie castle in the midst of the winter season? And despite the significant amount of time the man spent riding at Sister Anne's side, the monk did believe that Gamel's offer of a blanket was rooted in nothing more than charity.

Had she not been a nun, some might have concluded that the pair had found a delight in each other that exceeded the pleasure of a traveling companionship. Yet Thomas had no doubts about Sister Anne's virtue or her good understanding of a man's ways. The woman might be vowed to God, but she had also been a wife, mother, and a well-regarded apothecary before she left the secular world in her third decade to heal the sick in God's name.

She was quite capable of dealing firmly with Master Gamel if he had done or said anything against propriety. And if the physician's conduct went beyond her ability to correct, she would have told both Thomas and Prioress Eleanor. She had not done so. He himself had ridden close to the pair for most of the journey and noted only the routine of innocent conversation. Although appearances could belie the truth, the monk thought all had been seemly between nun and physician.

Gamel twisted around in his saddle to look at the nun. "My fears for her health grow, Brother."

A wind surge struck them with force. The horses whinnied nervously. The whites of their eyes showed fear.

"This weather will surely kill the good woman!" Extending his hand in supplication, Gamel shouted: "Would she accept something from you that she dare not from me?"

"I shall speak with her," the monk replied. With some effort, he urged his horse away from the warming flank of the physician's mount.

As he approached the nun, Sister Anne raised her head with evident reluctance. Her eyes narrowed in the icy air. "Have I caused some difficulty?"

"If my hands and feet have grown numb, yours must have too."

"And Master Gamel cannot understand why I rejected his offer to wrap me in a blanket." Her mouth was hidden, but small wrinkles at the corners of her eyes deepened with gentle amusement.

Thomas chuckled. "Since I would have welcomed it, I wonder myself!"

Another malevolent burst of wind slashed at them, forcing the pair to turn their backs against it and curl inward to conserve body heat.

"My mother bore me during a North Sea gale, Brother," the nun shouted. "This woman's skin has been hardened by long exposure to these storms. You and Master Gamel are London men and own far more tender flesh." She straightened and urged her reluctant mount to turn around.

Teeth gritted, Thomas tried to grin. "How many years must I reside on the East Anglian coast before my soft youth be forgotten?"

"Never, I fear." Her kind eyes softened the retort.

He nodded. "Master Gamel has cause for concern. Your face is very white, and you have taught me…"

She touched her cheek. "I can feel my fingers…" Suddenly, she pointed to the thick mist. "Is Sir Hugh returning?"

At the front of the company, a tall rider drew up next to a tiny figure.

Thomas strained to see. "He is speaking with Prioress Eleanor."

The knight raised his hand and gestured for the travelers to follow him.

"We shall have the relief of hearth fires before long," Anne said, then directed her horse toward the waiting Master Gamel.

Struck with vague apprehension, Thomas hesitated and patted his mare's neck as he watched the nun and physician ride off together.

His mount sensed the journey's end had finally come and snorted, indicating impatience with this unwarranted lingering.

Thomas smiled. "Did I not promise you a warm stall and a good meal to follow?" he whispered. When her ears flicked, he signified agreement with her desire and let her join the other horses on the road to comfort.

The party moved slowly, no more than two abreast. The path to the castle gate was narrow, just wide enough in places for one supply wagon to pass.

A few horses danced nervously in the howling wind.

Grateful that his mare was focused on what awaited her within the castle walls, Thomas forced himself to emulate her lack of interest in what lay below them, although he was quite aware of the jagged drop to the sea on either side. Where the road dipped, he felt the rising spray from the waves as they attacked the rocks like a besieging army, intent on destroying fortress walls.

Uncomfortably reminded of the collapsing walls at Jericho, he shut his eyes and tried to imagine a more pleasing event. The *Play of Daniel,* a liturgical drama recently performed at Tyndal, came to mind. That memory of sweet singing distracted him briefly.

Then the road inclined upward again, and the ground beneath him felt more solid. Closer now, he soon made out the castle itself. The outer curtain walls were as circular as the rocky terrain would allow. The keep within, black with damp, soared into the high mist.

He shivered.

The place was fearsome. Some, he had heard say, called the fortress *le château doux et dur.* Perhaps it was sweet in the softer seasons when breezes caressed men with the warm scent of wildflowers. Now, the castle loomed like Satan's shadow: gloomy, impenetrable, threatening.

As the party approached the open gate, Thomas saw the lowered drawbridge that spanned the void between mainland

and island. "The sea has won one battle here," he muttered and squeezed his eyes shut.

When his horse walked onto the wooden planking of the drawbridge, her hooves made a hollow sound. To keep from thinking about the abyss beneath, Thomas opened his eyes and stared at the high walls of the keep which rested on the firm earth inside. He looked up at the higher windows and concluded that was where Baron Herbert's family must live.

Then he saw a dark figure leaning out of one of them.

Thomas instinctively tensed with apprehension.

The figure bent forward, spread his arms like wings, then slid, headfirst, from the window.

Crying out, Thomas covered his eyes with a hand.

The man's scream cut like a knife through the roar of the sea and wailing wind.

Chapter Two

Prioress Eleanor clutched her mazer of sweet mulled wine closer to her chest. If only her hands would stop shaking from the cold, she thought and bent her head forward to sip.

Standing on the other side of the Great Hall hearth, Sir Hugh stared into the leaping flames, lost in thought as if pondering the nature of fire. A burning log cracked, scattering bright sparks around his feet. The prioress' brother did not flinch.

A grey-bearded servant scuffled toward them, paused at a respectful distance, and bowed.

Eleanor glanced at Hugh but he seemed oblivious to the man's presence. "We desire nothing more," she said.

The servant's eyes brightened as if grateful for the dismissal. Bowing again, he departed. The bottom of his shoes grazed the rushes as if he did not have the strength to step higher.

Slowly, the fire's warmth began to penetrate into her bones. Eleanor relaxed her tight grip on the mazer and studied the profile of her silent brother. Hugh had changed since he sailed for Outremer with Lord Edward. Although he bore few observable battle scars, the once pink-faced lad, possessed of irrepressible enthusiasm, was now a hollow-cheeked man with changeable moods.

She shut her eyes. When he first retuned, she heard him tell entertaining stories about his journey home from Acre, tales that provoked much laughter and not a little awe at table. Then she had looked into his eyes and saw a soul draped in mourning.

Footsteps from the outer corridor shattered the musings of both brother and sister.

A lean young man strode through the doorway.

Sir Hugh blinked, then offered a fleeting smile.

There is less warmth and more caution in that look, Eleanor noted, before turning to greet the arrival.

"I came to beg forgiveness for our rude greeting." The youth bowed to the prioress and ignored the knight. "I am Raoul, youngest son of Baron Herbert." He shrugged. "Or perhaps I should say youngest but advancing in rank with unseemly speed."

"The Prioress of Tyndal." Hugh gestured with courtesy toward his sister, and then hesitated with evident confusion. "I am Hugh of Wynethorpe, a friend of your father. He and I were close companions in Outremer."

Raoul responded with a barely civil nod before turning his attention back to Eleanor. "I speak for all my family in welcoming you here. Your prayers on our behalf are sorely needed."

"We are much grieved by the unfortunate accident. The man who fell…" Hugh spread his hands.

"Gervase? He had become the heir to our father's fortune, the second son of five. To his parents' grief, he learned today that God did not intend for him to fly." Raoul scratched at some faint bristles on his chin. His expression shifted between amusement and unease. "The current heir, Umfrey, has now locked himself in the family chapel. I think he would have been happy enough to become the family's oblate to the Church. To his grief, that role falls to me while my prayerful brother shall be obliged to learn how to wield a sword." His tone was jesting, his look impudent. "Perhaps your timely arrival means I am destined to find a monk's cell at Tyndal Priory."

Eleanor swallowed a sharp retort. "I shall bring God's comfort to your father and mother as well as prayers," she replied, choosing to respond only to the request for her pleas to God. The youth's demeanor was somewhat impertinent, but grief and shock often produced strange, inappropriate reactions. Some wept at the news of a loved one's death, others might laugh, but this was the first time she had met a man who considered a brother's horrible death as little more than an inconvenient change in his own vocation.

"I'm told my father is with the corpse. My mother is in her chamber with our cousin, Leonel." Raoul pointed upward. "The dead one may have been her favorite, or so I have heard. I am amazed that you cannot hear her wailing." He shrugged. "Leonel will have found a way to comfort her. He could soothe a soul on the way to Hell."

Raoul might be the Benjamin of this family, so young that his beard was more promise than fact, but his words suggested that this youth was never anyone's favored child. Eleanor felt her annoyance dissipate, and her heart softened a little.

"I remember that Baron Herbert had five sons. You claim that only two remain?" Turning his back on the youngest one, Hugh poured himself some wine from a pottery jug and failed to offer Raoul any of it. "'Tis a pity that your mother did not bear a worthy son soon after your father left England."

The baron's son flushed. "You said you were close by my lord father's side, yet you did not hear of his eldest son's death? I am surprised."

Eleanor set down her mazer on a nearby table, slipped her hands into her sleeves, and waited for her brother's response. Raoul may have spoken with mockery, but Hugh had goaded with stinging words.

"Baron Herbert left for home soon after he heard. I stayed longer with King Edward and had little opportunity to offer comfort."

"Ah, yes!" Raoul's mouth twisted into a sneer. "Until after the assassination attempt against our king. That I had heard."

Eleanor grew uneasy. What quarrel lay between these two?

Hugh stiffened. He said nothing, but his expression betrayed a fury that matched the intensity of the wind outside.

As if suddenly aware that he was gravely offending his father's guest, Raoul stepped back with a sheepish look and continued in a softer voice. "Then you could not have learned that the third eldest brother recently drowned. He was called *Roger*." His tone was painstakingly courteous.

Hugh's was not. "I received word."

"Which accounts for the honor of your visit?"

"If you were not told of any particular reason why your father may have desired our company, then the fact that he simply wished it should be sufficient for you."

With that prickly rebuke, the color in Raoul's face deepened into burgundy, but he held his tongue.

This sharp exchange between her brother and Baron Herbert's youngest resounded in her mind like the crashing of lances on shields. This was a house in mourning, she thought, not some tournament. The dispute between these two had gone on too long.

Turning to Raoul, she said, "Your grief over these recent family deaths must be profound, my son. Our visit may be sadly ill-timed, but Brother Thomas and I are here to give what consolation we can. Please tell your mother that I shall visit when she wishes. Brother Thomas awaits your father's summons."

Before turning to face the hearth, Hugh unexpectedly gave his sister an appreciative nod.

Raoul bowed to the prioress. "Then I shall leave to convey your kind words. In the meantime, I pray that all comforts have been provided you and your fellow travelers. If not, tell me at once. My father would have no guest lack any desire or need."

Before Hugh could say a word, Eleanor quickly assured Raoul, on behalf of the entire company, that all was as it should be.

The prioress waited until the sound of Raoul's footsteps had faded down the corridor before walking to her brother's side.

"Well done, sweet sister!" He grinned and offered wine. "If God be willing and the king need one highly skilled in the art of making peace, I shall mention your talents. To separate two men so hot for battle took courage."

"Why do you dislike Raoul?"

"On the voyage to Acre, his father told me that his seed must have been too weak when that boy was bred. If the lad was denied some desire, he sniveled like a babe denied the teat. If reprimanded by his father, Raoul whined like a beaten dog and ran off with tail between his legs. Herbert complained that his son seemed incapable of facing adversity like a man must." He sighed. "As for my own knowledge of the boy, I spent as little time as I could with him during my early visits here. He was too young for companionship, and I cannot recall that he was ever welcome company for anyone."

"He could not have been much more than a child when his father left."

"That child is now a man. He still whines."

Eleanor playfully swatted her brother's arm. "He was rude enough to you. I have known boars to show more courtesy to their hunters, but you did provoke him."

"You cannot excuse his boorish behavior for that reason. He may be trying to grow a man's beard, sister, but he is nothing like his father." Hugh made a point of rubbing the place his sister touched as if she had hurt him, then laughed. "Men are flawed creatures, sometimes cruel and often ill-mannered, yet we must all exhibit courage and restraint. A few have learned the lesson so well they have become saints."

A log burst in the fireplace. Sparks flew like shooting stars.

Eleanor stepped back a safe distance from the hearth. "Unless God performs a miracle, Raoul will not be one of them." She looked up at her brother with an amused expression. "I do not defend him. He lacked all sympathy for his parents, cared little enough about the deaths of his brothers, and suggested that taking vows was much like establishing his proper place near the salt at table." She hesitated. "The only one to whom he bestowed a meager compliment was a man he called *Leonel*. Do I correctly remember the man's name? Raoul called him *cousin*."

"Even Raoul could find little for which to fault Sir Leonel. The man is Baron Herbert's nephew, son of a brother who died many years ago. The baron and his wife gave a home to the boy and his mother, a woman who sorrowed so much over her dead husband that she soon sickened and died. I know the nephew. Leonel accompanied the baron to Outremer and showed such bravery that he was knighted."

"This man finds favor with you?"

"On Herbert's behalf, many of us grieved that Leonel was not his heir."

Nodding, the prioress fell silent and watched as her brother's thoughts seemed to drift away. "Do you not like any of the baron's sons?" Her voice was soft.

He blinked as if she had just shaken him out of a dream. "Baron Herbert must have been born with a sword in his hand. He never turned his back on danger and inspired greater courage in all of us during battle. Should it surprise that he expected sons of equal merit? Aye, he was disappointed in his offspring. The first, however, was a good steward of the land, and his father was content to give at least one to the Church, saying that the family needed a holy man to pray for their souls. As for the second who just fell to his death, the third who drowned, and the fourth, now hiding in the family chapel, he never spoke much about them. I've told you what he said about Raoul."

Hugh rubbed his hands and walked to the table where he considered pouring another mazer of wine. "In truth, I knew none of them well," he said. Deciding he would drink no more, he faced his sister. "What cause had I to doubt the baron's judgement on his own children?"

"Why take his nephew with him to Outremer? Surely he would have been happier bringing one of his sons? Were they disinclined to war, they still would have understood the service to God in reclaiming Jerusalem. Even the one bound for the Church would agree, although he might have chosen not to wield a sword." Eleanor knew that bishops had often used maces to avoid the prohibition against shedding blood when they decided to go into battle. The fine distinction between mace and sword had always escaped her.

"Leonel was the best choice for more than one reason. The nephew inherited nothing from his own father, a man most imprudent and cursed with foolish vices. What land he owned as the second son was sold by Baron Herbert to pay off gaming debts. The babe and mother would have starved, had the uncle been a less honorable man. With five sons of his own and those debts to clear, he had nothing to give his nephew except horse and armor. He hoped Leonel would acquire enough wealth for himself in Outremer."

"And the baron's sons were content to stay in England, rejecting the glory of taking the cross?"

"The eldest did complain, but his father refused his request. He trusted him to guard all he possessed, then accepted the plea of the second-born to remain in England as well. The other three were too young to go. Since the eldest died of a mortal fever, Herbert was wise to leave two sons of mature years to safeguard his lands. As we all learned, a crusader's lands may have been placed under God's protection by Rome, but men do not always honor God's will. Too many men who took the cross came home to nothing." He shook his head. "Apart from the eldest, only Raoul demanded to go with his father."

"Raoul?"

"Puppy that he was, he whimpered and moaned. When Herbert wearied of the noise, he stood the boy on a table in front of witnesses, stripped him, and felt between his legs. The baron declared the lad still a babe and sent Raoul off to find his mother, wailing like a newborn."

A cruel story, Eleanor thought, and noted that her brother's expression revealed no joy in the tale either. When Hugh's own son, Richard, came to him in like manner and begged to be taken on the voyage with Lord Edward, her brother denied the child's request with gentle words and then convinced him he would be a braver boy for staying home.

In the firelight, Hugh's face was grey with fatigue.

"It is late," Eleanor said. "Sister Anne has long since sought our quarters to rest. I should join her."

Hugh took her hand and kissed it. "I must seek my own bed as well. Ask your good nun to pray for me, sweet sister." Then he vanished into the corridor to find the winding staircase leading to the chambers above.

Eleanor's own eyes grew heavy with weariness. As she walked through the windy corridor, the stone floor damp from the storm, she wondered how troubled her dreams would be in this place so devoid of peace.

Chapter Three

Baron Herbert looked down at the bloody corpse. Was there anything in the mess of battered flesh he still recognized as his second child?

Squeezing his eyes shut, he tried to remember all that this hollow shell had once been, and, although his heart screamed in agony, his eyes remained dry, refusing to grieve. He opened them and reached out to caress his son's twisted neck. His fingers touched skin, but he felt nothing.

"Of course I would not," he whispered, turning his callused palm upward. "This is not my son, only inanimate clay."

He knelt by the body and took a deep breath. The odor of death was little different from that of a slaughtered deer.

Rage filled him. Like a possessed man, he began to pound the stone floor until his hands bled. "This is still my boy," he roared, then stared at his torn fists.

Death, violent and irreverent, was well-known to him. In war he had seen countless dead bodies: some slaughtered in combat, others in villages by soldiers still crazed with battle frenzy. He watched as men were burned to charcoal, screaming for their mothers, and walked past bodies of women raped with spears while their wailing babies were smashed against walls.

Many of these were infidels, for whom he felt no sorrow. Their death agonies were paltry aches compared to what their benighted souls would suffer in the eternal flames of Hell.

Others were known to him, men with whom he had shared wine before battle or a fire on a bitter night. For these, he felt a prick of grief, yet any sadness was offset by the knowledge that their souls were in Heaven, freed of worldly imperfections or any care.

"But this is my flesh and blood, made with my seed," he wailed, shaking his fist at God. "My son!"

Slowly he reached up and touched the torn clothing that covered the corpse.

"Nothing," he whispered. "Nothing."

In utter despair, he bent double and howled like a wolf under the full moon.

◇◇◇

A woman stepped back from the chapel's open door. For a moment she stood, eyes raised, and listened to her lord husband's wild keening.

Then Lady Margaret turned her back and walked slowly away.

Chapter Four

The wind bit like a nipping dog, but the morning sun struggled to bring warmth, albeit with a feeble touch. The scudding clouds, a mix of white and dark, promised uncertain weather.

Brother Thomas grasped his thick cloak and pulled it closer, then bent forward to look down into the cove through one of the crenels along the curtain wall near the entry gate. "I am glad we were surrounded by mist when we arrived yesterday," he said, gazing at the narrow path leading to the drawbridge.

The cliffs on either side of the road were steep and bristled with sharp rocks. Watching the surf batter at the narrow promontory, he believed it was a miracle that even that vestige of land-bridge remained between mainland and island. Not that it would be long before the castle was irrevocably separated, he concluded. The edge of pale rock against which the drawbridge rested looked precarious, although the castle itself was settled on very solid ground.

Growing numb with the cold, he walked on, keeping close to the stone wall to avoid the full force of the wind. When he reached the protective mass of the watchtower, he paused and looked down again.

Now that the storm had abated, he could see that the cove was a rounded bay, protected from the full might of gales. There was even a sandy beach. In the summer, fishermen's boats might be dragged up on shore to keep them safe, he thought, although the dark markings on the cliffs suggested that very high tides would render that impossible on occasion. Looking more carefully, he saw the boiling of riptides.

"No wonder the place is called Lucifer's Cauldron," he muttered. "There may be safety from the winds, but the incoming tides must be fierce."

Perhaps fishermen did work along the coast in the milder seasons, he thought. When the castle was finally separated from the mainland by too great a distance for a drawbridge, provisions could be brought in by boat. For a moment, he amused himself by trying to imagine how supplies might be lifted from the bay before deciding there must be some location on the island that would prove better suited.

In this weather, he had no wish to seek it out.

A wind gust whipped around the tower and struck the monk with such force that he momentarily lost his balance. Reaching out for the wall, Thomas righted himself and then scurried toward the wide, stone staircase leading to the courtyard below. As he descended the stairs, he was passed by soldiers on their way up to take a turn on watch. He pitied them on such a bitter day.

Emerging into the bustle of castle life in the bailey, he was grateful for that comparative warmth provided by humans and animals crowded together. As he walked back to the keep, he avoided the thickest mud, mixed with manure from the various herds of long-horned goats, grunting swine, and lean-sided cows.

Briefly, he stopped to talk with a man mending a harness. Although the fellow's fingers were red and swollen with the cold, he owned a cheerful disposition and was eager for a bit of idle chat.

When Thomas finally reached the stairs to the keep entrance, he felt a sharp pain and stopped to look at his hand. The palm was scraped from his fall against the stone wall. He shrugged. A little blood, but the wound was minor—unlike what that poor man suffered yesterday, falling from the high window.

Thomas shuddered with sympathetic terror.

He gazed up at the walls of the baron's residence. Tilting his head, he studied the few narrow windows of the keep. How had the man fallen?

Whoever had built this fortress understood the coastal storms, as well as defensive concerns, and considered both in the design of those windows. The worst winds might drive mist, snow, and rain into the corridors of the upper halls, but the narrow windows were mostly on the leeward side, and the outer curtain walls gave the keep some additional protection. Those walls were also several feet thick.

With the thickness of the stone, the small openings and the position of the windows, Thomas could not imagine how any wind had caused the man to lose his balance. Even if he had slipped on the wet stone floor, the windows were at least waist-high. Considering all, it would be very difficult for a conscious, healthy man to accidentally tumble through the openings to his death.

Thomas knew the man might have jumped. No one had suggested such a thing when they took him to the corpse, laid out in the chapel, and asked that he do all he could for the man's soul. If the family had suspected self-murder, none would have dared to mislead a priest about such a matter. God would know the truth. Fearful for their own souls, few would risk a lie.

Or the man could have been pushed.

Thomas hesitated, shocked at his reaction to this possibility. He ought to be distressed that the man might have been murdered. Indeed he was. He was also intrigued.

"I should be ashamed," he muttered.

He wasn't.

"If I long so for violence, perhaps I ought to have gone to Outremer as a soldier on pilgrimage to wrest Jerusalem from Muslim hands or become a mercenary. I am no peaceful servant of God," he whispered to the wind, but he knew he had never truly yearned for horse and armor.

Not once had he ever wished to kill others for glory, profit, or even to serve God. If he hadn't been caught in bed with Giles, he might have been content to remain a clerk to some high-ranking churchman.

He shook his head at that option as well. If he had stayed a clerk in minor orders, he would have become quite dull-witted with boredom. Instead, he had been forced to take monastic vows and was sent to the remote priory of Tyndal where he found himself in service to a woman. No man rejoiced at the chance to bring God's justice to those who murdered more than Prioress Eleanor of Tyndal, a tiny woman who never let Thomas' wits grow fat for want of exercise. Few other liege lords could have filled his life with quite so much adventure.

He smiled. "Since I am in her holy service, perhaps I need not rebuke myself too much," he said, lowering his gaze to the muddy steps, "yet I should assume the baron's son fell by accident and be prepared to offer what consolation I can to the family. Surely, this is what my prioress will send me to do."

Holding firmly to that thought, he entered the keep and climbed the steep, curved stairway to his small room. Once the chamber of the family priest, recently deceased, it was near the small chapel where the current heir cowered for protection near the altar. Knowing the frightened Umfrey would appreciate soothing words, Thomas decided to go to the man after the next Office.

As he opened the door to his guest quarters, Thomas looked back over his shoulder and down the dark, narrow corridor that led to the family chapel. Despite good intentions to set thoughts of murder aside, he could not easily shake his doubts that any man could have fallen from those windows without assistance.

Chapter Five

Prioress Eleanor stood in the doorway of Lady Margaret's chambers.

The shutters had been opened for light, letting in the brisk sea air, and a fire crackled in the small fireplace. Although the burning wood struggled valiantly, it only just succeeded in blunting the chill. As for the welcomed light, that was a pallid guest.

"Please," Lady Margaret said and, with courtesy, invited her visitor to a place near the hearth. "There is Ypocras to drink for warmth and health." While the white-haired servant heated the proffered mulled wine, Herbert's wife fell silent and turned with an absent gaze to the window.

The lady has a hardened face, Eleanor decided as she accepted the cup. A sparkling glance or merry laugh might have softened the sharp bones and hollow cheeks, thin nose and narrow mouth, but there was no evidence that joy was common, at least not in recent times.

Yet the high forehead, silken skin, and blue eyes suggested Lady Margaret had once possessed beauty enough. Eleanor wondered when it had vanished. As Sister Beatrice once told her, youth wraps most young women with beguiling loveliness, which then flees after the first babe is born. Since Lady Margaret had borne her husband many sons, the allure must have faded only with the baron's departure for Outremer. Try as she might, Eleanor could not name any by-blows sired by him, at least none known in England.

Eleanor winced at the injustice of her observation. The day after a son's sudden death was not the time to seek joy or beauty in any mother's face. Grief equally scarred hearts and brows with scouring ash. Recalling Raoul's callous indifference to his brother's death, the prioress found herself relieved that sorrow had at least touched the mother.

Lady Margaret turned back to face her guest, her eyes unfocused. She blinked as if surprised to see this stranger so near, then cleared her throat with embarrassment. "Forgive my discourtesy. I was distracted."

The aged maid offered her mistress a cup of mulled wine. The lady accepted it, cradled the cup in her hands, and stared at the steaming liquid as if demanding the drink dispel her living nightmare. When it surely refused, her brow furrowed.

"Our arrival was sadly ill-timed," Eleanor said. "If speaking of your grief would bring ease, my ears are your servants. I bear God's comfort."

Shutting her eyes, the lady bit her lips as she fought against emotion, but tears defied her will.

The prioress bowed her head in sympathy and waited for Margaret to speak.

"Then tell me the reason God has chosen to curse me. I bore all my sons in agony. That is a woman's affliction, and I never complained of it. Instead, I rejoiced that I had given my husband so many strong boys. Most women are not so fortunate."

Eleanor nodded and sipped her wine.

"Why now must I watch my sons die? God burdens me with more pain than Eve ever suffered, and she committed the greatest sin." Margaret raised her reddened eyes and stared at the wood-beamed ceiling.

Eleanor said nothing, knowing the lady was not finished.

"Our five sons stood at my side when my lord knelt at the bishop's feet and took the cross." She gestured toward the chamber window. "We stood on those very walls and watched him ride away with his banners and his knights, proud to precede the Lord Edward in Outremer."

Eleanor glanced at the elderly maid and noted a glimmer of sympathy before the woman quickly turned away. *If this aged one has served the baron's wife for many years,* the prioress thought, *the Lady Margaret may be a kind mistress who inspires affection.* Now quite dismayed by her initial, unsympathetic impression, her heart softened with greater compassion.

"When our eldest died of a fever, the priest reminded me that one child's death was an expected sorrow, more were common enough. At least we had had joy of him until he was old enough to take on a man's burdens, the man of God said." Her lips curled with contempt. "Must this bring us comfort, even happiness?"

Eleanor bit her lip and refused to concur with such icy consolation as the baron's wife seemed to expect from her. Instead, she tilted her head in a gesture of commiseration.

"After much prayer, I softened my stubborn despair, although the memory of my boy refuses to fade." She shot a glance at the prioress. Her look now held more anguish than ire. "Is that my sin? Does God punish me for refusing to rejoice in my lad's release from wicked mortal flesh?"

"If God marks the fall of a sparrow, He surely mourns the death of any mother's child." Eleanor grieved that a woman might conclude that God deemed her maternal sorrow to be without reason.

The baron's wife blinked, then her lips twisted with renewed bitterness. "When my husband arrived home, four sons still greeted him."

Hearing the pitch of the woman's voice rise, Eleanor was alarmed at the force of her enmity.

Lady Margaret spun around and threw her cup of Ypocras against the rough wall. The metal clanged in discordant protest. Splattered wine painted the stones crimson.

As if Death had just entered the room, Eleanor trembled.

The servant bent to retrieve the cup, then fell to her knees and took a cloth to the dark puddles of liquid.

Covering her eyes, Margaret gasped for breath. "Forgive me, Prioress Eleanor! I have never before railed against God, even while my lord fought the Infidel and I endured bitter chastity in an icy bed. When my eldest died, I did not curse Him but learned to pray that my son would find favor amongst the angels. I may be a flawed and sinful woman, but neither am I more wicked than others of my sex."

Eleanor murmured sympathy, words she knew to be inadequate in the face of so much pain.

"I came to my lord with an unbroken maidenhead, bore sons, and sated my lust only with my husband. Tell me where I have sinned so grievously that I deserve more anguish than any mother ought to suffer!"

"Remember the story of Job, whom God first blessed above all other men and then burdened with more curses than any shameless sinner. This man also suffered the death of all his children. Afterward, God touched his flesh until there was not a spot on his body where a festering boil did not weep. Yet Job cursed God not and was rewarded with even greater wealth and more children for his faith."

"Job was a saint," Margaret hissed. "And his wife remained fruitful and bore other children because he slept with her. My sons are dying. My lord refuses to share our marriage bed. Now my courses begin to fail me." She turned away. "Our old midwife says this is a sure sign that my womb grows barren and shall soon fail to provide the nourishment needed for a man's seed." A thick tear wove a torturous route down her cheek. "She has given me fennel but…"

"Are you not still blessed with two living sons?"

Raising her eyes heavenward, Margaret began to wail.

Eleanor wished she could have taken back what she had just said. Walking to the weeping mother, she laid a comforting arm on hers. "My words were thoughtless but not meant to be unkind. There is no child's death that does not cut away part of a mother's heart."

"Our former priest said I must forget the dead ones." Margaret spat out this advice as if the words were made of wormwood. "My firstborn had time to confess before he died, but the soul of my Roger may be in Hell. He drowned without making peace with God. Had that priest been alive yesterday, he would have claimed the same fate for my Gervase, blaming him for his own death."

"In Hell? Surely not with a priest in residence to urge him to frequent confession!" The full meaning of Margaret's words about Gervase now struck Eleanor. She stepped back in shock. "Do you believe your son's death yesterday was a deliberate act of self-murder?" She looked at Margaret's face.

The lady turned away.

Eleanor shivered and reached down to retrieve her drink. The warmth of the Ypocras had dissipated, and she set the cup back on the table. "What has led you to think that the fall was no accident?" she whispered.

Beginning to shake uncontrollably, the baron's wife said, "Your priest may have rescued my son's soul. He tried."

Eleanor urged Margaret to sit, then gestured for the servant to reheat the wine with the poker near the fire.

The earthy smell of cloves mixed with sweet cinnamon filled the air.

Taking the cup herself, the prioress put it into the lady's hands and braced them so the mother could sip. "Drink a bit more," Eleanor said and waited until natural color had returned to Margaret's face.

"I was there," the lady whispered.

Eleanor ached with compassion.

"My husband's nephew was with me. Leonel and I stood in the corridor just outside this room, looking out the window. Since we knew your party was expected to arrive before nightfall, we wished to greet you below as soon as you rode up."

And why was the baron not with his wife, waiting for their guests to arrive? The question flashed in her mind, despite the tension of this moment, and Eleanor was perplexed. It was a strange discourtesy from a man who had asked such a great favor from them all.

"My son called to us from the stairwell. We watched him approach." Margaret put a hand over her heart, her widened eyes signifying she was reliving the event. "He staggered, laughed and shouted nonsense, as if he had drunk too deeply of wine."

"Was this common with your son?"

"Boys, learning to be men, often do, but my son was neither very temperate nor too fond of unwatered wine. To see him drunk that early in the day was a surprise. Leonel was as shocked as I and whispered that he would take his cousin off to bed before he disgraced himself. He swore he would discover the cause for this behavior."

"Your nephew is close to his cousins?"

"He has lived with us for many years. He was like an elder brother to my sons and was well-loved by them before he left for Outremer with my lord. If anyone could have persuaded my son to sleep off his indulgence before exposing himself to ridicule, it was Leonel. His heart is as kind as his manner is firm."

"So your nephew went to your son…"

"He called out, telling Gervase that he must show manliness, that even angels would be angered if he failed to do so. My son replied that he had sworn an oath and would honor it, then slid onto the bench of the window seat. Leonel turned to ask me if I knew what his cousin meant, thinking my son had promised me something. When he did, my son leaned out of the window. He spread his arms and shouted that God had made men masters over birds. He would fly with the mews. Leonel and I stared at him in confusion, then my boy went head first out of the window. I screamed."

Eleanor knelt by Margaret and took the forgotten cup from her hands.

"As my son fell, I saw his face from the window where I stood. For an instant, he was joyful, then understood he was falling to his death. He screamed for help. I reached out. Leonel dragged me back, fearing I would leap after my boy. The last thing I remember is Gervase's horrible shriek…"

Margaret grasped the prioress' hands with a painful grip.

Pulling the woman into her arms, Eleanor whispered words of comfort she knew were not heard. Perhaps it mattered not what she said as long as the sound of her voice silenced the memory of the son's howl as he plummeted downward, knowing his body must shatter on the unyielding earth below.

"He did not mean it! He did not," Margaret cried out.

Surely Gervase did not intend to kill himself, Eleanor thought, but there was something wrong about what had happened. If the young man did not make a habit of drinking too much, why had he chosen this time to get drunk? She knew that mothers were often willfully unaware of their sons' vices. Perhaps the lady suffered this loving blindness. It was a question best answered by someone else who knew the habits of these family members and owned a clearer eye.

In any case, too much wine might cause men to do foolish things, but rarely did it make a man believe he had been gifted with impossible flight. And what oath had the son sworn? Was that pertinent to his actions or were his words meaningless babble? There were too many oddities for her to set aside. Eleanor grew increasingly puzzled.

For now, her duty lay in giving what comfort she could. Later she would speak with her brother. Perhaps he knew more that would settle her uneasy questions. Barring that, the baron's plea for help might contain a detail that would explain why this family had been so burdened with this much tragedy.

Chapter Six

Thomas walked out of the corridor's grey light and down a step into the small family chapel located on the floor above the Great Hall.

As his eyes grew accustomed to the gloom, shapes slowly formed. He sought the one owned by a frightened son but saw no one at all. The only sound came from the wind whistling through the tiny barred window high in the stone wall.

How odd, he thought, looking around this place dedicated to God's worship. The baron's family had been long graced by God with wealth, yet the altar was made of grey stones, little different from those forming the walls of the castle and not even more finely chiseled. The thick beams in the low ceiling lacked any carving or painted images. The floor was laid with wood, roughly hewn. Only the cross on the altar suggested a donor who wished to share his worldly fortune with God. The bright gold glittered in the thin shaft of dim light.

This austerity seemed at odds with a man whose actions suggested a rigorous faith. Baron Herbert had not only felt compelled to take the cross but unlike many of his rank, also promptly honored the vow and spent several years in Outremer. Yet this chapel resembled a monk's cell in its plainness. Men of fewer means or even less faith filled God's house with greater riches than he had done.

Thomas frowned, then reminded himself that he had not come to find fault with decoration but to seek the baron's son.

Peering around again at the chapel, he saw no alcoves or hidden corners. There seemed no place for a man to hide. Perhaps the heir had recovered his courage and rejoined the family in their quarters.

Someone sneezed.

Thomas saw movement in a small gap between altar and wall. "I accompanied Sir Hugh of Wynethorpe, a friend of Baron Herbert," he said, "and reside at Tyndal Priory where I serve Prioress Eleanor and God."

There was no response.

Thomas waited.

"Prove you are no imp."

The monk brushed back his hood and raised both hands, his open palms facing the cross. "If you can see me, you will observe that I own neither horns nor hooves." That he could honestly claim. In his opinion, there were men with tonsures and soft hands who served Satan better than any imp. Thomas did try not to be one of them.

"Approach the altar and honor the cross on which God's son was crucified."

He accomplished that in three steps, then knelt, crossed himself, and clearly recited a prayer.

"What is your name?"

"Brother Thomas of the Order of Fontevraud. I have learned of your brother's death and bring God's consolation for the grief you suffer."

"Remain where you are." A man pulled himself up by the side of the altar. Clutching the stone as if unable to stand otherwise, he peered without blinking at the monk.

"And you are called *Umfrey*?"

The man grunted in response, then squeezed his thin body through the narrow space until he got to the front of the altar. Sliding into a crouch on the floor, his right hand reached back to touch the stone as if seeking reassurance that he still had God's protection.

"How did you know where I was?" With only a couple of feet separating the two men, the son's musty sweat was rank and potent.

"I learned that you had come to pray for your brother's soul." A small lie but a kind one, Thomas thought. The man mending the harness in the bailey had called Umfrey a coward, hiding in a chapel when he should have taken a sword to do battle with Satan's army. Whether the son had come here out of fear or devotion, the monk knew he must be pleading to God for something while he was in His sanctuary.

Baron Herbert's current heir whimpered.

"The prayers of two men are stronger than those of one."

"If this family is to escape the Devil's grip, we shall need all of England to kneel on our behalf!"

"You believe the Prince of Darkness has chosen your family for special torment?"

"Satan has most certainly taken residence here since my father's return."

Did Umfrey believe the baron had brought the Evil One with him? That would be an unusual accusation against a man who had taken the cross, Thomas thought. "Why conclude such a thing?" The answer, he hoped, would be illuminating.

"The last honest death in this place, Brother, was that of our eldest brother who died of a winter fever when my father was in Acre." Umfrey began rubbing the altar with the back of his outstretched hand. "After our father's return, my third oldest brother drowned. Some say that Roger's death was an accident. Others whisper self-murder, but I don't agree with that. Now the second son, Gervase, has fallen from a window, shouting that he could fly." He snorted. "Fly like some bird? Would it not be unnatural for a man to emulate a soulless creature? God would never allow such a thing. The Devil must have promised it. Surely you would agree, even though you know nothing of us?"

"I might well." Thomas had not learned enough to conclude anything, but he did not want to cut short further confidence when the son seemed so eager to talk.

"My brother, who died yesterday, had hoped to serve the Church before he became heir. Do you think it likely that such a man would claim he could fly like one of Satan's imps? There is too much evidence that God has forsaken us! Although my father served Him in Outremer, he now avoids honorable light and walks abroad only in Satan's hours. That must be a sign too."

The monk nodded encouragement.

"As for my brother who drowned, he was afraid of the sea. He neither swam nor went out in any boat. Had he not been too young, he might have begged to go with our father on crusade, but only if he could have taken a land route. His worst dreams involved spending an eternity bobbing in some hellish lake. Why would he go near enough water to drown in it? Self-murder is a false conclusion. The only logical explanation for his act is that evil rules here."

Although Thomas was inclined to agree that something troubling was happening, he knew that men often did strange things out of fear, grief, or guilt. We are rarely reasonable when our fondest hopes are dashed, he thought.

In this instance, the heir had longed to serve God. The third may have desired, with equal fervor, to avoid that vocation. As one who had once lost all he loved, Thomas understood how despair might so ravage a man that the torments of Hell seemed mild compared to the agony suffered on earth. He would venture the question.

"Might both your brothers have suffered a profound grief, a sorrow so dark that it drove them to self-murder?"

"They had no reason to commit such a vile sin! Roger may not have had a calling to serve God, while Gervase did, but some satisfactory resolution with our father's blessing could have been reached. It is true that he never granted them any audience after his return, but I see no rational cause for them to despair. Leonel was always ready to help us. Nay, the only conclusion is that the Prince of Darkness has put this castle under a spell, and God allows it because we have gravely displeased Him."

Thomas' attention was caught by one remark. "You say that your father did not speak to those two sons after his return from Acre. How could he have ignored his heir?"

"They never spoke together. None of us did."

"Was there some quarrel?"

Umfrey folded his arms, although his back still pressed against the altar stones. "On the day our father returned to English soil, he sent word ahead that separate quarters must be prepared for him. When he rode into the bailey, he bowed to our mother but refused her welcoming embrace. As for his sons, he dismissed us without so much as a blessing and has since denied all pleas for any audience. There was no occasion for any disagreement to take place, Brother. All four of us, Gervase excepted, were mere boys when he first left us."

Thomas was mystified. To say that no quarrel had occurred was ridiculous. Something must have happened to make the baron shun all contact with his family, whether or not the event occurred before he arrived home. Rather than argue, the monk opted to remark on the obvious difficulty in this situation: "Your father must communicate with someone, else his orders and wishes could not be honored. Perchance his steward?"

"Only to Leonel. Our cousin gives orders to the servants and takes messages to our father when need requires. When a reply is requested, he brings it. As always, he shows kindness by the swift delivery of our particular wishes."

"And this cousin has been long with you?"

"Since the death of his own father. He is older than all of us, excepting the eldest, and took the cross with our father. He fought in Outremer with distinction."

Thomas frowned. What had caused Baron Herbert to behave in such a strange way? Was it fear that someone in his family might wish him harm? Or was all this due to either a misunderstanding or true quarrel? There was yet a third concern. Although he hesitated to suggest such a thing about a man who had vowed to recover Jerusalem, he knew he must ask.

"Do you think your father is possessed?"

"He is my sire, one who slaughtered many in God's name. How can I believe that the Devil has found any place in such a Christian heart?"

Respectful though this reply was, Thomas heard doubt in Umfrey's tone. Possessed or not, the baron was a troubled man. His behavior toward his family was baffling. Added to that was the issue of why he had begged Sir Hugh to bring healers of both body and soul to this castle, a question yet unanswered.

Hearing a scratching sound, Thomas nervously glanced over his shoulder.

A small, round shadow raced across the floor and vanished into a gap in the wall.

He sighed, grateful that it was not the Devil he had heard, scraping his claws on the stones. Nonetheless, he wondered if the Evil One was about as this baron's son believed.

Like Umfrey, Herbert might fear that Satan had spread his foul embrace around this castle. Or did he think some unnamed plague was raging here? When he sent for Sir Hugh, one son had died in an unusual manner, if Umfrey were to be believed. The baron could have some reason to think that death meant an exorcism should be done. With this second death, the baron might either be convinced of the need for godly intervention, or else he suspected that an unknown illness was driving his sons mad.

Umfrey was now staring at the ceiling, his lips moving in silent conversation with some invisible entity.

Thomas hoped it was God.

Why had the baron refused any contact with his wife and sons? Why was he reportedly seen only at night? Despite taking the cross, Herbert could have subsequently committed an unspeakable sin. As punishment, God might have inflicted his sons with wild frenzy so they lost all reason, the one drowning despite his fear of the sea and the other believing he could fly. Thomas had his doubts about this but concluded that the need for healers of souls was clearer than why the baron had also called for medical help.

Sin was always the most common worry. Rampant plagues, particularly confined to one family, were infrequent. The secular healers might have been requested for the baron himself, but if Herbert had suffered a grievous wound in Outremer, he would have felt no shame in admitting to it. It would have been suffered in God's service.

Shaking his head, the monk decided that the baron must fear that some illness, requiring the most knowledgeable physicians, had infected his family. In any event, Thomas could see no rational answer to what was happening. He knew too little.

"Brother?"

"Aye."

"Although I do not know how he did it, Satan has killed two of my brothers." Umfrey's voice trembled. "And I believe the Evil One lurks just outside that door, waiting to murder me next." He reached out a hand in supplication. "Save me! I do not want to die. I do not want to spend eternity in Hell." Leaning his head back against the altar, he gazed at the ceiling and began to wail. The despair in his choking sobs was unbearable.

"I promise that I shall seek out this evil," Thomas replied. "There are three of us here who serve God, one of whom is Prioress Eleanor. Her service to His justice has gained enough respect that even the Devil must surely quail when he sees her." Then the monk stepped closer to the cowering man, put his hands on his shoulders and urged him to pray.

By the time Thomas left, Umfrey had slunk back into the gloom surrounding the altar. When the monk shut the door to the chapel, he looked down the narrow, dark corridor and shivered.

"I hope I have not made a promise that is impossible to keep," he whispered and hurried back through the changing shadows to his chambers.

Chapter Seven

Supper that evening was a dreary affair. None of the baron's family joined their guests in the Great Hall, although the servants were attentive and the kitchen had provided ample fare for all who cared to sit down at table.

Master Gamel showed some appetite. No one else did. Sir Hugh picked at the little he had placed on his trencher. Those under monastic rule ate sparingly of the rich sauces and dripping slabs of roasted boar. More accustomed to an austere diet of fish, aged fowl and many vegetables, they were overwhelmed by this secular bounty. Under different circumstances, they might have found pleasure in such a rare feast, but Death blunted it.

Glancing at her fellow religious, Eleanor concluded that their feigned attention to the generous meal had long ago exceeded the requirements of expected courtesy. She rose, and they followed with evident relief. Even Sir Hugh took advantage of the chance to escape, and Master Gamel swallowed one more mouthful of red wine before abandoning his soaked trencher. With a courteous bow to his table companions, he left to seek his bed.

While the servants removed the food and plate, stripped the linen, and began folding the trestle tables against the wall, Eleanor walked to the fireplace. At least the poor will benefit from our meager appetites, she thought, convinced that the kitchen would have an abundance, even after the servants ate, to hand out the next morning for charity.

Sister Anne joined her and asked if the prioress wished to come to the chapel. Eleanor knew she should accompany the nun and Brother Thomas, but the time was apt to seek more details from her brother about Baron Herbert's family. She promised to join the pair later.

Looking around for Hugh, she found him leaning against a window in the corridor just outside the hall. He stared down at the bailey, his expression indicative of a mood no brighter than the coming long night. As Eleanor approached, he turned to greet her with a distracted smile. It was manifestly contrived.

She told him her concerns and pretended not to notice his darkened spirit.

"I am as ignorant as you about the reason for these tragedies. Even though this current one should have added to his urgency, Baron Herbert has not yet chosen to summon me." His tone was rough with impatience. "Because his missive spoke of great need, I endangered your health, that of your sub-infirmarian and a noted physician by urging this perilous winter journey. Forgive me for begging you to join me in this folly." He threw up his hands in disgust.

"My decision was freely made, as was my choice to bring Brother Thomas, but I do wonder why you asked for Sister Anne if you intended to bring a physician." That her brother had omitted mentioning the monk struck her as odd. She gave him a questioning look. "I might have chosen another nun to accompany me for modesty's sake and left her to care for the dying."

He looked sheepish. "I do owe you an explanation and must add a plea for forgiveness. Even now I think of you as my young sister, a child whom I must guide and protect."

She laughed. "Since I remain much shorter than most women, you are easily forgiven for considering me your *little* sister."

His grin was instant, then he grew pensive. "Baron Herbert is a man of strong opinions. Having little confidence in those not trained at a university, he asked for a physician of high repute. He considers apothecaries, and any woman amongst them, as mere grinders of powders and mixers of strange potions. They are lesser talents to him."

"Then why bring Sister Anne at all?"

"Surely you know that many at court praise her skill as God's gift. Although Master Gamel is a learned man, I believed she might be the better healer, but the baron would never have accepted her judgement on any illness. Her observations and conclusions might be invaluable but accepted by the baron only if spoken with the tongue of a physician."

"I wonder that you imagined this man of medicine would be agreeable to the deception. Even if he were willing to discuss matters with Sister Anne, his own opinions must take precedence with him."

"Master Gamel is a scholar, one whom I have learned to respect. He, too, has heard of your sub-infirmarian's reputation and expressed eagerness to meet her." He fell silent and looked back to the window.

Tucking her hands into her sleeves for warmth, Eleanor decided to drop the subject. "Then feel no more guilt over bringing any of us here, my brother. God often guides us into inexplicable situations only to reveal His purpose later." Even if Hugh's handling of this situation turned out to be misguided, his intent was founded in love and charity. "Should this journey not prove instructive for our souls," she continued with a gentle smile, "I shall find joy enough spending time with a brother I have not seen in far too long."

With evident affection, Hugh put a hand over his heart as he looked back at her. "Such words are like the balm of honey to your unworthy kinsman, my lady."

Eleanor was about to reply when she heard footsteps. Bending to look around her brother, she stared down the shadowy corridor.

Hugh spun around.

A tall man greeted the pair with a deep bow. "You would be justified in feeling anger over how this family has ignored your arrival," he said. "On behalf of Baron Herbert, I wish to apologize for our lack of hospitality and beg your forgiveness. The circumstances may be unusual, but we still owe our invited guests courtesy."

The prioress was struck dumb by the man's beauty. His eyes were the color of violets, shoulders broad, and his golden hair was cut short in the fashion of most fighting men. There was one deep scar along his left cheek, but that did nothing to mar his appearance. A battle wound was a mark of honor and courage, she thought, and found she quite liked it.

"You have no need to apologize," Hugh said. He embraced the man, then introduced Sir Leonel, the baron's nephew, to his sister.

Eleanor realized she was staring and quickly bowed her head when the man smiled at her.

"You have been most kind to my aunt." His soft words were like a caress. "She told me that your counsel and prayers were deeply comforting."

Feeling her cheeks grow hot, she hoped the bright color would be mistaken for modesty. "You were at her side when your cousin fell to his death," she replied, willing her thoughts to a loftier purpose. "If you have not yet done so, I implore you to seek God's comfort with your priest. Grief over Gervase's death must be sharp indeed."

A muscle twitched in his jaw.

She briefly wondered what that meant before logic abandoned her, vanquished by her wayward passions. Even her eyes burned. She shut them.

"We no longer have one. Our family priest died just before you arrived, my lady. It seems that God demands many souls from this place. Although my wish may be wicked, I do pray He is satisfied at last with the number He has gathered."

She looked up at him.

His mouth twisted with a hint of bitterness.

"Brother Thomas is here with us," she murmured. "God understands anguish when too many of our beloved ones die. He would want you to find solace." Sir Leonel's lips were full, she noticed. In another, that might be considered feminine but not in this very masculine nephew. "I urge you to seek our priest's counsel."

Without warning, Leonel fell to his knees in front of her, his hands folded prayerfully.

Her heart pounded so hard she feared both he and her brother would hear it.

"Bless me," he begged.

Eleanor did not remember what phrases she spoke but knew how her voice trembled.

Jumping to his feet, his eyes glowed.

She stepped back as quickly as if he had been flames leaping from the hearth.

Then Leonel abruptly turned grave, thanked her for the grace, and turned all his attention to her brother.

"We came at your uncle's behest," Hugh said, although no question had been asked.

"And I have also come at his. He asks that you attend him."

"I shall come whenever he wishes."

"Now, if you would be so kind."

This is welcome news, Eleanor thought, and was relieved that her reason was returning. She turned to her brother. "Before you leave, Sister Anne must be summoned to my side for propriety. I may not linger here alone." She was also much in need of the steady, comforting companionship of her friend and fellow religious after this unsettling encounter with the baron's nephew.

A servant was dispatched to bring the nun from the chapel. Within a few moments, the sub-infirmarian arrived, and the two men left.

Eleanor willed herself not to watch Sir Leonel walk away. He is a man of decided charm, she concluded as she forced her gaze in the other direction.

As prioress and nun walked back to the briskly dancing fire in the hall, Anne leaned close to her friend's ear. "I sense something amiss," she murmured. "Have you cause to be troubled?"

Aye, Eleanor thought, then firmly cast aside all thoughts of Sir Leonel. "These deaths. They have multiplied," she said. "When my brother asked me to accompany him here, he confessed that Baron Herbert had said little about the reason for his plea. I understood that one son's death must have caused deep melancholy, but I was perplexed by the request to bring healers of both body and soul. Nonetheless, I took Hugh's word that the baron would never have begged the favor without cause."

"Brother Thomas' spiritual consolation added to my experience as an apothecary would serve the baron's need, as you reasonably assumed. Have you learned something that proves your conclusion erroneous?"

"I should have questioned my brother further. I fear that you may have suffered this long journey without cause."

"I confess I was startled to see a physician riding with Sir Hugh's company of soldiers."

Eleanor rubbed her hands to enhance the fire's warmth.

Aware that the servants were still about, Anne bent closer for more private conversation. "You have no cause for regret. I am always pleased to come with you on your travels, whether or not my humble skills are needed. On this journey, however, I have learned so much. Master Gamel has generously shared some of his knowledge with me on the road. The time I have spent learning from him will bring great benefit to our hospital at Tyndal."

Eleanor suspected that her sub-infirmarian had taught this fur-cloaked London man more than he had her, but she did not speak her thoughts. "With those words, you exemplify the meekness required of us all."

"I did ask Master Gamel what your brother told him about the baron's concerns." Anne's eyes twinkled.

"And how did he respond?" As always, her friend had guessed what the prioress might want to know.

"The baron specifically asked for a skilled doctor, one with particular experience in treating soldiers returning from Outremer."

The prioress raised an eyebrow. Hugh had not mentioned this to her. Perhaps the request was of no significance to him, but it aroused her curiosity. "What reason was given for this?"

Anne shook her head.

Might this physician be interested in a particular injury or malady, an affliction found primarily amongst those coming home from the holy wars? "I am surprised that Master Gamel agreed to leave his patients. Something about this request must have sparked an interest."

"Sir Hugh has done him many favors, he said, including the opportunity to consult with this man in your brother's service." She hesitated. "The one from Acre?"

"Lucas," Eleanor replied.

"I was not quite sure how he served your brother."

Eleanor was uncomfortable with the question. "He is a convert from Islam, a physician in his own land," she said. "I know little more than that." Rarely did she lie to Anne, but now was not the time to reveal the rumors surrounding her brother's companion.

"*Lucas?* That is an unusual name for an infidel."

"He took the name at baptism," Eleanor said. "My brother explained the name change was to honor Saint Luke, the physician, companion to the sainted Paul." And that was all she wished to say about the man. Quickly she changed the subject: "Even if he did wish to repay my brother for past kindness, surely Master Gamel has many patients who will suffer in his absence."

"He has a son, one who followed him in the study of healing arts. The physician is proud of his son's talents so had little hesitation about leaving the suffering with him." Anne smiled. "His only concern was that many might learn to prefer the younger man to the father. He told me that he is not so old that his only desire is to sit by the fire and play with his grandchildren."

"Master Gamel is a good man to offer his services so generously to the baron." If this physician was willing to discuss medical theory with a man from Outremer, she thought, he might even ponder the opinions of a woman as her brother claimed.

Anne hesitated. "He does hope we may all soon learn the purpose for our journey."

"As do I." Eleanor shivered and began to pace. "I am uneasy about this place. There is something amiss, and I am beginning to fear that Satan has taken residence in the castle."

Anne gasped.

Eleanor knew it was not like her to make such statements, believing as she did that mortals were more likely to be the Devil's henchmen than tailed demons. "I have just met the baron's nephew, Sir Leonel, and believe he is right when he says that Death has been vigorously plowing this field for souls. One son drowned. Since then, the castle priest has died. Yesterday, the heir tumbled to his death from a keep window." She stopped and stared into the writhing flames. "Death has been too merry here."

"Perhaps Brother Thomas should perform an exorcism."

The prioress' expression darkened.

"I mention this only because you fear that Satan…"

"I do feel a malign presence," Eleanor said, "and conclude the baron may well have had cause to call for a priest. Indeed, if there is a plague of imps, he might be most grateful now that he has three of us vowed to God's service. That noted, I still wonder why he asked for a physician. We know not whether the disease in this place is of the soul, the body, or both, and it may well take the wisdom of us all to find out."

"Have you spoken with anyone else here about this matter?"

"The baron's wife. Unfortunately, she knows nothing of her husband's wishes or concerns because of some unexplained estrangement from him. As for the sons' deaths, Lady Margaret witnessed her Gervase's fall, as did Sir Leonel."

Anne winced, horrified by what the mother must have felt.

"The baron is not the only one who smells an evil stench. The lady does as well, but I was unable to learn anything of import. Her anger against God was so hot that I saw no value in questioning such a grieving mother." She frowned. "The happy news is that Sir Leonel has just taken my brother to see the baron."

"Then Sir Hugh will soon learn the specific reasons for this visit."

Eleanor looked back at the corridor window and grew alarmed. Night had vanquished day. It was now Satan's hour. "Let us pray that he does," she said, suddenly filled with irrational anxiety. In this moment she felt as if imprisoned in this castle and feared she might never be able to escape.

Closing her eyes, she asked God to forgive her weaknesses of flesh and spirit. For once the world felt too ominous for her, and she longed for the safety of her priory. Did she have enough faith and courage to deal with whatever evil might be in residence here, or would it destroy her?

Chapter Eight

One guttering candle struggled against the darkness of the room. Looming shadows mocked the effort.

Sir Hugh began to sweat despite the chill air. Those things that unman us may be secreted from other mortals, he thought, but we can never conceal them from either God or the Evil One. Despite having faced combat with courage enough, he trembled now. Night belonged to the Devil.

"Where is your heathen underling?"

Hugh swallowed a sharp cry, took a deep breath, and willed himself to calm.

A man stood, silhouetted against the light of the entrance.

Or at least it seemed a mortal shape. Choosing caution, Eleanor's brother said nothing.

Then the man slammed the door shut and walked close to the wall, circling Hugh like a lion after prey. "Have I changed so much that you no longer recognize me? We were like brothers in Outremer." The voice was hoarse.

Hugh bowed to Baron Herbert. "My lord."

A shadowy hand waved the courtesy aside. "You did not answer my question."

"In truth, I could not see your face…"

"My other question."

"Do you mean Lucas?"

"A fiendish infidel who mocks the true faith. When he took the name of a saint, he committed yet another blasphemous act."

His face growing hot with anger, Hugh took a moment to reply. "He remains in my manor near London. I knew he would not be welcome here."

"You may find that King Edward has mounted his head on a spike by the time you return to court."

"Lucas was judged innocent in the assassination attempt against our king."

Herbert snorted.

"May we cease this debate, my lord? I have no stomach for arguing with you, and we have never agreed on this matter."

"There is wine, Hugh. I beg your forgiveness when I ask that you serve yourself."

Hearing an odd hesitancy in his old comrade's voice, Hugh's anger fled. He walked to the pitcher of wine and poured. "May I bring you some of this?" His question was gently asked.

"I brought a cup with me. Will you sit over there?" He pointed to a chair some distance away.

The two men fell silent and drank.

Then the baron dropped his cup. It clattered as it rolled across the stone floor. "The servant will retrieve it later," he muttered. "I have drunk more than enough this evening."

Perplexed, Hugh wondered if the baron's habits had changed since his return home. Herbert had always been temperate. Even so, there was no evidence that the man was drunk. His words were not slurred, nor had he stumbled in the dim light.

"Do you ever long for Acre?"

The question surprised Hugh, and he hesitated before responding: "Sometimes." The truth was less ambiguous. Had he not been Baron Adam's eldest son, he might have stayed. Coming back to England had been difficult for him, but that hint of wistfulness in Herbert's voice, when he mentioned Outremer, was unexpected.

"To you, I may confess this. After taking the cross and leaving my wife and sons, I cursed the day I took that oath. My faith drove me to do what was right, but each night on that ship I

dreamed that I was sleeping by my wife's side. When I awoke…"
He coughed.

"Although I have no wife, I did leave my beloved son behind."

"A good lad, I have heard, who serves as a page at the king's
court."

Sipping his wine, Hugh waited.

"We did not recover Jerusalem."

Although the darkness in the room may have hidden the
gesture, Hugh silently nodded.

"Yet I almost remained in Acre."

"Although you loathed the land and its people?"

"The Muslim usurpers? Of course." Herbert grunted. "Many
Christian men did settle there to purify the land."

Those soldiers cared less about cleansing the earth than
acquiring property, Hugh thought, and most married local
women. He had heard too many discuss the opportunity to gain
wealth. Knowing how much his friend condemned the marriages
in particular, he wondered that his friend had even thought to
remain. "Not long after you sailed home, King Edward left
Acre as well. If you had stayed, you would have been cruelly
disheartened. He was Christendom's strongest leader. With his
departure, we lost all hope of regaining the holy city."

"Dare you doubt that God would lend His hand to another
of true faith?"

"If he were also talented in the art of war, there would be no
question. Besides King Edward, did you ever see such a man in
Acre? I never heard you speak of one."

"You have always placed cleverness above religion's power,
Hugh. Had you not shown great courage in God's battles, your
laxity in matters demanding faith might have been questioned
more often."

"Why did you want to remain in Outremer, my lord?"

Herbert did not reply for a long moment, then cleared his
throat. "I had become very different from the man who left wife
and sons in England."

All of us did change, Hugh thought, but no one discussed the transformation any more than they did their wounds and scars. "Then I am surprised you chose to return." He knew his words held a sharp edge, but he still struggled against the hurt he had suffered when the baron left Acre. Although the two men had fought together like brothers, his friend left for England without sending even the briefest word of farewell.

"I was no longer worthy of gazing on Jerusalem's walls. I am a sinner."

"Are not we all?"

"Most certainly." He pointed at Hugh. "And you were the greater one, or so I told you once. God has since proven me wrong." His voice cracked. "I cannot yet point to what unspeakable transgression I committed, but He is punishing me beyond endurance for something."

Herbert rose from his chair and walked over to the window. For a long time, he stared outside. The silver moonlight cast an eerie glow around him, then clouds the color of soot extinguished the light.

"I understand why you required a priest from me, although there must have been many who could have consoled you on the road back from Acre."

The baron stood in silence, running the palm of his hand up and down the stones of the cold wall.

Another cloud, trimmed grey with moonlight, scudded across the backdrop of night sky.

Hugh grew impatient. "Out of friendship I came in this winter season, although you gave little enough reason for your plea. Master Gamel, one of the most respected physicians in London, awaits your pleasure. In deference to your rank, Prioress Eleanor agreed to leave Tyndal Priory and bring her own priest to serve your particular spiritual needs. Her sub-infirmarian, Sister Anne, also accompanied her, a renowned healer whose skills are highly praised by many at court."

"Be not angry with me."

Hugh heard a catch in the baron's voice. Was he weeping?

"For all our disagreements over certain matters, I knew I could trust you, not only to come to my aid without question but also never to betray me."

"Each of us was always the other's shield in battle, my lord."

"Let me bury my son tomorrow. Afterward, I shall explain, to the best of my ability, what is happening here. Aye, I have begged much from you, but I fear some hideous plague has struck my family. Whether God has cursed them for my sins, or Satan has taken residence in this castle because it delights his corroded heart, I fail to comprehend. Do you not feel a malign presence here?"

In reply, Hugh put a hand to his heart and nodded.

Chapter Nine

"Identify yourself!"

Brother Thomas uttered an oath and jumped back from the creneled curtain wall.

A soldier emerged from the shadows. His spear glittered in the moonlight.

"Brother Thomas." Despite the cold, Thomas pushed back his hood, hoping there was enough light to reveal his tonsure and give strength to the honesty of his claim.

"A monk? Where did you come from?"

"I am with the party of Prioress Eleanor and her brother, Sir Hugh of Wynethorpe. We arrived yesterday."

"An ill-timed visit." The soldier stepped companionably close to the monk like any creature seeking precious warmth in a biting wind.

Thomas swiftly pulled the hood back over his head and nodded.

"I advise you not to stand still, lest you become a pillar of ice. I'd not like having to explain to my sergeant how a monk came to resemble Lot's wife, albeit in a more frozen form." He laughed at his own humor.

There was enough truth in the poor jest, Thomas decided, and walked on.

The soldier kept pace beside him. "As I said, the arrival day was badly chosen if the prioress and her brother sought merriment and feasting. You're a welcome enough sight though. We need God to save us from the Devil's claws, Brother."

Thomas stopped. "All mortals do. Are you suggesting there is more reason than usual here?"

"Demons abound."

"Satan's legions are always about. Why conclude there is a more formidable invasion?"

"Unnatural deaths." The soldier's voice trembled more than the cold would explain.

"Surely not murder?" Growing increasingly numb, Thomas resumed walking at a brisk pace toward the watchtower.

The soldier trotted alongside. "Not by any human hand."

"Truly?"

"Nor is this current death the first here committed by the Evil One."

"You would serve God well if you helped me understand what you mean. I have only heard that another son died not long ago. Drowned, was it?"

"Or so some say." He lowered his head. "And then our old priest. After that, we'd none of God's servants until your party arrived. Doesn't that tell you something?"

Caught by the implications in this news, Thomas slowed his pace.

"A little faster, Brother?" The soldier rubbed his hands and broke into a jog.

Obliging, Thomas hurried after him.

When he reached the entrance to the high watchtower, the soldier pointed at the top of the structure. "We could both find shelter from the wind, Brother. I've done my round of the wall for now. It's time for a stint up there with the falcons, although they're wise enough to find refuge inland for the winter. Fortunately, the good baron built some protection there for us sentries." He pulled opened the entry door and gestured for Thomas to go inside. "Up the stairs. Should be ale. Warm us both."

The wind whipped sea-salted air against his face. It stung. Needing no further urging, the monk hurried through the door and raced up the narrow steps.

The round space on the top of the tower was chill enough, but the walls and a short overhang of wood held the wind at bay. Near the staircase, a poorly crafted table had been pushed against the wall. A jug rested precariously on top of the unevenly hewn wood.

Grabbing two ill-shaped pottery cups from the floor, the soldier poured.

Thomas drank. The ale was rough but served its purpose of sending warmth through to his bones. "You think the priest's death was not a natural one?" Although he was interested in what this man might say about the deaths of both sons, he was more intrigued by the soldier's apparent belief that the Devil had killed a priest.

"If Satan kills a man, is that not unnatural?"

The monk agreed. "How did you learn the Devil did it?"

"I found the corpse." He shuddered and downed the contents of his cup in one draught, then poured another. "More for yourself?"

Thomas placed his cup close to the pitcher.

"It was morning. A couple of months after the drowning." The sentry took a deep breath and leaned against the tower wall.

Glancing into his cup, Thomas hesitated, then gulped the drink down and reached for the jug. The man's beginning did not bode well for a story much shorter than some ecclesiastical history. If he were fortunate, the tale might prove as entertaining as anything by the Venerable Bede. He doubted he would be so lucky.

"Lady Margaret and the sons had waited a long time for the priest to come to the family chapel for Mass. He was an old man, she finally said, and perhaps he had fallen ill. Never considered whether he might have drunk too much wine the night before." Raising his own cup, he gave it a significant glance, then chortled. "She commanded me to seek him out."

Thomas was struck by two things. The soldier had not mentioned that the baron was with his family, and the priest's immoderate drinking seemed to be common knowledge if this sentry knew about it. If the latter were true, it was odd that the Lady Margaret would be ignorant of the priest's vice, unless she was being charitable. These details had implications, but he held back on questions, choosing only the one that would hurry the tale along: "What did you find?"

"A dead man. He was lying in bed, hands modestly folded as if he had been praying when Death came for his soul."

"Your description suggests he died at peace. Why conclude he had been staring into the Devil's face?"

"His eyes belied any calm, Brother. They were wide open and streaked with red. They looked like the Devil had sucked blood through the man's eyes. The last thing the poor priest must have seen was the fires of Hell in the maw of the Evil One."

The monk swallowed more ale and nodded as foreboding increased.

The soldier leaned closer. "I've seen men killed in many ways, Brother. Never have I seen a corpse with eyes like that!"

Thomas had. One of the softest paths to death was with a pillow. It leaves no marks, except for the eyes which are streaked with red. He had seen this once before, when a clerk died in his bed a few nights after beating a mere youth for a minor error in transcription. The man had severely whipped others for equally small infractions. This time, his latest victim seemed likely to die or be crippled by his wounds. When Thomas found the body and asked questions, another had taken him aside and whispered that he would be well-advised to let matters be. Thomas had regretfully heeded the caution, realizing that no one would cooperate in bringing any killer to justice, but later overheard how the clerk had been smothered.

Misinterpreting the monk's silence to mean he had revealed something better left unsaid, the soldier turned pale. He waved away his words, then clasped both hands together to keep them from betraying his fear. "Now I never really meant anything about actual murder, nor did I claim the good priest was wicked, only that some devilish creature may have stolen his soul. Maybe the priest was caught unprepared because he was sleeping? But I'll leave any conclusions about imps to others, especially a man of God like yourself."

The monk started to allay the man's fears.

Now the soldier leaned forward and lowered his voice. "Whatever you do decide, Brother, I beg you to say nothing about where you heard this. I'm just a simple man who honestly believed he smelled the stench of hellfire near the priest's corpse."

Thomas looked at the soldier with sympathy. "I never asked your name." He grinned. "I probably overheard the tale, shared amongst men standing in shadows. How could I point out the one who told it?"

The soldier poured them both more ale.

After a companionable silence, Thomas decided to ask his unspoken questions. "You said that only the Lady Margaret and the sons were waiting for the priest. I wondered if Baron Herbert had not yet returned to England, or was he in the chapel as well?"

"He was home, but no one sees the baron much, least not in daylight. He walks the walls when darkness falls, just like you were, although he prefers those that look out to sea and not these closer to English soil. I might have mistaken you for our lord, except he's much thicker around here." He pointed to his chest.

"He does not attend Mass?"

"Before the priest died, he did. Not with the family though. My lass, who washes the linen, told me that our lord never shares his lady's bed, nor does he break bread with her. He's never seen in her company. My lass thinks Lady Margaret must have committed a grave sin while her husband was fighting God's war, although she can't imagine what. The lady's always been a kind mistress." He nervously rubbed at his cheeks, waiting to see how the monk would react.

Thomas nodded encouragement to continue.

"Mind you, all that is only woman's talk. They're sweet things, but they do cluck away like all hens. Being a monk, you might not give credence to their rumors."

"Does Baron Herbert never speak with his sons?"

"I don't know. They are a sad lot compared with Sir Leonel. Not that they're bad ones, but they lack their father's fire. Now that nephew is a man, fought in Outremer, and has the scars to prove his mettle. I think the baron has always favored his brother's son over his own."

Thomas started to ask another question

The soldier leapt to his feet. "I'm due back on watch, Brother."

Perhaps it was just as well, Thomas thought. Despite the ale and the shelter, the damp cold was too bitter to continue talking. He would have to leave the details of the sons' deaths for another time and had probably gained enough of the soldier's confidence to query him later. There was one last thing he could do to guarantee that.

He rubbed the cup dry on his robe and put it down on the table. "Since I was given the old priest's chambers near the chapel, while my prioress is a guest here, I should search the place. If I find any hidden wine, I will bring it to share with you another night," Thomas grinned.

"That's charitable of you, Brother. Considering how much he drank, I doubt you'll find any. If there had been a drop left, he would have fought the Devil before he let him steal his soul. Forgive me for saying this, but I could have wrung the priest out and gotten wine enough to drink for supper if the cellar had been empty of it."

Thomas laughed and slapped the soldier's back, before retreating down the stairs. As he hastened toward the steps leading to the bailey, he wondered if he should tell Prioress Eleanor what the soldier had told him.

"Perhaps not until I have learned more," he whispered to the pummeling wind. "Although some foul deed may have been committed, I have no proof, except this one soldier's word. He seems a good man, but I do not know him well enough to conclude that he actually saw what he claims."

The evidence was thin, and, as a guest in this place, Thomas knew he had no right to cry *murder* quite yet.

Chapter Ten

Prioress Eleanor and Sister Anne emerged from the common chapel just off the Great Hall. Although the body of Herbert's son was no longer there, removed by the family to prepare for burial tomorrow, the wretchedness of his death had given a sad direction to their prayers.

Without uttering a word to each other, they both stopped at a window in the corridor and looked down into the bailey. Such was the nature of their friendship that their spirits were bonded even when each was preoccupied with private thoughts.

Eleanor stole a glance at her friend. She was worried about her.

In repose, Anne often bore a solemn expression but was still quick to laugh or raise spirits with her clever wit and shrewd observations. For several days now, Anne had fallen into unusual silence, her jests and insights halting or absent as if her thoughts had fled to some distant place.

Of course winter was a bitter season, filled with little joy, and this journey in particular had been a hard one. All this was cause enough for anyone's weary sadness, yet it was quite unlike her sub-infirmarian to succumb to such emotions for long. It was also rare that Anne did not confide troubles.

Puzzled and unable to put a finger on the exact nature of Anne's distraction, Eleanor turned her attention to what little she could see from the window.

Despite this being the family home of Baron Herbert, the prioress found little beauty in the fortress. Grey snow lay against walls and was pushed into corners, well-stained with the yellow-brown effluence from the living. And thus it remained, in stubborn defiance of any hope of spring. During the day, people and animals scurried to and fro in the bailey, noisily occupied with the demands of their lives and duties. She found little joy in their activity.

Were she honest with herself, she knew that such was the state of any castle in winter, when the cold made outside work a misery. Had she been at her father's fortress in Wales, she would have seen similar sights and thought nothing of them. Here, she found fault.

What illogical creatures we mortals are, she thought, then concluded that a prioress, obliged to strive toward God's perfection, had no excuse for such irrational and unacceptable failings.

Although a dying sun never meant that all activity ceased, there was little enough to see in the courtyard now to distract her. Torches flickered in the hands of soldiers. One blacksmith beat red-hot iron with a rhythmic clanging, and sparks flew like fireflies. The pungent stench of animals, too long in one spot, rose in the wind and assaulted Eleanor's nose.

As she well understood, a castle was built to accommodate war, not the comfort of women and children, yet this fortress did seem uniquely grim, even when she tried to exile her bias. She understood how it had earned the name of *dur*, but what reason was there to ever call it *doux?*

Melancholy tugged more forcefully at Eleanor's soul, and she quickly cursed whatever dark spirit resided here that seemed so determined to destroy all gladness in the heart. Thou shalt not win, she swore with fierce determination.

To drive away the morbid feeling, she turned her thoughts away from herself. It was time to draw her friend out and try to heal whatever burdened her. Her first question addressed the most likely problem: "Are you well?"

Anne flinched, but her expression softened with affection. "Did I not ask you much the same question earlier? Maybe we are both infected by some vile fetor hovering about?"

Eleanor stepped away from the window, her cheeks stinging from the sharp wind. "You have been so quiet of late. I feared that the journey may have been too great a hardship and that you had sickened. Knowing your concern for others, I wondered if you refused to confess ill-health lest you cause us difficulty." She touched her friend's arm and smiled. "None of us would ever think such a thing, and I speak as both friend and prioress."

"My mother suffered to give me birth on this coast. Winter presents little that I have not endured before. I suffer no corporal illness, but I do confess that my spirit is uneasy." The nun folded her hands and pressed them against her heart. "Do you truly think this castle is haunted by some malevolent force?" She turned her head so any expression was hidden by the folds of her wimple.

"Lack of knowledge is like a fertile land where the flowers of evil thrive," the prioress replied. "When Hugh returns from seeing our host, we shall learn the reason for the baron's summons. God's intent shall be made evident, and He will give us the guidance needed to resolve the problem. Then demons may no longer torment us with those unsettling thoughts born of ignorance."

Anne turned with a smile bright with enthusiasm. "Master Gamel said much the same yesterday about ignorance and evil, although he was referring to a proven treatment for an open wound. Some reject his preferred technique because they believe God has only sanctioned another way." Suddenly, her face reddened.

The prioress raised an eyebrow.

The sub-infirmarian again hid her face. "He did consult with a priest, who determined there was nothing sinful in the remedy," she said softly. "As you said, God provides enlightenment when the need exists. Ignorance, so beloved by Satan, soon vanishes." Anne bent forward, rested her forearms on the stones of the window, and stared down into night.

Rarely had she ever seen Anne discomfited, Eleanor thought. As if listening to the sounds below, Eleanor said nothing and studied her friend out of the corner of her eye. After a moment, she asked: "Is the physician married? If so, this journey must be an especially long and lonely one for him."

"His wife died a few years ago. He blames himself for that, claiming that his skill was too poor to save her. As I mentioned, there is a son, the only child to thrive of the eight borne, and the young man shall soon marry the daughter of a family friend. Master Gamel is delighted that the match has proven a happy choice for all."

The two had discussed much more than medicine on the road, Eleanor thought, then become aware that there was no joy in Anne's words. Although the nun had suffered the death of her only child before she took vows, she always found pleasure in hearing about the offspring of others.

"There should be grandchildren soon to cheer his heart."

Eleanor nodded. Perhaps Anne's last remark revealed the source of her pain. With her own babe dead, Anne's arms must feel even emptier without the hope of grandchildren she could never embrace. "A son's marriage?" Eleanor eased the subject away from that of children. If she wanted to pursue this cause of her friend's pain, it should be done in a more private place. "A good enough reason to pray for a swift return home…"

"I hope my company does not offend?" The man's voice was soft with misgivings and intended courtesy.

The two women spun around.

Sir Leonel bowed.

"Not at all," Eleanor replied with more fervor than was required. She knew her face must be glowing and that the cause was not attributable to the surprise of his arrival.

"I was in the chapel too. You did not see me."

Indeed she had not, the prioress thought. God must have blinded her to this man's presence so she could concentrate on the state of his dead cousin's soul.

"I did," Anne replied. "With all you have suffered over the death of your cousin, Gervase, it seemed a kindness to let you pray in peace."

Eleanor looked into Leonel's eyes. How many men had eyes that color of a summer flower, she mused, then realized that he was standing so close she could feel his warm breath.

She willed herself to retreat until her back was against the wall. "You were sad witness to his tragic fall," she said, pleased that her voice did not tremble this time even if her knees did.

"And I grieve deeply, my lady, but his mother suffers far more. Lady Margaret and I were standing at the window in the corridor above when he approached." Leonel bent his head. "I still cannot understand what caused the accident. Perhaps he was bewitched, yet we had spoken together not long before and shared some wine. At that time, I observed nothing untoward." He frowned in somber memory.

To keep her mind focused on something other than his musky scent, Eleanor commanded the arrival of cool reason while allowing her curiosity free rein about the circumstances of this death. "I remember the bitter wind when we arrived and how much comfort mulled wine gave us. Might the chill air have caused him to drink more than he ought?"

"I tarried over my cup longer than he, but we did not talk together for long. He had planned to meet with Raoul. His youngest brother had something he wished to discuss, he said. My cousin soon left me." He tilted his head in thought.

What a fine profile, Eleanor thought then cursed her distraction.

"I remained in the Great Hall and did not seek the company of Lady Margaret until she sent for me."

"Raoul? Who is…?" She blinked, trying to remember where she had heard the name, then quickly felt very much a fool. "Oh yes! He came to greet my brother and me after our arrival." She glanced up at the baron's nephew, carefully avoiding those violet eyes. "You believe your dead cousin was bewitched, not befuddled with drink?"

Leonel frowned. "My aunt might have believed that, and perhaps she has cause. I thought *bewitched*, yet I truly do not know what caused this tragic accident. My uncle does ask if some spell has been cast, for he has now lost three sons. One death may strike the heart like a sharp mace, but three wound so deeply that any father might long for death himself. He cries out in his sleep for relief."

She nodded, bracing herself against the wall for strength that she did not own.

"Had my cousin been under a wicked spell, my uncle might find a little consolation in knowing that Gervase died at Satan's hand, not God's."

"I do not understand," Eleanor said, confused by his words and her own sinful failing. "Why would he find solace in that?" She hesitated. "And why would anyone think that God had struck down your uncle's son?"

"It would be best if he himself explained his fears, my lady. Forgive me for speaking out of turn." He bowed. "And I have kept you far too long from rest. Pray forgive my selfishness, but your company has given me courage and reassurance. Thank you for offering this wretched sinner such charity and succor."

Not trusting herself to speak without betrayal of her emotions, Eleanor lowered her gaze and prayed that he saw only soft benevolence in her face and not reprehensible desire.

"Before I leave," he said, "I have a message from Lady Margaret who grieves that so little courtesy has been shown to you and all who journeyed here with your brother. She begs that you and your company join her for a light supper tomorrow before Compline."

"She has suffered the death of a son and yet provided for our comfort most generously. We shall be pleased to accept her invitation."

He murmured pleasure on his aunt's behalf, then walked away.

Anne leaned close to the prioress' ear and whispered, "That man's smile was warm enough to heat mulled wine, was it not?"

Fearing that her friend had discovered her weakness for the man, Eleanor stiffened.

But Anne had not noticed her reaction. A puzzled expression on her face, she was watching Sir Leonel depart.

Chapter Eleven

The morning winter light was weak as if the sun cared little about rising that day, even to cast warmth on the entombment of a baron's son.

Thomas walked back from the grave, head bowed and eyes moist. The burial had been ill-attended. Since there was no other priest here, Thomas had offered to perform the rites. He may never have met the young man, but he grieved that so few cared about his death. Even the father had not come to see his son returned to the earth.

"Brother Thomas!"

The monk stopped and looked over his shoulder.

The physician hurried toward him, cheeks bright with exertion and breath white in the frosty air.

Thomas raised a hand in perfunctory greeting. In his present mood, he did not wish the company but smiled as if he welcomed it. At least Master Gamel had been at the graveside, although there was no reason for him to come. The monk appreciated the kindness, a quality he increasingly suspected was part of the man's nature.

"It was a sad event, Brother." Gamel was puffing when he reached the monk's side. "His mother was dry-eyed and fled early. Neither his father nor his younger brother, Umfrey, appeared. Only Raoul and Sir Leonel remained to join you in prayer for the man's soul. The latter at least shed a tear." He shook his head.

"When my beloved wife died, some said I could not possibly weep more than I did at her death bed, yet I lamented over her grave so long that my son had to drag me from it." He looked up at Thomas, his eyes suggesting embarrassment over revealing such emotion. "A father would surely feel no less grief at a son's death."

"Sorrow wears many disguises. The Lady Margaret may have wept herself dry of tears. As for Umfrey, he hides in the family chapel to escape demons and fears for his own life."

"And what news of the father?" The question was brusque.

"Sir Hugh met with him last night, and Baron Herbert sent word that he wished to have this son buried before he met with us. Prioress Eleanor conveyed the news to me after prayer today and confirmed that was his only message."

Gamel looked confused. "A reasonable request from a grieving father, yet he was not here to say a farewell to his boy this morning?"

"I must assume good cause."

"I cannot be as charitable, Brother." These words were sharply spoken. "I would feel differently had the baron come to watch his son's corpse laid in the ground. His actions suggest no grief at all, and now I begin to suspect little need for our presence. A patient does not urgently call a physician to his side, only to leave him waiting outside the chamber door."

The monk agreed but said nothing. Adding fuel to Gamel's vexation would serve no purpose, and, until they learned what troubled the baron so profoundly, tolerance was better advised. He nodded with appropriate solemnity, hoping his silence suggested the need for forbearance.

In the distance, a sea bird shrieked, the cry only adding to the present gloom.

Thomas did not dare speak of what he had heard. Whatever the baron's specific reasons for summoning them, there was cause enough for concern. A priest may have been murdered, and now two sons were dead, the circumstances unusual and the deaths in rapid succession. As for Baron Herbert's lack of overt grief, Thomas refused to conclude anything. He had never met the man.

"Forgive me, Brother. My words were callous. I have little cause for complaint. The delay is such a minor thing, compared to this tragedy." Gamel bowed his head with regret.

"You left many behind in London who still have need of your skills. Some impatience to return is understandable." Thomas chose to be gentle. Mortals often inflated themselves with self-importance; few admitted when they did so for petty reasons. Gamel had shown a rare humility.

"My son is skilled enough to take my place." He brightened. "I am proud of the lad, although I take care not to praise him too highly. When I was his age, I thought I knew everything there was to know. Now I fear I know very little indeed." His eyelids drooped with sadness. "Not only did I fail to keep Death from wresting my cherished wife from my arms, I was also unsuccessful in persuading the dark creature to take my soul as well."

Growing pensive, the monk looked around. This was the hour when most daily labor had begun, yet all activity was muffled as if any boisterous din would offend the dead. Blacksmiths muted their hammering. The laundry maids whispered. Even the cattle lowed softly. In grief, this physician wept while Baron Herbert refused to watch his son's body consigned to the earth. Gervase's mother railed against Heaven. He himself had never found a way to lament over the death of his own father. Who dares to measure the depth of anyone else's mourning?

Thomas turned back to Master Gamel and said, "Sometimes God's purpose differs from any mortal's wish. When this is the case, we shall fail despite the skills we possess. You cannot blame yourself for your wife's death or your own continuing life."

Thomas turned away and avoided meeting the physician's eyes. His statements were conventional, and he did long for them to be true, but God knew how often he failed to see any purpose in the suffering of innocents.

Gamel grunted.

Perhaps the physician had the same doubts as he, Thomas thought, but neither would admit to the impiety except to a confessor.

"May I ask after Sister Anne? I feared for her health because of the chill she suffered."

Brother Thomas raised an eyebrow, momentarily bewildered by the unrelated subject. "If our sub-infirmarian had fallen ill, I would have learned of it. You would have been called as well."

Gamel smiled with relief. "You have removed the weight from my heart, Brother. Indeed, I was grateful for her company on the way here. She is well-educated in the healing arts, far more than most that have practiced the apothecary trade. Although she is also a woman, she taught me many things I did not know. Her father was a physician, I believe, and she learned from him. And her manner is so modest that I did not even realize at the time that she had given me knowledge I lacked…" He stuttered to a stop, his cheeks flushing as he realized he had been chattering on with unseemly enthusiasm.

"I did notice that you spent much time by her side." The monk winced at his poor phrasing. He had meant to banish any hint of disapproval

Gamel clasped his hands until the knuckles turned white. "The nun is most virtuous! I have never met any woman of her vocation more chaste or humble. Sometimes I did wonder if I was in the presence of a saint."

Bowing his head in acknowledgement of Sister Anne's virtue, Thomas no longer doubted that this man had lost his heart to the sub-infirmarian. He tried to feel outrage over Gamel's transgression but utterly failed to summon indignation. To his knowledge, no sin had been committed except in the heart. Surely God would deem such relative innocence a minor failing.

Although faithful to her vows, Thomas knew that Sister Anne had only come to the religious life to follow her husband who had forsaken the world after their son's untimely death. Perhaps God preferred her choice of religious vows, however reluctant, but he was sorry that she might not find the comfort of a more earthly love in the arms of a good man—like this physician. Silently, he growled at God.

"Master Gamel!"

Startled, Thomas turned around.

Sir Hugh loomed just behind him.

Thomas stepped away from the man and wondered how often this knight had slipped behind a foe, then slit his throat. The monk had not heard his footstep and was grateful he was not Hugh's enemy.

Or was he? The man had never uttered a word to him unless obliged. Even then his demeanor was invariably glacial.

"Surely Prioress Eleanor requires your presence, Brother." Hugh's tone was barely civil. "I seek a private conversation with Master Gamel."

Willing his features into feigned humility, the monk strode off until he could take a deep breath and calm his rising anger at the knight's discourtesy. What had he done to make Sir Hugh dislike him so?

He found himself by the stables and walked inside. The smell of warm horse flesh and dry hay soothed his spirits. He leaned against one of the stalls.

One fear was that Hugh had learned of his work for the Church as a spy. That would cause the knight to doubt the monk's honest fealty to Prioress Eleanor, a concern Thomas could well understand.

As he considered this more, Thomas decided it was unlikely that the knight had discovered the secret. Father Eliduc was too careful to let the information slip out, and, had his prioress learned of his dual allegiance, she surely would have banished him from that trusted circle of counselors she called upon for advice.

A horse nickered at him from the stall. Bending over the wooden frame, Thomas recognized his mare. "Eat," he said. "You'll need the strength for our journey home." She gazed at him with liquid-eyed disdain.

Stroking her neck, Thomas then wondered if Hugh knew of his imprisonment. Although the story had been hushed, it could be learned, even if few would speak loudly of it. He might only be his father's bastard, but too many owed his sire respect to defile his name with any son's transgressions.

"The trip home will be easier," the monk whispered to the mare. "And may it come soon. We shall both be happy to see the walls of our priory." She shook and turned back to her fodder.

As he pushed away from the stall and walked out of the stable, Thomas doubted the revelation of his sodomy would even matter to Hugh. After all, he had atoned for the deed. The Church had accepted him as a religious, which meant he had done acceptable penance or else payment of some form had been exchanged to ease the process of total forgiveness. If boys could become bishops and bishops fathered babes, Thomas knew his own father was of high enough secular rank to permit one bastard son a place in a remote priory as a simple monk.

A little girl tugged at his robe, and Thomas stopped to give his blessing. With an understanding smile, he assured the red-faced mother that he had not been offended by the child's innocent assault on his clothing.

As he continued on toward the keep, he realized that the thing troubling him most in this matter was not so much Sir Hugh's cold manner as the recent change in the knight's young son, Richard.

A few years ago, he had met the boy at Wynethorpe Castle and developed a father's love for him. And since the lad's own sire had been in Outremer, Richard often turned to Thomas for advice in matters he felt uncomfortable discussing with his grandfather, Baron Adam. In short, affection between monk and lad was mutual.

Soon after Sir Hugh's return, all communication abruptly ceased.

Thomas lamented the loss. On this journey, he had been tempted to confront Sir Hugh and seek the cause. Since the lad still sent messages to his aunt, Prioress Eleanor, courtesy would have required him to at least add that he included Thomas in his daily prayers. Richard no longer mentioned him.

He was not sure why he hesitated to ask Hugh the reason the contact had been severed. It may have been the knight's coldness toward him or else some niggling fear. In any case, Thomas had not spoken of it. A father must take precedence in a son's heart, he repeated often, and the boy's sire was now home. It was a poor argument, but he consoled himself with the knowledge that Sir Hugh loved Richard beyond measure.

He paused and glanced back.

Sir Hugh was gone, and Master Gamel was now talking with a servant who was pointing to a spot on his outstretched arm.

Did the knight really need to discuss anything with the physician? The monk decided it was petty to conclude that Hugh had dismissed him solely to banish the monk from his presence.

Thomas rubbed his cold hands together and decided he had best seek hot, mulled wine to warm his bones and silence this troubling chatter of his uneasy spirit.

Chapter Twelve

"Where are you hiding, Umfrey?" Raoul peered around the chapel but could see no one, let alone his timorous brother. "I am not an imp, although you have called me one often enough in time past."

A shadow quivered near the altar.

"Let go of the altar. I've not come to slit your throat."

Silence.

"You are not that well-hidden." He sniffed loudly. "I smell your sweat."

Not even the intake of breath.

After a moment of waiting, Raoul shouted that he had come to butcher the sibling who was now their father's heir, detailing two uniquely violent acts he was contemplating. He stopped and waited.

Someone opened the chapel door and peered in.

"It is I, Raoul, youngest son to Baron Herbert. I have come to talk with Umfrey, not bludgeon him."

The man slipped away but left the door noticeably open.

"As you have heard, I announced myself and my purpose." He motioned toward the door with an exaggerated gesture. "Be comforted. That man will return after I leave. Should he find you dead, all will know who did it. Ask yourself if screaming bloody intent is the rational act of a brother who wants to inherit your eventual title and land."

Umfrey thrust his head above the altar. "If you meant that as a jest, it was a vile one." He now rose and shuffled to the dim light, cast from the window into a puddle by the altar. "Even pretending that you might commit violence in God's place is impious."

"Since our brother's death elevates you to heir and me to a religious vocation, it becomes my duty to say that your stench must offend God. Surely it is blasphemy to piss so close to the cross. Could you not have left long enough to use the latrine?"

"Satan lives in this castle. I dare not leave Our Lord's protection."

Raoul studied his cheerless brother. Umfrey was hunched over, head bowed, thin arms hugging his sides as if to keep his heart from beating its way out of his chest. "Although we have never loved each other," he said, "I pity you."

"Neither of us was ever favored. You and I should have grown closer as brothers."

"The former I'll grant you." He spat.

Umfrey opened his mouth to protest this latest churlish act, then changed his mind. "Our mother was fondest of the one buried today," he muttered instead.

"In recent days, that could have been true. Mother always was changeable about her affections within the brood. But our father remained consistent. I was born last yet have heard it said that he looked on none of his sons with love after Leonel arrived. Do you remember anything about that?"

"Our father did not show me favor, but then Leonel came here before my birth. I am not that much older than you."

"Yet we never banded together against our cousin. Why do you think that was?" Raoul leaned against the wall and peeled off a torn fingernail.

"We all liked Leonel. When our father discovered that one of us committed some offense, our cousin would plead for mercy on behalf of the guilty one."

"And didn't our sire always seem to find out our crimes, no matter how clever we thought we were! I, for one, needed much advocacy for the many times I was caught out." Raoul snorted. "And I was oft given lesser punishments when our cousin pled my cause. Leonel must have learned how to cast charms, considering his success in halving the beatings I was due."

"Charms?" Umfrey gasped. "Surely you do not suggest that our cousin is an imp?"

Raoul sighed and slid down to sit on the planked floor. "I shall make a poor religious, for I do not think men need imps to prick them into evil. All the Devil need do is sit and watch as men devise wicked deeds to perpetrate on others." He chuckled. "Maybe we were created in Satan's image, not God's?"

Umfrey crossed himself and stepped back from his brother. "I shall listen to no more of your blasphemy!" His voice shook with fear. "Now methinks you are an imp, dressed up in Raoul's image. Tell me why you came here." Once more he made the sign of the cross. When his brother did not vanish in the expected puff of malodorous smoke, he looked relieved.

"You were not at our brother's grave this morning. That was noticed."

"I prayed for his soul. Here."

"Some suspect you feared his corpse would sit up in its shroud and point you out as his killer."

"He fell, unless the devil pushed him. But no man did! Leonel and our mother were witnesses."

Raoul shrugged. "I only repeat what I have heard. When are you leaving the chapel?"

"When Satan is sent back to his own domain. Until then, he fiendishly works to destroy our family line."

"Whether the Devil or God intends to obliterate this family, I cannot say, but I do know that only you and I remain alive of the sons." He stood up. "Shall our parents survive, do you think? Maybe good-hearted Leonel is also on the list of those condemned. Who do you think will die next? There is no logical order to the deaths as far as I can see." He waited.

His brother gagged as if something had stuck in his throat.

"If you are lucky, your time may come before you starve here. Are you praying that you be killed before our father, or mother, or…?"

Umfrey sobbed piteously.

"Hush! Father slapped me often enough for weeping. Did he not do the same to you? How could you fail to learn the art of swallowing tears when sorrow kicks you in the groin?"

"I may weep before the cross," Umfrey whimpered.

"Like a woman." Raoul snorted, then waited until his brother's snuffling ceased. "Have you had anything to eat or drink since our brother's death?"

"That monk from Tyndal Priory left me something." He waved at the door leading to the corridor.

"A kinder deed than many others here would have thought of doing," Raoul muttered and he reached for his pouch. "I shall make sure you are fed, brother. The family must care for its own, not by the good grace of a stranger, monk though he may be."

"Dare I…" Umfrey did not finish his question.

"Trust me? No, but you have little choice unless God mistakes you for a sparrow and drops seed at your feet for nourishment. And you could drink your own piss… As for that, I shall send you a pot." He grasped something in his pouch, then tossed it toward his brother.

Umfrey stepped back in horror and let the item drop at his feet. The thing glittered in the pale light.

"That is a cross to take with you for protection when you must leave the altar to set the pot outside the chapel for the servant to remove." He rubbed his nose.

Umfrey bent down and snatched it up, kissing the object in penance for failing to catch it. Then he stared at the object. Quite large, it was ornately crafted in gold. "Where did you get this?"

"I found it. That is all you need know."

"Then you have let kindness enter your…"

"I have done no such thing, Umfrey. I'd rather like to stay alive myself. If you survive as well, then I am content. But I have a price for my care of you."

"Never will I agree to anything sinful!"

Raoul sneered. "Tell me all you know about our two dead brothers. Did you see or hear anything that could suggest why they died?"

The man shook his head.

"Treasonous plots? Thievery?" He pointed in the general direction of the baron's chambers. "Even patricide?"

Covering his eyes, Umfrey groaned.

"Do you refuse to speak because you were also involved? If you confide in me, I promise to protect you from hanging, even if it means lying to the king's men." He waited a moment. "Since you are frightened enough for your own life, I suspect that you are not their murderer. But I may be wrong. At least your opportunities to kill again are limited if you remain in this chapel." He gestured at the stone wall. "I ask once more. There is something amiss here, and the evil bears a man's face. Confess what you know."

"About murder?" Umfrey squealed the question like a piglet with a pinched tail.

"Surely you do not believe Roger drowned by his own hand or accidentally? That night, he was in my room, drinking wine and bragging about how many women he could swyve before Mass. I do not think he meant mermaids."

"God must have so terrified him with a vision of how he would burn in Hell for those boasts," the brother whispered, "that he threw himself…"

"Your logic is faulty if you conclude he would have set aside his terror of the sea and committed self-murder by swimming too far into the ocean from Lucifer's Cauldron. You believe in God's grace. Would He not want Roger to cleanse his soul first rather than go straight to the Devil's arms without confessing and doing penance? Nay, brother, he was sent to Hell by a mortal hand."

"Then Satan killed him. Otherwise, it was an accident!"

Raoul slammed his fist against the wall. "You have grain for wits, Umfrey. He was terrified of the water, would never go swimming in the sea, and there was no boat found. Besides, who would swim here in the middle of winter? He may have shared your lack of cleverness, but he was not a complete fool."

"Dare you deny the Devil's hand in this? As for Gervase's fall, he was either driven to leap by an evil force or it was truly an accident!" Umfrey's voice rose to an unnaturally high pitch.

"Mother says he acted drunk." Raoul rubbed his chin. "Our beloved brother did love his wine, but he had always hidden his excesses well. He and our priest not only shared a fondness for the grape, they also feared that they never measured up to God's expectations for those who take arduous vows. After a few flacons, they were more at ease with their failings. In sympathy with Gervase, the priest convinced our mother that her son was possessed of both great faith and a frail constitution when his head ached too often." Raoul hesitated. "Maybe he did fall because he was drunk, but I see no reason for him to approach our mother in such a state after so carefully hiding his vice."

"Then the Devil pushed him."

"*Something* pushed him. I am ignorant of how it was done." He fell silent.

Umfrey folded his arms in triumph. For the first time, he smiled with confidence.

"What do you know?"

"Maybe you did something to cause the death. I have heard that he was going to meet with you just before he fell."

"If I did murder him, I must have very long arms. Has anyone claimed that I was present at his death? Or maybe you think our mother or Leonel pushed him?"

Umfrey wilted. "There can be no reason for these deaths other than the presence of the Evil One."

"Very well," Raoul threw his hands up in exasperation. "Besides food, drink, and a pot, is there anything else you need, sweet brother?"

Umfrey slunk back into the shadows. "I long to see my father," he murmured.

Raoul gasped. "Father? If I were facing death, I'd rather choose a whore to distract me from my sorrows."

Hissing, Umfrey stepped forward.

"That was a jest. I will seek out Leonel. Maybe he can plead on your behalf since I have been banned from our sire's chambers."

"Tell our father that I shall kneel and kiss his feet if he will only come here."

Raoul grinned as if eager to mock his elder brother, but instead he turned away and walked to the chapel entrance. As he reached to shut the door, he looked back and peered into the gloom.

Umfrey squatted by the altar and clutched the corners like a drowning sailor might a spar.

He shut the door, then leaned against the stone wall and laughed.

Chapter Thirteen

Lady Margaret's intended feast of hospitality soon became a burdensome thing.

The lute player's string snapped, cutting his finger and ending the diversion. The ballads had been melancholy, but the music did mask the absence of conversation. Only the shuffling of servants' feet, the clunk of platters, and an occasional cough now echoed through the Great Hall.

Sir Leonel offered Eleanor a choice slice of cold rabbit.

After a graceful refusal, she looked away. Her prior attraction to him had been swiftly countered with painful sessions as she implored forgiveness on her knees in a damp chapel. Tonight, when she saw he was seated next to her, she was unhappy. His presence had initially rekindled uncomfortable pleasure before the memory of aching knees ended it. Mild annoyance replaced desire, but she was not certain how long that would last.

Her longing for Brother Thomas was difficult enough, but the monk had shown such virtue in women's company that she doubted any could ever tempt him into bed. She felt safe with him, no matter how wicked her lust. Glancing up at Sir Leonel, she was not as sure about him. She shivered.

"Are you chilled, my lady?"

"A draft," she replied and said no more.

Instead of pursuing conversation, Leonel grew quiet. Reaching out with his boxwood-handled eating knife, he speared a thigh from the platter and concentrated on tearing the meat into small bits on his trencher.

She watched him out of the corner of her eye and was perplexed that he had so quickly chosen to honor her assumed preference for silence, born of habit from priory meals. More likely he has been infected with the settling gloom, she concluded. All others had been this night.

The gathered company was a small one. Although she was surprised that Raoul had not attended this supper, she took no umbrage. He had been wise to avoid it. As for Umfrey, Brother Thomas told her that the current heir was still cowering in the chapel. Eleanor did not think the cold rabbit enough to tempt him forth. As for the baron, she had learned his habits and expected his absence.

Eleanor stifled a yawn. She had little appetite for food, drink, or even company, but courtesy demanded she remain until Lady Margaret rose. Nuns might be excused for additional prayers; prioresses had secular responsibilities. This was one occasion when she regretted that obligation.

Closing her eyes, she recalled Naaman's story, a man healed by Elisha. Although he wished it otherwise, Naaman continued to bow before idols because his king, an honorable man, required his support. She sympathized with his grief over not taking the more righteous path as much as she understood his predicament.

A woman's laugh shattered her reflections. Surprised by the unexpected levity, Eleanor looked up to discover what had amused the Lady Margaret.

Sitting next to the baron's wife was Sir Hugh. When they first took their seats for supper, the prioress noted that her brother had tried to engage the lady in conversation. Margaret responded then with minimal courtesy, but now he had apparently succeeded in lifting her melancholy mood.

Again, the lady laughed.

Few sisters believe their brothers to be captivating, yet Eleanor had been well entertained on the journey by Hugh. He had become a fine teller of tales after his years in Outremer. With so many adventures behind him, he could draw upon countless stories to inspire wonder, delight, and even terror in his listeners. As she studied Margaret's face, however, the prioress feared that Hugh had done more than amuse. There was a new sparkle in the lady's eyes.

Eleanor frowned. Surely Hugh had not meant to seduce the wife of his friend, yet Margaret was responding as if that had been his intent. The lady turned her head to expose the smooth whiteness of her neck. Her face colored a pleasing light pink as she gazed back with half-open eyes at the knight.

This was not the conduct of a virtuous wife. Perhaps the baron's wife had been trying to seduce Hugh? Eleanor wished she had paid more attention to their conversation.

Sir Leonel muttered something under his breath.

Stealing a look at this nephew, she saw him scowl in disapproval at his aunt and her guest. Eleanor knew she must devise a way to warn her brother against continuing on this dangerous path. Cuckolding a friend was always dishonorable. Doing so after the death of a son was unforgivable.

She could think of nothing to do. Frustrated, she reminded herself that Hugh was no callow youth. He was several years older than she and had fathered at least one child. Sister though she was, Eleanor knew he was handsome enough to attract women into his bed and was probably skilled in the arts of both pleasing and rejecting them.

She shut her eyes and sat back in the chair. May he be wise enough not to pursue the seduction of this one, she prayed, then picked up her short eating knife and pretended to find something on her trencher of interest.

Sir Leonel mumbled an apology, rose, and left the hall.

She watched him stride off. Had she not been worried about Hugh's behavior, the prioress might have sighed with relief at the man's departure. Again, she cautiously looked over at her brother and the baron's wife.

This time the lady sat with her eyes modestly lowered. Hugh was talking to the guest on his other side.

Perhaps she had misjudged what was happening between the two. Assuming lack of virtue based on a moment or mere glance was ill-advised. Eleanor gritted her teeth, chided herself for making rash assumptions, and turned her attention to Sister Anne who was on the other side of Sir Leonel's vacant chair.

The sub-infirmarian's head was bent, her eyes half-closed. She coughed.

Seated next to her, Master Gamel looked startled and bent to softly ask a question.

Giving him an equally hushed reply, the nun looked up and, with evident disinterest, studied a group at a lower table.

Had some wizard cast a charm on this place, causing otherwise honorable people to succumb, one after another, to mortal failings? Or was it Satan who was sending his imps with hell-lit torches to enflame lust in them all? Eleanor looked up at the heavy wooden beams across the ceiling as if expecting to see a fork-tailed creature exuding a foul reek. Looking back at Anne, she swiftly made the sign of the cross as her heart began to ache with growing concern.

Although the sub-infirmarian served God honorably, she had confessed to Eleanor how much she missed the comforts of the marriage bed with the man they both now called Brother John. Eleanor knew Anne had not come to the religious life with a profound vocation, but this was the first time she feared that her good friend's obedience to her vows might be sorely tested.

As she looked at the expression on Master Gamel's face, both tender and worried, the prioress suspected the man had touched her friend's heart with his own affection. If so, it was her duty to condemn this, but surely God's compassion would permit her to be gentle about it—unless, of course, the physician had said or done something to compromise Anne's virtue.

Eleanor hoped nothing untoward had happened. When the two healers were introduced, both seemed eager to share information. The nun had always welcomed conversation with those who might teach her more of the healing art. On this journey, the pair had ridden together, often lost in dialogue, but in clear view of everyone in the party. The prioress had not seen anything unseemly in this.

Brother Thomas would know best, she thought. Since he had ridden close by the physician and nun for propriety's sake, he surely would have intervened had he seen or heard anything improper. As another who respected Sister Anne and loved her chastely as a friend, Thomas would never let anything occur that might harm her. Eleanor was equally certain he would have told her in confidence had he felt any doubt.

Stealing another hurried look at Master Gamel, Eleanor now perceived nothing in his expression except a physician's concern. Maybe he feared the nun was ill and would not admit to it. He raised one hand to his mouth, bit a finger, and carefully studied his quiet companion. His eyes glittered with moisture, but the air was heavy with smoke from burning candles.

Eleanor reached for her goblet and sipped the excellent red wine. I had best cleanse my own heart of sin, she decided, before I start accusing anyone else of lust. It may be that the Devil has so filled my soul with unchaste thoughts that I see the fault in all others.

Another burst of laughter exploded in the hushed room.

Eleanor looked up in time to see Lady Margaret rest her hand on Hugh's arm. The baron's wife put her other hand on her breast and let it slip down her body with a caressing gesture.

Hugh sat back, his face flaming red.

That might answer the question of which is seducing the other, Eleanor thought with some relief. Hugh is a frail mortal like us all, she thought, but I am grateful that my brother seems to be resisting the temptation to swyve the baron's wife.

Then Eleanor's anger flashed. How dare Lady Margaret try to deceive her with fine declarations of unyielding virtue? Hadn't this woman proclaimed just yesterday that she had maintained her chastity under the most trying conditions during the baron's absence? Now that her husband was home, she seemed eager to wallow in another man's bed and right after her son had died. This was sin beyond imagination.

Or had grief and the rejection of her husband so weakened her resolve that temptation found her an easy prey? Eleanor shook her head in confusion. There might be more to this strange behavior than wickedness, unless, as she feared, her own sins were coloring her observations.

The prioress searched out Brother Thomas at the table to see if he had also witnessed what was happening between her brother and Lady Margaret. Were he as perplexed as she about the interaction between the pair, she would feel more confidence in her conclusions.

But the monk was lost in thought. The food on his trencher remained untouched. His brow creased, he slowly rocked a wine cup back and forth.

Everyone seems bewitched, Eleanor decided. Mortals might be the usual perpetrators of evil in her experience, but she was uncomfortably aware that this occasion could be the exception. Each of them acted as if enchanted by some strange charm: she with lust for Sir Leonel, the lady for Sir Hugh, and perhaps Master Gamel and Sister Anne for each other. Brother Thomas, whose virtue had always been strong enough to withstand the lure of women, appeared to be in a trance.

Eleanor squeezed her eyes shut, but not before the pressure of a throbbing headache begin to build over her left eye. She pressed her fingers against her brow. Not since she was a child and learned of her mother's death had she felt so vulnerable.

Chapter Fourteen

Lady Margaret stood at the window and cursed herself with more vehemence than God ever could.

No woman had acted more the fool. Cats in heat offered themselves with more dignity than she had done tonight with Sir Hugh. Resting her forehead against the unyielding stone, she wept. The transgression she might have committed was a sin she had not even truly desired. "My most beloved husband, why have you forsaken me?" she murmured. "How did I offend?"

Lifting her head, she looked out on the black night and let the darkness slide into her empty heart. She grasped her breasts. "When these were still sweet to suck and my flesh bore the blush of roses, men begged to lie with me. I rejected their pleas, not even allowing a single kiss. Why? When you rode through the gate, you turned your back on me, refusing to grant even one kind glance. Shall I pay for cleaving to my vows as God required? Was my constancy so great a sin that I must writhe alone in my bed like the Devil's whore?"

A squall of hard rain hit the open window, stinging her face. She laughed.

A servant, passing through the corridor, abruptly halted in alarm. The tray in her hands tilted. Struggling, she righted it before the vessels tumbled to the floor. "My lady, are you ill?"

Spinning around, Margaret pressed her back to the wall and screamed maledictions at the woman.

The maid gripped the tray and ran down the corridor, not stopping until she had reached the safety of a door. Only then did she dare look back, her eyes wide with terror.

Margaret slid to the floor and bent forward, fists pressed into her womb. "I can bear this no longer," she whispered. "My sons are dying. My husband refuses to lend me the comfort of his arms. My loneliness eats into my soul where it rots like a rat's corpse. What grave transgression have I committed to deserve these curses?"

The wind howled in reply.

"When I was young," she whispered to whatever spirit might care to listen, "our union was blessed. I was as fruitful as my lord was virile. Then he left to take the cross. Should I have abandoned my children and taken holy vows myself? Is that my sin?"

She waited for a response but could feel no warmth of God's love in the icy air.

"Am I to be condemned for lust because my womb begins to wither?" She looked up at the unrelenting darkness outside the window, then screamed: "Is it just, my lord, that I must suffer because we grew old apart?"

◇◇◇

At the end of the corridor, two servants peeked around the corner. The wizened maid drew the sign of the cross; the young one shook her head in dismay.

"I see the Devil himself hovering over there. See? Just behind the mistress," the former whispered and pointed toward Lady Margaret. "He'll be riding the mistress tonight in her bed for cert, leaving our master to walk the ramparts alone again."

The young one shuddered.

Hastily, they both scurried away.

Chapter Fifteen

Hugh nodded to the soldier on watch.

The man was eager to talk, but Hugh's spirit begged for silence. With a terse reply, he passed the man by, then grieved that he had not been kinder. Sentry duty on windswept nights was a lonely task, one he understood well. How many nights had he stared into the blackness, fearing a muffled sound was the enemy and wishing it so in equal measure?

Turning around, he shouted encouragement and a jest to the motionless shadow behind him.

The soldier raised his hand and resumed his slow walk along the wall.

The coming storm confirmed Hugh's troubled mood. The wind was wild, the air so cold it nipped painfully at his face. He knew he should not be here on these exposed ramparts; neither could he bear any longer the softer company he had escaped. As the untamed elements lashed him, he doubted that any effort to retain his reason would last. He surrendered to failure. His warm, fur-lined cloak might protect his body from those elements, but his maimed spirit trembled.

He had been foolish to leave Lucas behind, the only person who could pull him out of the whirlpool that often threatened to drown him in memories of blood. But the baron hated the very sight of the man, and, when Hugh received Herbert's message and discerned the man's evident suffering, he had chosen to honor the baron's prejudice over his own need. Tonight, he feared the consequences of that decision and begged God to hold back the madness clawing at his soul.

The brutish wind's high shriek against the stone wall echoed a dying soldier's scream. The waves crashed on the shore below like a trebuchet-flung rock smashing a fortress wall. The world was at war again. He could never quite escape it, even in sleep when the memories of battle rushed back in dreams.

Herbert was right. No one could comprehend this mix of terror, excitement, madness, and triumph except a man who had sliced another in half, then seen the expression as the dying man realized what had been done to him. No one else could understand how it felt, at the end of the battle, to be the one who remained alive, surrounded by the mutilated bodies of other sons of Adam. He was not the only one who had raised his sword and roared, the orgasm of feeling never quite matched by the bedding of any woman.

But with peace came the ghostly horsemen: skeletal, pale, and dotted with clots of gore. They drove away the bloodlust and burned into his soul the images of what he had done to mortals like himself. Now the dead men came to him in dreams or, like tonight, slipped out of shadows on lonely walls. That was one reason he had spoken so abruptly to the soldier: he had briefly mistaken him for a ghost.

He paused and walked over to the crenel in the wall. Staring out into the darkness, he forced himself to remember, as Lucas taught him, that it was the sea crashing against the shore, not some giant engine of destruction, and it was the wind howling, not men dying too slowly of unimaginable wounds. Tonight the effort failed. The fear remained and his stomach knotted. Breaking out in clammy sweat, he bent forward and vomited away from the wind.

As usual, God failed to bring him peace.

Hugh sought a sheltered spot under the watchtower and shivered. Soldiers never spoke of these things. When a man's dreams bled into daylight visions, driving him mad, his comrades called him *possessed*. He remembered when one had been slain by friends as he swung his sword at phantoms. Afterward, the men claimed they had killed the demon, but Hugh suspected their act had been a kindness. He had never seen any soldier recover his reason when he ceased to distinguish between shimmering bright images and the paler world.

Clutching his body to still his shivering, he cursed and willed himself to other thoughts.

He would not become one of the mad.

This was a fine castle, named *Doux et Dur* by those who built it. As he knew from years past, the island on which it stood could be sweet in the summer season. Seabirds inhabited the cliffs, some singing like an angel's choir, while others, the puffins in particular, laughed with the merriment of a king's fool. The earth bedecked itself with flowers, their colors flashing in the sunlight as they swayed in gentle breezes. On Hugh's earliest visit here, a spindly-legged boy with spotted cheeks, he had lain with a servant girl in a bed of tender grass and soft petals. She had been his first.

Although he could not recall her name, and he had not seen her on this visit, he held that memory of their coupling in his heart, a tender corner that he kept protectively enclosed, sometimes even from himself. Perhaps she had died of some fever, but he hoped she had married a youth with a sweet smile, one who loved her more than himself.

He backed up to the stones of the watchtower and pressed his head against the rough wet rock.

Yet this place was still a fortress, its stones hard and unyielding, and cast a long shadow on the mainland that only dared touch this island with one bony finger of earth. The man who was now his king argued that it was not unassailable, although Hugh said otherwise. In the end, Hugh had conceded the debate to Lord Edward.

Hugh's lips turned into a thin smile. Had Edward known that Hugh deliberately lost the argument by twisting his logic into an untenable position? With this king, few ever knew what passed through his mind, including his friends.

"Have the night demons shattered your sleep, Hugh?"

Reaching for his knife, the knight spun around but quickly realized that the shadow bore the hooded shape of Baron Herbert.

He released his weapon back into the sheath.

The baron chuckled, wandered a short distance away, and leaned against the tower wall.

Hugh remained silent.

"Or was sleep banished in favor of time spent swinking my wife?"

"You have no cause to so foully besmirch your wife's honor, my lord." Hugh knew he hesitated an instant too long.

"Do I not?" The man rubbed his hand against the stones, then stared at his palm.

"If any man claims she is aught but virtuous, he lies."

Herbert sighed. "You have never shown skill in the art of deception, Hugh. I learned what happened at supper. Dare you deny your sin when God sees everything we do?"

Hugh's mouth became too dry for swift response.

The baron waited, then laughed with brittle merriment. "There were once five vigorous sons to prove how hard I rode her before I took the cross. Ah, but she was a fine lass to handle in those days, spirited and eager." The last words were almost lost in the rising gale.

"No honest man will claim that the Lady Margaret has done other than honor her vows to you at the church door and in God's hearing."

The baron spun around, the hood hiding both his face and expression. "She laid her hand in your crotch. Is that what you call honoring vows? If so, then you speak of the Devil's virtue."

Hugh grasped his knife, lifting it slowly from the sheath until the hilt was clearly visible. "On this, as it stands for the cross we bore in Outremer, and on the sacred vows we took, I swear that I did not touch the Lady Margaret, nor did she touch me, in any sinful way."

"Leonel came to me from the supper, and, when I asked how our guests fared, he let slip a hint of my wife's behavior. I pressed him for details." Blunted by the wind, the baron's voice was hoarse.

Hugh's heart pounded. Although the lady had not fondled him as the baron claimed, nor had he himself attempted any hidden pleasuring, they had excited each other with imagined joys by looks and smiles. Closing his eyes, he recalled how her nipples had pressed against the cloth of her gown. He felt himself stiffen with remembered lust. "He could not have seen what he claimed from where he sat," Hugh replied, willing his body to a softer virtue.

"You call Leonel a liar?"

"Never, but I believe that he misinterpreted some innocent gesture. As you have lost a son, your lady has also suffered from that death. I sought to amuse her with stories of my travels home and did succeed, for a moment, in lightening her spirit. Once, she tapped my arm and smiled when I told of an especially merry adventure. There was no wickedness in that."

Herbert said nothing and turned again to look out across the wall and into the darkness.

"Leonel has always been your most loyal liegeman, my lord. He was right to tell you of his concern even if he mistook the intent."

"I should know you too well to fear that you would put horns on my head, Hugh, and grieve that I have even grown distrustful of my proven friends. As for my wife…" His voice broke. "I pity her. In the name of God's mercy, she has not deserved…" With that, he fell silent.

Shame enveloped Hugh like fire. Leonel may have been wrong in what he reported, but he had not erred in other respects. Hugh had been Herbert's comrade in arms, his friend, and yet tonight he had shamelessly wooed his wife. He may not have made the baron a cuckold, but he had reached for the horns.

As for his treatment of the Lady Margaret, he had committed sin enough, walking away from her without speaking as if she had been a whore he had paid to give him a frisson of pleasure. Now he saw the depth of his self-deception and dishonor. He had lusted after the baron's wife, beguiling her until her frail woman's nature might have weakened enough to join him in bed. His sole virtue in this disgraceful evening? He had not actually coupled with her.

"Hugh?" Herbert's rough voice spoke of tears and grief.

"My lord?"

"Ready the priest and physician you brought as I begged you to do. Before the next Office, I shall send Leonel to bring the three of you to my chambers."

Chapter Sixteen

The light vanished.

Curious, Thomas turned to the soldier beside him. "Did you just see anything in the cove?"

"Demons," the man said. "I've seen them down there before tonight." He made the sign of the cross, hesitated, then quickly repeated the gesture.

As Thomas left the narrow watchtower window, he was unsure himself about the exact nature of what he had seen. He reached for the pitcher of wine he had brought as a gift and looked back to ask if the soldier wanted more as well.

The man, grinning sheepishly, was right by his elbow.

The monk filled their cups.

"So you saw the fires too. At least you believe me, Brother?" Keeping an eye on Thomas, the man raised his cup with two hands and gulped a mouthful.

Nodding, the monk took time to drink before he asked, "When did you first see the lights?"

The soldier scowled with such concentration that he might have been trying to decipher the mystery of Latin script. "Not long after the baron came back from Outremer. I'm sure of that, but as to day or time I cannot say. I'm on watch most nights, usually after supper. At first, I thought the Devil had created some phantasm to jest with me, so I stopped the next time to shake a fist at him for his mockery. The fires didn't disappear, and I began to think they were no imagining. I watched, like you did just now, and had no doubt about what I saw. You think they're demons with hellfire torches, dancing on the beach?"

Walking back to the window, Thomas looked out toward the cove. No more lights relieved the darkness, but he was sure he had seen something. "Did you tell anyone?"

"Oh, aye! My sergeant. What if he had awakened to find some soldier in the service of…" He waved his hand. "…the French king, Phillip the Bold, grinning over him, and I had said nothing about lights in the cove? He'd have had my guts for sausage."

Although he knew the seriousness of such a danger, the monk was also amused by the soldier's image. "The invader would have cut your sergeant's throat before he had time to punish you."

The man pointed his cup toward the stairwell. "You don't know my sergeant. A minor inconvenience, a slit throat. He'd have tucked his head under one arm and used the other to lash my butt with the flat of his sword."

"Now that's a dutiful servant any liege lord would wish!" Thomas laughed. "What did he do when he heard your report?"

"Took several of us down to the cove to search for the cause."

The wind lulled momentarily. Voices rose from below the tower window. Curious about who might also be on the wall tonight, Thomas leaned into the window to peer down into the night.

There must be at least two men just below him, but the thickness of the wall around his window prevented Thomas from seeing any just beneath him. From his voice, the monk suspected the hidden man was his prioress' brother. The other he did not know. Had they seen anything in the cove?

Sliding back from the window, he turned again to the soldier. "What did you find?"

"Nothing. It must be as I said: Satan's imps."

"If you found no torches, footprints, horse dung…" Thomas touched each finger as he pretended to consider the possibilities aloud. He did not want to insult the man, but he feared the investigation might not have been thorough. Just how seriously would this unknown sergeant have taken the word of a man, cold and lonely, who might be prone to imaginings as he paced a deserted wall?

"There had been a high tide, but the Devil is too clever to leave any evidence if he wishes to keep his antics secret. He doesn't need a tide to wash it all away."

Thomas grinned in concurrence as he nodded at the soldier. The man was not as naïf as he had feared. "So your sergeant decided there was nothing amiss?"

"Aye and told me plain enough that I shouldn't drink all the ale between watches." He snorted. "Like any man, I'll not turn away a warming cup, but anyone can speak to my lass about how much I drink. Never take too much that I can't please her in bed." He flushed.

"Well, we both saw the lights tonight," Thomas replied and lifted his cup. "We'd only drunk this one to fend off the chill." He finished the drink. "Did any of the others on watch see these fires?"

A disgusted look crossed the man's face. "One might have done, or else he feigned it. He said a thing or two on the way down to the beach, suggesting he expected to share in any praise. After I was rebuked, he changed his mind and mocked me like the rest."

Thomas shook his head in sympathy.

"Might this man admit to seeing anything if I talked with him?"

The soldier spat his contempt. "I cannot be sure he was a witness to anything. He's fast enough with an open palm if coin's offered, but I won't vouch for his honest telling once paid."

That conclusion Thomas had already reached, but now he wondered about those two men on the wall tonight. If one of them was Sir Hugh, the monk knew he could not approach him and ask questions about what he might have witnessed in the cove. Not only was the knight's animosity a factor, there was another reason the monk hesitated.

A castle wall on any winter night was a cold place for both a casual meeting and companionable talk. Thomas himself had paced the walls, meeting only this soldier on watch, and they had retreated to the tower for conversation. What if Hugh had reason not to want any witness to his meeting with this unknown man?

He decided to avoid his prioress' brother entirely. Somehow he must find a way to acquire any information through her. Surely there was a way to phrase his request and avoid revealing that he had witnessed any meeting between Hugh and another man.

Nothing was coming to mind. He turned around to ask the soldier a question.

The man was very quietly pouring more wine into his cup.

"Is that where Roger, the baron's son, drowned?" Thomas asked, looking back at the window and gesturing toward the cove as if he had not seen the act.

"Aye."

When Thomas looked over his shoulder, the soldier gestured politely at the pitcher. The monk courteously refused, suggesting the man drink instead. "If those lights were demons, they might have killed him," the monk said, not believing that such had been the case but hoping to elicit an interesting response.

The man's face grew noticeably pale.

And that was an intriguing reaction, Thomas thought, and decided to pursue this line of questioning to see where it might lead. "You have nothing to fear from me. I am only a guest here and not known to the baron. Whatever you tell me will never be traced back to you. I swear it."

This time the soldier did not wait for an invitation and poured himself more wine. "I confess I did not like the son much." He shrugged. "He followed after my lass and once pushed her against the wall."

Thomas saw the remembered hot anger surging through the man's cheeks.

"She jabbed him with her knee though." Then he grinned. "Said he didn't have much between the legs, yet he did howl as if he did and never troubled her again."

"He was the baron's third son?"

"Aye. Gervase, the one just buried, was the second. He became heir after the first died of a fever."

The man did love a story, but, on the hope he might learn something pertinent that he did not know enough to ask, Thomas opted for the wiser course of letting the soldier talk for a while.

"He'd been promised to the Church, and had professed a liking for the religious life. Still he seemed to have taken to the change in vocation well enough, or at least he didn't speak ill of it. He drank a lot though. Would have made a merry enough priest, like our old one. That seemed his only vice and probably why he and our priest got along so well."

"Celibacy was not his problem unlike the one who drowned?"

"Gervase liked to keep the wine close and women at a distance. But that third-born? He was the opposite in his vices. Women were his drink of choice, not that he didn't like a cup or two. When he inherited the religious vocation, no one thought he'd be easy with celibacy. There were so many of his by-blows around that several prayed that God would geld him. None here grieved when he died, except his parents."

"Then he had many enemies who might have killed him."

"He did have enough of them amongst fathers, brothers, and at least one husband." The soldier thought for a moment. "But I doubt any would have murdered him." He straightened and tucked in his chin. "Had he managed to swink my lass, I'd have thought about it, for cert. Never would have done anything though, and not because I'd be afraid of hanging either. My soul would have flown straight to God's hands on the grateful prayers of everyone here. Still, I'd not want to bring pain to the baron's wife, nor would anyone else. She's earned our love with her kindness during her husband's absence."

Thomas thought for a moment. "Not a single man? Some stranger, perhaps, or an infrequent merchant?"

"For all the man's failings, he was strong, built like his father. He'd have squashed most men's heads like a handful of sand."

"A difficult man to drown then?"

"I'd say! It would have taken more than one plus careful planning. Besides, he hated the sea. When he was a wee lad, he fell out of a boat. Would have died if his cousin hadn't saved him. So he believed the sea was the Devil's creation and never would go too near it again. Nay, Brother, you'd best look for demons in this death."

"Where was he found?"

"In the cove. He went missing one night, although that was common practice if he had some woman. The next day someone saw a body on the beach. When we went down to investigate, we recognized him. No one could discern what had happened. There was no boat, although he'd never have set foot in one."

This was a strange story indeed, Thomas thought. "No evidence that he might have been killed by a blow, for example, and not by drowning?"

"Sir Leonel was with us. He asked the same question and examined the body but found no strange wound. The corpse was battered. He thought that was from the rocks. We all assumed drowning."

"Had any woman gone with him that night?"

"None of ours. As for the servants of any guests, the baron has welcomed no one until Sir Hugh and his party arrived."

The monk grunted. He was at a loss for any more questions.

"Maybe he saw the lights too and was lured down by the Devil. That's what I believe. Then the riptide might have caught him, pulled him out to the island rocks, and Satan spat him back on the beach." He looked longingly at the pitcher.

Thomas walked over to the table and poured what remained into the man's cup. Although it was clear that something villainous was happening, his logic could not discover the root of it. If only they had come here sooner, the bodies of at least one of the two sons might have been examined by Master Gamel or Sister Anne. Now all evidence was lost to them, buried in the earth blessed by God.

"Imps," he muttered, watching the man swallow the last of the wine. That was as good an explanation as any for the moment and might even be true. He shuddered.

"I had best be back on watch, Brother." He looked up at Thomas, his eyes just unfocused enough to suggest the wine might keep him quite warm on this next round of the wall. "Your gift of wine was charitable." His smile was lopsided, but honest gratitude shone through.

Thomas promised to return soon with another pitcher, then let the soldier descend the stairs ahead of him. Before following, he looked out the window one more time but saw nothing of note.

Now he felt obliged to tell his prioress what he had learned, but, before he did, Thomas had one more thing he wished to do.

Hunched down in the shadows near the next watchtower, a hooded man wrapped his thick cloak tighter around him and waited. When Baron Herbert and Sir Hugh left the windbreak of the other tower for the bailey stairs, he stood, looked around, and scuttled along the wall, taking care to remain in deep shadow.

Just as he reached the place near where the two men had met, he heard a sound above and drew back against the wall. Looking up at the watchtower, he saw someone lean out of the window. Although he could not identify the man in the darkness, he concluded it was the usual sentry, taking more time than usual with his ale on a cold night. He waited until the man retreated, then walked to the fortress wall and slipped far enough into the crenel to look down with safety into the cove.

Raoul wondered if either his father or Sir Hugh had seen the lights, but, from what he had overheard, he doubted it. They were too concerned over the state of his mother's virtue. He snorted with contempt.

Perhaps that was just as well, he thought. He knew the incident had been investigated once. The cause was determined to be a drunken soldier's imagination, although he was surprised that his father had thought no more on it.

As for tonight, Raoul decided that his father and the knight would have dismissed the sight if they had noticed it. The lights had been only briefly visible and had not reappeared. Even he could have concluded they were nothing more than the moon shimmering on the water before a storm cloud quickly cast a veil over it.

He hesitated long enough to make sure the men could not look back and see that he was following them down the same stairway into the bailey. Still amused at their foolishness over his mother, he grinned. His father must soon acknowledge that he, the despised youngest son, was a man worthy of respect.

Then he disappeared once again into the shadows and down the bailey stairs.

Chapter Seventeen

The chapel's darkness weighed down on Umfrey like cold ash.

He squirmed in distress.

As his brother and the monk from Tyndal had promised, a servant brought him both food and drink. He had eagerly devoured and imbibed but now regretted such lack of restraint. The chamber pot was full, and he needed to piss.

Cursing the sinful weakness of his aching bladder, he remembered Raoul's mockery and touched the large gifted cross he now wore. He would have to leave the altar since he dared not defile this sacred place again. "Protect me," he whispered, fondling the cross.

Then he pulled himself to his feet, scurried away from his sanctuary, and out the chapel door. As he splashed urine against the far outside wall of the corridor, his relief was immense, but terror returned with greater force. Not even pausing to secure his braies, he clutched at them and shuffled back through the door toward the altar.

A tall shadow stood between him and comforting asylum.

Umfrey whimpered.

The shadow stepped aside and gestured for him to come forward.

"Who are you?" Umfrey fumbled with the ties on his braies and willed his bowels not to betray his fear.

"You asked to see your father, lad." The hoarse whisper cut the silence like a dull saw on wood.

His teeth began to chatter, all words sliced to bits before he could utter them.

"What reason do you have to fear? Come closer."

Umfrey took two steps and stopped.

"Why did you summon your father if you have nothing to say?"

"I don't want to die!" Tears began to flow down his cheeks.

The shadow said nothing.

"There is evil in this place." Umfrey's tone was beseeching as he gestured to the creature. Was it man or spirit, he wondered. "What have any of us ever done to deserve assassination? We have always been loyal sons. In your absence, we protected and served our mother as you commanded us to do. We did nothing to dishonor you and greeted your return with joy. What have we done to displease either you or God?"

"Nothing."

Rubbing at his nose, Umfrey peered into the darkness. His legs shook so that he feared he might collapse. "Then why?"

The shadow spread his arms. "Be comforted in my embrace!"

The son hesitated, then uttered the sob of a small boy seeking a parent's soothing, and rushed forward.

But the hug he received had a sharp sting. His eyes widened in horror as the knife pierced his chest and grated against his ribs. Without a sound, Umfrey slid to the floor, his body bending as if praying to the altar that now failed to grant him refuge.

"Indeed, none of you committed any sin at all," the shadow muttered, "except for that of living." Then he quickly placed Umfrey's limp hand around the knife and left the chapel as silently as he had arrived.

Chapter Eighteen

Thomas looked around the simple room that had once been home to the dead priest.

There had been no cause to search here before. Even now he wondered if he should bother, but the priest had probably been murdered. Although the monk had much to report to Prioress Eleanor, he would not do so until he investigated all he could without further direction.

Running his fingers along the wall, he walked quickly around the room.

The quarters were tiny, the only luxury being nearness to the family chapel. The furnishings were plain. There was a small bed, hard enough for any man of God, and a crudely made chest. On the wall a badly carved cross was hung. That was askew.

Thomas straightened it.

He knelt on the floor and examined the stones. None were loose. Sitting back on his heels, he looked carefully at the wall but saw nothing within reach that suggested a hiding place. To make sure, he walked around a few more times, studying the stones and touching a few suspicious ones. All was as it ought to be: solid, austere, and proper for a priest whose concerns should not have included earthly comforts.

"Except this one did not lack interest in a worldly pleasure or two," Thomas muttered. Where, for instance, had the man kept his supply of wine?

Briefly he poked at the mattress, finding no odd shapes or lumps. Not that he had expected to find a wineskin there, but he felt better having made sure.

Sighing, he leaned against the wall, shut his eyes to exile all assumptions from his mind, and then studied the room anew.

Near the door and against the wall sat that wooden chest. He stared at it with forced interest.

When he first arrived, he rejected the object instantly as possible storage when he saw that the corners were gnawed. Knowing that he did not want to provide castle mice with fresh nesting material, he had hung his few possessions on a peg high in the wall. He had never looked inside, having no curiosity about what might have moved into it after the priest's death.

Now he walked over to the chest and gripped the lid. There was no lock, and the hinges were red with rust. As he raised the top and gazed at the interior, one fragile hinge disintegrated into gritty fragments.

There was little enough to see, and nothing to spark curiosity. In the center lay a robe, threadbare and carelessly folded. A large, chipped pottery jug sat in one corner. Although a stranger might have puzzled over that, Thomas believed its purpose was to store ale or any wine the priest could get. An equally battered cup lay tilted against the side.

At least the priest took the time to pour his drink into a cup instead of gulping it straight from the pitcher. There is a sad dignity in that, Thomas thought.

He straightened. None of this was informative, nor were the wood dust and mouse droppings. The man may have been too fond of drink, but he seemed to have honored his vow of poverty.

Thomas started to lower the lid but, on a whim, reached down instead and picked up the discarded robe, shaking it open. Amidst a flurry of dark lumps and bits, something fell to the floor. Dropping the robe, he retrieved it.

His first impression was that the item was a pilgrimage badge. Then he saw it was made of wax and concluded it was more likely to be a seal. "Yet it is attached to nothing," he said, perplexed.

Looking into the chest again, he found no parchment, or fragments of same, and turned back to study the image in his hand.

The figure was faint yet clear enough to be that of a seated man in a bishop's miter, giving a blessing. Below him was a figure, perhaps a monk, hunched in the attitude of profound reverence. What struck Thomas most were the clappers in one of the bishop's hands.

He frowned. "Saint Lazarus?"

This saint was the man raised from the dead by Jesus. Legend held that Lazarus of Bethany and his sisters, Mary and Martha, later fled to southern France where he became a bishop in Marseilles. Although the poor and sick often prayed to him, the most frequent supplications for relief came from lepers.

Where had this seal come from, and why keep it? The old priest had so few possessions. Shaking his head, Thomas assumed that the seal must have had especial meaning for the man. Perhaps a brother or another beloved kinsman had suffered from leprosy.

In England, there was a religious order, founded in Jerusalem, called the Order of St. Lazarus. Many referred to the members as the leper knights. If the priest were of high enough birth, someone in his family might have begged entry after discovering he had the tragic affliction.

"When the reply came," Thomas murmured, "the priest must have kept this seal in remembrance." How sadly anonymous this man and his life had become, the monk thought. Men spoke of his fondness for drink, not the sorrows he suffered.

He picked up the discarded robe, folded it, and returned it to the chest. As he started to tuck the seal back into the garment, he glanced at the floor.

The odd lumps of dark material intrigued him. He picked one up. It was not wood, most certainly not mouse droppings, and it had a faint peppery scent. He reached down for more.

Some of the bits crumbled into his hand. He sniffed again. Slightly sweet as well as peppery, he thought. Were he to guess, he'd conclude it was a strange vegetable or herb. The kind was unclear.

Suddenly he stiffened, thinking he had heard something. Were those muffled voices in the chapel?

Although Umfrey did move about, his footsteps were silenced by the thick walls. Thomas now realized he could have heard a door open just as he began to search this room. He had ignored the sound then. After all, the chapel belonged to the family, and someone might have come to comfort the terrified son.

A chill swept through him. Stuffing the lumps and seal into his pouch, he raced out the door and immediately collided with a large servant passing by in the corridor.

"Quickly!" he said, pointing to the chapel entrance behind the man. The servant froze and stared at him with utter lack of understanding.

A hooded figure emerged from the chapel.

Thomas called out, but the unidentifiable being rushed away without speaking.

The monk hesitated, longing to give chase, but the immobile lump of a servant blocked his way.

Fear for the well-being of the baron's heir gave him strength, and Thomas grabbed the servant by the arm. Dragging the man toward the chapel, the monk dreaded what he might find inside.

He pushed open the door.

"Umfrey?"

No one replied.

On the floor near the altar was a huddled shadow.

Thomas rushed in and fell to his knees beside the figure.

Herbert's son was bent double, his hands clutching at his chest.

Thomas grasped the son's shoulder. The body fell over, and the monk realized that his own hand was now wet and sticky. "May God have mercy on your soul!"

The servant screamed and ran from the chapel.

Tenderly, the monk eased Umfrey onto his back. A pool of blood was on the floor. A knife lay near the heir's hand.

Thomas looked back toward the chapel door. If he had not seen the unknown creature leave, he would have concluded that Umfrey had killed himself. Now the monk was certain this was murder.

Gently holding the man's head, he started to whisper absolution into the dead man's ear.

A light fluttering of warm air caressed his hand. "Is it possible?" Thomas whispered.

Putting his hand on Umfrey's chest, he confirmed his rising hope. The son still breathed.

"If You are merciful," he cried out, "I will not have to tell this family that one more son has died."

Tearing cloth from Umfrey's garments, Thomas pressed a handful into the bleeding wound and tightly bound the padding against the gash with the man's belt.

Then he leapt to his feet and ran for help.

Chapter Nineteen

Prioress Eleanor followed the servant through the narrow passageways of the castle keep. Perhaps the sea breeze cooled this place in summer, she thought, but the wind from the winter sea, howling through the windows, pierced her to the very bone this night. She ached so painfully from the cold that she longed for the moment when it numbed her.

With the unexplained deaths of the baron's sons, there had been much talk of Satan residing here, but now she doubted it. The Prince of Darkness might be foul; he was not witless. Preferring heat, he resided near Hell's flames and would therefore eschew this place, leaving the castle to those disgraced imps he had banished to realms of eternal ice. Would she ever be warm again?

The servant stopped at a wooden door and knocked.

A voice from within gave permission to enter.

Opening the door, the servant bowed and gestured for Eleanor to proceed inside.

The chambers were brightened by flickering candles impaled on two tall iron candlesticks which rested on minutely detailed lion's feet. A raging fireplace provided heat. Despite the chill she suffered, the intensity of the dancing fire struck the prioress with uncomfortable strength. She turned away and sought her hostess.

The remaining shadows struggled against the light and teased cruelly with the gaunt face of the woman sitting in a deeply carved chair.

"You are kind to see me." Margaret's words were devoid of warmth.

"I was told your plea was urgent." Eleanor replied with gentleness, hoping to soften the wife's clearly troubled spirit.

"Come closer to me. I would speak in confidence."

Eleanor walked to the lady's side. Some might say those words were haughty, she thought, but she heard profound suffering hidden within the command.

Lady Margaret began to weep. The jagged sound of her sobs confirmed she was a woman unaccustomed to emotion breaking through her resolve. "I have sinned most grievously." She spat out the words.

Eleanor took the lady's hand and cradled it gently in her own. "You are not alone in this. Be comforted, for God brings solace to those who wish it."

The woman showed no sign of being soothed, yet neither did she flinch from the soft touch. Her unblinking eyes stared at the prioress.

For a moment, Eleanor wondered if she was looking into two black holes leading to Hell.

"I long to die."

"Why?" Although she ought now to call for Brother Thomas, and urge the lady to seek penance for such a desire, Eleanor had learned from the anchoress at Tyndal that a woman's hardest confessions often flowed more easily into repentance when she could speak first to another daughter of Eve.

"Look at me! I am a woman beset with lust, unfaithful in spirit to her husband, and the lowest of all God's creation. This wickedness must be why God is slaying the sons of my womb!" Tearing her hand away, she pressed both palms against her eyes and wailed.

Eleanor saw a servant hovering near the fireplace. It was not the lady's usual maid. "Leave us," she commanded. The despair of their mistress should not become the subject of gossip.

As soon as the girl slipped away and had shut the door, the prioress found the pitcher of wine and poured a small measure into a cup. Returning to the baron's wife, Eleanor lightly touched the woman's arm. "Drink," she said, leaving no doubt she expected obedience.

Lady Margaret's face reddened, and then she nodded. With a swift gesture she brushed the moisture from her cheeks and took the proffered drink, sipping at it until the mazer was empty.

Eleanor refilled it and handed the cup back. "We all suffer lust. It is one of several curses with which God burdened the first woman. Yet you told me earlier that you came to your husband a virgin and did refuse all temptations while he was gone. Did you speak the truth?"

Margaret looked away. "I'll not deny temptation, but I fled from it. Now that my lord is home, I have lost all strength to resist." She glanced back at the prioress. "I saw your expression at supper. You recognized my wickedness, and I do confess that I longed to lure Sir Hugh into my bed."

"Did my brother join you there for sport?"

"He is more virtuous than I."

Eleanor said nothing. Many proclaimed that a woman so lacking in virtue must be denied all sympathy. God forgave, however, and so would she. As for her brother, men were often called the victims of woman's rampant lust. It was conventional wisdom she had cause to doubt, and she hoped he had been kind in his refusal. The shame Lady Margaret suffered from such public longing was humiliation enough without a man treating her like a common whore.

As for her own right to condemn, Eleanor owned none. She herself had itched with lust for Sir Leonel and had coupled often enough with incubi disguised as Brother Thomas in her dreams.

"My brother is not a saint," she said, "and may well have been tempted, but your virtue is renowned and he would have assumed that tonight was God's test of his own. Being a soldier, not a poet, he cannot transform lust into verse, praising your beauty like Solomon did. His only recourse is to turn his back and walk away. Knowing my brother, he would choose to suffer rather than insult your honor by approaching your chambers. He was well aware that your door would have been barred to him had he tried."

Margaret hid her reaction by drinking more wine.

"There is another matter at issue here. You said your husband has refused to honor his responsibility to the marriage bed. Even though the Church might long for us all to remain celibate, it recognizes that it is better to marry when we are incapable of choosing the higher virtue. Thus it is the obligation of both husband and wife to embrace each other in mutual satisfaction. His failure to honor this obligation encourages sin." She raised a questioning eyebrow. "Might he have decided to take vows?"

Margaret shook her head. "He has not said so." Her lips twisted into a sour smile. "That means nothing for he has refused to speak to me since his return."

"Even so, if entrance into a monastic life was his wish, he would surely have sent a message informing you of those intentions." At least he should have done so if he felt any affection or a scrap of kindness toward his wife. Eleanor tried not to betray her disapproval of the baron, but Brother John, a man of unquestioned faith, had wept bitterly over the pain he was inflicting when he told his wife of his longing for the cloister. "Was your marriage a happy one in the past?"

"Before my lord took the cross, it was." Margaret's eyes became unfocused with wistful memory. "We found deep joy in each other and were blessed with many sons…" She began again to weep, but these sobs were muted.

"How long was Baron Herbert gone?" Eleanor asked the question as much out of mercy as curiosity.

"He left England before King Edward and set sail from Outremer in advance of our lord's return. He did not travel directly home. He first stopped in Solerno, and then Rome before going to Paris."

An interesting journey, Eleanor thought. The stop in Rome was understandable for anyone of Christian faith. Solerno was a more curious choice. Paris suggested troubling reasons of a more secular nature.

As for the stay in Solerno, the renowned medical school was a likely cause. The possibility that he had become impotent did occur to her, but surely the excellent physicians there would have told him whether or not his condition was hopeless. He would not have needed to seek medical advice elsewhere, especially in Paris. Since Baron Herbert had not shared a bed with the Lady Margaret since his return, however, there was no reason to ask her if he was still virile.

After Rome and Solerno, he could have sailed from Italy, a much faster route to England. If he did not need the services of doctors in Paris, there was one other reason men went there. That was to sell their loyalty to the French king.

Yet the baron had made no attempt to hide his visit. This fact boded well, leading the prioress to doubt he had any intent that reeked of treachery. The many relics available in Parisian churches suggested he was probably satisfying a vow made during his sojourn in Outremer.

All considered, nothing about the baron's journey home explained why he had banished both wife and sons from his favor. Eleanor was left with the same obvious conclusion with which she had started: Baron Herbert had an unknown reason for delaying his return for as long as possible.

"My brother also traveled by land rather than sailing," she said at last. "Our family may have regretted the choice, but he had many adventures as a result. Our patience has been rewarded with his fine tales."

"You are fortunate. When my lord arrived at our gates, he counted the number of sons awaiting him, then turned his back on us all with no explanation. He lives apart, and although we have begged audience with him, he always refuses. Any messages are sent through Sir Leonel." She looked away. "That is a harsh task to demand of the young man. Yet he balances his duty to my husband with respect and compassion toward us."

"Sir Leonel seems a worthy man. I have heard that he fought valiantly at your husband's side. Was he not knighted for his valor?"

Margaret nodded. "My husband was rightfully proud when King Edward chose to honor our family by including our nephew in the ceremony." She sighed. "I fear my lord has found his nephew to be a better son than those I gave him."

"If he found fault with any, surely it was because most were unformed boys when he left. With such a noble sire, they must have grown into worthier men."

"Before he left for Outremer, he called them all sniveling creatures because not one showed any longing to wield a sword." The lady's laugh was sharp. "Only our eldest, the heir who died of a fever before my husband's return, inspired any praise and that was faint enough. My husband said of him that he might wield accounting rolls well enough, but they would be soft swords were this castle attacked."

A hard man, Eleanor thought. Although her own father was an experienced and skilled warrior, Baron Adam never condemned his youngest son who had always preferred farming to battle. His only other son, however, had proven his mettle in war.

Unlike her father, this baron had not known most of his sons as men, first because of his absence in the cause of capturing Jerusalem for Christian sovereignty and next because of his inexplicable delay in returning. His knowledge of them remained that of babes clinging to their mother's robe. Did he fail to understand that boys eventually matured?

"I had hoped that Raoul at least might find favor with his father when he came home. He has grown into a man who reminds me much of my husband when I first knew him."

Eleanor raised an eyebrow at this unexpected remark. "How so?"

"Our youngest keeps his own counsel, then acts with swift, firm purpose. Although his demeanor is stern, this mother knows he owns a loving heart. I fear he mocks what he should not, but his father's faith deepened only after God had proven His favor with so many sons."

An interesting assessment, the prioress thought, and quite different from my brother's. This Raoul was no sniveling creature, yet the lady's opinion was softened with a mother's vision.

Margaret frowned. "It is a pity that Umfrey is now my husband's heir. He has no love for swords and is best suited to a place in the Church. With only two sons left, and Umfrey ill-suited to the task, Raoul may have to remain here, providing his brother with the strong arm and wily spirit needed to survive in this sinful world. That grieves me. We had wished to give one son to God's service."

"What of Sir Leonel? Will he remain with this family that raised him?"

"Unless he finds a place amongst the king's men, he has few choices. Leonel's father, my lord's only brother, gambled inordinately, and my husband was forced to sell Leonel's lands to pay the sire's debts. Truth be told, my husband sold some of his own patrimony as well to save the family honor. Since this meant there was less to give to the Church, the call to take the cross won my husband's heart more firmly. If he could not buy fine plate for God's altar, he knew he should give his soul to the cause in Outremer."

"Your husband is a worthy man, generous to both kin and God."

Margaret turned her face away.

Eleanor suspected the lady had disagreed with both the baron's choices but also concluded that the opposition was never given voice. If she did not speak of this to the baron, she would never admit it to any stranger.

"As for the future," Margaret said, "Umfrey will find some work for his cousin to perform here, after my husband's death, unless my lord begs the king for a small favor. Although Leonel did bring wealth back from Outremer, it was too little to buy enough good land to support the needs of a knight of his rank."

Eleanor was reminded of a young man she met last summer whose father lost all by supporting Simon de Montfort. It is difficult, she recalled, to be sired by a father of noble birth, then be left nothing with which to provide a suitable living. Leonel had shown only grace, from what she had heard, but he must still suffer from the loss of his estate.

"Perhaps the king will grant him more than a simple living," the prioress said. "Unlike his father, your nephew has behaved with honor and showed bravery in God's cause."

"For the time being, he shows no inclination to leave my husband's side, nor, it seems, does my lord wish him to do so. Perhaps this is selfish of me: I do not long for the day when he must depart. The young knight lightens our cruel sorrow under the weight of my husband's silence."

Eleanor asked herself what else she could say to comfort this woman. Although there must be a reason why the baron had chosen to act as he had, she saw no cause. Nor did the Lady Margaret seem to know more than anyone else.

Unless the wife was hiding something, this treatment of Herbert's sons was unwarranted and illogical. Although the baron might have held his young, unformed sons in contempt before he left, most fathers would be willing, even eager to see how they had grown into men after such a long absence.

Was Baron Herbert so rigid in his expectations that he refused to grant them a chance to prove themselves? Had he learned something troubling about them, of which even his wife had no knowledge? Or had something else happened in Outremer to make him this unbending in his contempt? Hugh might know, but Eleanor doubted it. He had seemed as perplexed as she about what was happening here.

There was only one thing she might say, based on conclusions made after seeing her own brother so changed on his return, as well as other crusaders who had come to Tyndal Priory for healing. Her words might bring little comfort, but they could result in patience.

"From all you have said," the prioress said, "your husband has changed greatly during those many years of your separation. I have witnessed the same in my brother, although I saw him little enough after our mother's death. Greeting him when he returned from Outremer, I felt as if I were seeing his face in a mist. The image was recognizable, yet not as clear as it had been. Although I delight in my beloved brother, he has become a stranger in small ways. In the midst of conversation, for instance, he may fall silent and walk away as if he forgets that I am in his company."

Margaret tilted her head, listened, but said nothing.

"War is a man's lot. They grow up with it, learn the skills to survive, and then do battle. I overheard my father once say to a friend, that no one could understand what war was like except another man who had also fought."

"We suffer as well."

"My aunt agrees and once told me that women often do experience the havoc of war, but our pain is different and should remain unspoken. When husbands return from battle, changed beyond recognition, we must greet them with patience and charity. It becomes our duty to teach men the strength of the meek and pray they hear what God has taught us. If they do not, a wife is left with only the comfort God may grant, and she must pray for eventual peace in her husband's soul."

The lady looked away. "I do not have that fortitude you tell me the meek should own."

"I think you do," Eleanor said, reaching out to lightly touch the wife's wrist. "You have shown just such courage during the long years of your lord's absence."

Suddenly the door to the chamber crashed open.

Both women jumped to their feet.

A servant rushed in and gestured wildly, his mouth opening and closing without sound.

"Speak!" Margaret ordered.

"My lady, I have sorrowful news. Your son, Umfrey, has been found dead in the chapel!"

The baron's wife screamed.

Chapter Twenty

Raoul shook with terror.

From the hall, he had heard the servants chattering in high pitched horror over Umfrey's death. They might fear wraithlike imps and stinking demons, but he could feel a very tangible noose cutting into his neck.

Foul sweat dripped from his body. Baron Herbert's heir he might now be, but any rational sheriff would place him even higher in rank amongst those most likely to have committed murder. Did he not have good reason to kill his elder brother?

As the offspring of Baron Herbert, he would receive more courtesy than many others in similar circumstances, yet he doubted King Edward would allow him leniency. Cleaning up the lax judicial system inherited from his dead father meant too much to the new monarch. He had been ruthless in his handling of corrupt sheriffs. Raoul could imagine what he would do with a son who committed fratricide.

"I must flee now," he whispered to unsympathetic stone walls and tightened his arms around his chest to quiet his trembling. Any way to escape seemed impossible.

All reason fled. Tears stung his eyes. A pitiful whimper escaped his lips.

"How dare you whine like a castrated sheep! Either you still pretend you are a man or you had best borrow one of your mother's robes and learn to mince about like the woman you've become."

Raoul looked around, half expecting to see his father standing in front of him and mocking his fear. But the words had burst from his own mouth, even if he had borrowed the tone from his sire.

He cleared his throat. "Weapon. Disguise? Food and drink. A horse? Place to hide. Where to flee?" Recitation of the simple list calmed him and he began to plan how to avoid capture.

A weapon was required. He always carried a knife, but a sword might be well-advised. Even if he had little practice using it, others might treat him with caution if they saw it by his side. They would not know how much skill he actually possessed.

There was yet another advantage to the martial display. Should he wish to join a traveling party on the road, he would be welcomed as an additional defender against lawless men. Many soldiers also left England to sell their fighting skills as mercenaries. If he hinted that was his purpose, he would not have to elaborate further on the purpose of his journey.

He fell to his knees and reached under his bed. There he had hidden the sword he stole from his eldest brother's room after the man died of fever. "Thought to sell it someday," he muttered, pulling the weapon out. "Now it may be worth more in the salvation of my neck."

He checked the rough sacking in which he had rolled the sword. With luck, no one would suspect what lay inside if he carried it like a tool or a bundle of sticks. Once outside the castle, the weapon would be an advantage, but no common man owned such a thing. If anyone saw the sword within the fortress walls, they would either stop him for questions or remember seeing him leave when an organized search began for Umfrey's killer.

Standing, he reached over and lifted the lid of his storage chest and picked up a robe. He shook it out.

Well-worn and of rough material, it also had a hood large enough to cast his face in shadow. It had served him well enough as a disguise when he wished to seduce some servant girl without revealing his kinship with the baron. If the women mistook him for a common laborer in the dark, others might conclude the same when he mingled with the crowd in the pale winter light of the bailey. A purposeful stride should suggest he was engaged in honorable labor, one man of low rank indistinguishable from so many others.

He snorted as he dropped the robe over his head. Remaining anonymous should be an easy task. When in his life had anyone ever noticed him except when they looked for an object to mock or scold?

He went to the door and quietly opened it, then looked about with caution.

The hall was empty.

He slipped out and hurried down the corridor to the stairs. With luck he could filch bread from the kitchen and enough wine to fill his deer-leather wineskin. The servants were used to the baron's sons stealing bites and would pay no attention to him in the hustle of meal preparation. If these later remembered seeing him passing through, he did not care. He only wanted to escape the castle itself without leaving any hints as to where he might have gone.

And, he decided, he would have to walk. Riding might gain him distance from here more quickly but taking a horse from the stable was dangerous. One of the grooms could decide it would be to his advantage to stop him if rumors of his involvement in Umfrey's death were circulating. Taking the time to saddle the beast himself would slow him down, and he would be more noticeable on horseback as he left the castle.

He would have to find a local hiding place until the hue and cry was done. Once the assumption was made that he was probably far away, he could safely join a party of travelers down the mainland road and take on the guise of a battle-worn soldier with little patience for chatter. Until he reached the nearest city or, better yet, a harbor, his best hope of escape was to remain inconspicuous.

As Raoul flew down the steep steps, he thought of Umfrey and realized that he truly regretted his death. He had grown almost fond of his quivering cokenay of a brother since Gervase had taken flight from the window. As he thought more on it, he acknowledged that Umfrey had never been cruel to him like their father or even the other brothers. A little name-calling and that was about the extent of it.

In truth, Umfrey was more like a woman, having lost all claim to manhood. Raoul had seen this elder brother often enough, groaning with pleasure, as that soldier swyved him like a bull would a cow.

"A pity I never had sisters," he murmured. "I might have gotten along better with them."

But it was too late to think more on the past. Umfrey was dead, and Raoul wanted very much to live.

He pulled the hood of his cloak over his head and set his mind to quickly stealing the sustenance he needed to survive. Then he would slip into the bailey and become one more in a crowd of faceless people, coming and going, all of whom had some business in the fortress or with its lord.

As for a hiding place, he knew the perfect location.

Chapter Twenty-One

Sister Anne dipped her hands into the basin, turning the pale chill water into a glistening red. "We must send this joyful news to Lady Margaret and Baron Herbert."

Prioress Eleanor bowed her head. "We may not."

Anne spun around, stifling a cry of protest.

"I did not make that decision to be cruel but rather to save the parents even sharper grief." She put a hand against her breast. "I do understand that their anguish may push them beyond mortal endurance if they think Umfrey has been killed. May their torment be brief."

"Then why force them to suffer so?" Anne reached out in supplication. "Enduring far less than this, men have been known to deny the very existence of God."

"Had someone voiced to me what I have just uttered to you, I would have cried out in the parents' defense as well." The prioress grasped her friend's hand. "Consider this. The next victim might be Raoul, Leonel, Lady Margaret, or the baron. If the killer is not caught swiftly, others will surely die while we flounder in search of justice. Shall we allow the slaughter of all to give only a brief respite to any survivors?"

"You believe this attack was not the first against the family?"

Eleanor nodded. "A pattern is emerging. The death of the eldest was undoubtedly caused by fever. Although the second death might have been accepted as an accident, even self-murder, the third took place too close in time and was most peculiar in nature. This last death, being so curious, makes men begin to think too much on all the deaths. The murderer has begun to make mistakes. Not only was he careless in the stabbing of Umfrey, he has tried to kill too many, far too fast, and perhaps with too much cleverness."

"What is the killer's purpose?"

"I am not sure. The reason must be hidden in the baron's past, an act he committed that has led to this awful vengeance. Nor do we know how many deaths will satisfy the killer's longing for retribution. Until we know who he is, we may not understand why he is doing this."

"The rumor I have heard is that Satan cursed the family and sends his liegeman to collect their souls."

"A man is the more likely perpetrator even if wickedness rules his heart." Eleanor looked away. "I do not know his name but hope to trick him into revealing his identity. Umfrey's attacker may be emboldened to strike again soon if he believes he has murdered another successfully. He has already become imprudent. Greater arrogance would render him even less cautious, making him easier to trap. Were he to learn of Umfrey's survival, he might grow wary, more difficult to catch. Such reasoning forms the foundation of my plan."

"If postponing the message that Umfrey lives will stop the killing, the delay will bring more joy than sorrow. Please forgive my reaction. I spoke only as…"

"…any woman and mother would." Eleanor smiled with gentle sympathy. "I only pray that the plot shall succeed, bring swift justice and eventual peace, so the outcome may outweigh the cruelty."

"I join you in that hope."

Glancing at her friend's brief smile, Eleanor nodded, knowing well the dangers inherent in her ploy. After all, men not only denied God under such duress, they had slain themselves in despair.

"My lady?"

Master Gamel stood in the doorway, wiping his hands on a pink-tinted cloth.

Eleanor forced a cheerful look. "How does your patient?"

Gamel glanced at Sister Anne, his expression soft with evident affection. "He sleeps with a draught of mandrake to bring him respite from the pain I caused. I did not tell him what I was giving him because he had already refused the drink to numb the hurt of treatment. He said that his suffering would please God, yet men heal better when the torment is less acute. Or so I have observed."

The prioress squeezed shut her eyes, trying to banish the memory of Umfrey's piteous cries when the physician bathed his deep cuts in wine, spread honey around the edges, and covered the wounds with dry, clean dressings. Gamel's work was skillfully swift, but time slows to the speed of a worm's crawl when raw flesh is further abused.

"The potion was made by your sub-infirmarian. Had it not been for her knowledgeable assistance, I would not be as confident of the young man's recovery."

Anne blushed. "I did nothing, good sir. It is your skill that shall save him."

Turning to Eleanor, his manner grew shy. "Many quarrel with this choice of treatment, my lady. Most prefer cautery of all wounds, regardless of weapon, and ointments to draw forth the laudable pus, but I have had much success treating dagger wounds in this other manner."

The prioress glanced at Anne who answered her unspoken question with a nod. "Then God has given you wisdom," she said. "No man of faith should doubt His grace in doing so."

"Barring the wound turning foul, he has every hope of survival, although the injury will be long in healing."

"A careless killer, do you think, or one blessedly unskilled?" Although she suspected the former, Eleanor needed the physician's opinion to be more certain.

"More likely God's grace," he replied, "or so Umfrey believes."

The prioress raised an eyebrow in question.

"The assassin must have been in a hurry. A moment's reflection would have been sufficient to realize that the one blow could have been deflected." Using a palm to represent the victim's chest, he demonstrated the direction of the blow with his other. "The knife first hit the large gold cross the baron's son was wearing, then his hair shirt. Although neither would have been enough to keep a knife from a plunging into the heart, both skewed the direction just enough so the knife hit his rib and slid away into flesh. Added to that good fortune was the timely arrival and wise actions of Brother Thomas. If he had not found him so quickly, Umfrey's body would have emptied of all blood. Your monk saved his life by damming the flow."

Eleanor indicated understanding, then frowned. "Who knows that Umfrey still lives?"

The physician looked confused. He began to ask her meaning, then answered her question instead. "The servants who carried him here knew he was barely alive. They all told me that Umfrey was more in need of a priest than a physician's service. Umfrey did not regain his wits until after all had left. Only we must know that he is alive." He hesitated. "And Brother Thomas as well."

Anne concurred.

"The servant who entered the chapel with your monk certainly believed Umfrey was dead," Gamel said. "He hurried to tell Lady Margaret that news. After he left her, his progress was slower as he stopped to alert all he met of the latest horror committed by the Devil against this family. I have heard much whispering in the halls to that effect."

"Then we shall confirm the rumor, less with deceitful word than by sad demeanor," Eleanor replied. "We have little time to catch the attacker." Her jaw clenched. "I will tell my brother this tragic news of Umfrey's death, and he will be swift in gathering others for a discreet but organized search. Even though I trust his prudence, I must mislead my brother as well. A confidence, spoken in whispers, may still be overheard."

"The family will beg permission to prepare the corpse for burial," Anne said.

"And I shall dissuade them for a short time." Eleanor pressed her hand over her eyes, as if trying to hide her dismay at such devious tactics. "Brother Thomas needs time alone in the room to struggle with the Devil for the possession of Umfrey's soul before any burial can take place."

"There is one more matter, my lady." Gamel nervously twisted his hands.

From the physician's expression, the prioress knew he had held back a distressing detail. Impatient and uneasy, she beseeched him to share it.

"I should have told you this sooner, but the significance was so grave, so incomprehensible, I lost all ability to give speech to what I heard. This terrible thing may complicate your efforts to catch the killer." He spoke so softly his words were almost impossible to hear.

The prioress wondered what could be worse than these murders. "I implore you to speak plainly, good sir."

Gamel looked over his shoulder at the door. "While I was cleaning the son's wounds, he remained conscious. I grieved that he was alert to suffer so much, but I thought the memory of greater pain might distract him from my current work. I asked what he recalled of the attack."

Eleanor nodded approval. Whatever fearful news the physician had learned, he had had the wit to seek details soon after the attack.

"Umfrey told me that he had left the chapel to relieve himself. When he returned, his father greeted him by the altar."

"The baron never speaks directly with any of his immediate family," Anne said.

This was strange news indeed, the prioress thought. She gestured for him to continue.

"Earlier, he had asked that Raoul beg their father to come to him." Drops of sweat shone on Gamel's forehead. "At first, I assumed the baron had found compassion for the lad who was suffering so much. Whatever their quarrel, no father would want his son to bear such anguish. I would never..."

"Your conclusion is reasonable," she replied, keeping her doubts about Herbert's sympathy unspoken.

Gamel rubbed at his eyes as if trying to rid them of an irritant. "When the young man finished his story, my heart almost ceased beating with his appalling revelation."

Anne and Eleanor stared at him with dread-filled anticipation.

"Is it not an unnatural father who opens his arms to his child, only to stab him in the heart?"

Chapter Twenty-Two

Standing at her brother's side, Eleanor rued all the lies she had told and must still utter. Some were deliberate falsehoods, others the easy failure to add details. She suspected these omissions of fact were the same as any other deception. Did the purpose ever cleanse the sin?

She shook her head, then glanced at her brother and hoped he did not see how confused and troubled she was. "Surely you have learned something more," she said and instantly regretted her sharp tone. Knowing Hugh, she realized that he would have told her if he had and did not deserve a rebuke born of no cause but her frustration.

He clenched his fists, then cracked his knuckles.

She winced. "Never do that again in my presence! Such a reminder of the sound when bones and shoulders are set is loathsome."

The knight stepped back and stared at his sister. "You are no longer the little girl I remember!" He bent and held his hand about knee level. "You have learned the voice of command, my lady."

Eleanor knew he was trying to defuse the tension between them and was quite willing to allow it. With a forced laugh at his jest, she spun around and stared out of the window. "Oh, Hugh, what is happening here? Can you think of any reason for these deaths? Poor Umfrey!"

"If I did, I would not be standing here like that weak-kneed monk of yours."

Eleanor hid her curiosity at the remark. Now was not the time to question it, and she chose instead to wait for what else he had to say.

He cleared his throat with a growl. "We may learn something soon. A servant arrived not long ago and asked for Master Gamel and the monk. When Baron Herbert heard of his son's death, he called them to his chambers. I was not summoned."

Surprised and perplexed in equal measure, she asked him for more detail.

"Then you knew nothing of this either?"

"After I finished speaking with the physician, I went to the chapel with Sister Anne to pray for Umfrey's soul. She and I discussed the need to comfort Lady Margaret, then my sub-infirmarian left to wait upon that bereaved mother. I sought you. I have not seen Brother Thomas or Master Gamel since I left him."

Hugh scowled.

Although the prioress understood her brother's annoyance at being denied a place in the meeting with Herbert, she had greater hope that the baron might finally cast light on why these murders had occurred. Her plan to force the killer's hand might have yielded early fruit.

For so many reasons, she hoped the baron was not guilty of these crimes, but, until she knew more, she dared not discount Umfrey's reported accusation. It had been very difficult to keep her brother ignorant of this son's survival. Secrecy was one matter, but loyalty was another. Even though Hugh would share her horror at the possibility of filicide, Baron Herbert was his friend. She did not know the full extent of her brother's devotion to his battlefield commander.

He grunted. "Baron Herbert should have asked for you. On your behalf, I am offended that he chose the company of an ordinary monk over that of an esteemed prioress."

For a moment, Eleanor considered the tone of those words and concluded his meaning had little to do with concern over the difference in rank between a prioress and one of her religious. "He is a priest. When any mortal requires such a servant of God, there is no affront to my honor." In silence, she studied her restless sibling. "Has Brother Thomas offended you, Hugh? As his prioress, I must know of any insult."

He shook his head.

Eleanor's first suspicion was that her brother knew of Thomas' former work as a Church spy. If so, he might not wish to speak of it, fearing she was ignorant of the monk's dual loyalties. He would still be angry at the trickery and might wish to resolve the matter without alerting her to the problem. Despite his protestations, he did think of her as a little girl. She struggled not to smile with affection.

"We all have committed sins," she said, "but God forgives us when we confess our transgressions. Mortals are then obliged to do the same. Should you know of any recent wrongdoing, however, that may be whispered into my ear." She hoped her words suggested that she knew of Thomas' past and had forgiven him.

For a moment, Hugh seemed to mull what she had just said. "He has served you well, my lady, and I know of his kindness when Death danced around my son's bed that winter I was in Outremer." He grimaced as if those words had stuck like a fishbone in his throat.

She nodded as another reason for his evident dislike of Thomas occurred to her. This, she hoped, was the true cause, one that could be more easily resolved than perceived disloyalty.

"Are you angry that Richard grew fond of him? If so, chase that from your heart," she said. "The monk brought comfort to your son during the years you were gone. Now that you have returned, the boy will turn again to you as his father. Give the lad time. The bond of your mutual love is strong despite the long absence."

Hugh bit his lips and stared up at the ceiling. "You give wise counsel." He forced a smile. "Now that my son is at court in the service of our king, I see him often enough. Indeed, Richard has little enough time to…" He stopped. "Our father is proud of him," he hurried to say. "Says he rarely indulges in boyish mischief—or at least is not often caught at it." This time he grinned with evident pleasure.

Inclined to agree that anything her nephew did was a matter for pride, Eleanor laughed, sharing her brother's delight and choosing to accept the shift in the discussion away from her much-loved monk.

But memory of recent violence blew a chill breath on their levity, and they quickly grew more somber.

Hugh leaned against the wall and sighed. "I beg forgiveness for my sharp words. I have grown querulous over this delay in discovering Baron Herbert's need to call us here."

"The unfortunate deaths give cause enough for postponement."

"Your charity is a credit to you."

"You did say he was not a man prone to undue fears or exaggeration."

"He has been called severe, but he is hardest on himself. Even when suffering a near-mortal fever, he demanded that he be tied to his horse so he might join his men in combat." He shook his head. "That was one of the few times anything proved stronger than his will. The fever was so fierce it rendered him unconscious, and he was carried back to his bed. After he recovered, his hair dropped out, eyebrows as well, and he never recovered the feeling in one hand. Nonetheless, he still rode into battle. We honored him for his resolve and loved him for his courage."

"Your testimony to his valor is one reason I did not question his fears that some malign thing had taken residence."

"A prioress with your reputation would only honor his rank and be a match for any evil he suspected here." Hugh's eyes betrayed the love he had for this little sister who had grown into such a formidable woman. "You are much like our aunt at Amesbury," he said.

Eleanor flushed with pride at the comparison and turned away to hide that failing. "You praise me too much, sweet brother."

"And you are too kind to condemn me for my overweening pride, pricked because the baron did not include me in those he has called to his side. What I should pray for is enlightenment from Master Gamel. The baron may have slipped into deep melancholy after Roger drowned, but the subsequent deaths of

Gervase and Umfrey are beyond any father's endurance. Only Raoul is left now, a son who offers little comfort. I pray there is an earthly remedy to match the pain of such worldly woes." He hesitated as if about to say more but fell silent.

Eleanor was about to ask questions about the baron's relationship with his sons, when the sound of men's voices echoed down the outside corridor. Their actual words were muted by the invading wind and thick stone walls.

Brother Thomas and Master Gamel walked slowly together, their heads bowed in thought. As they approached, they looked up, evidently startled by the presence of the knight and prioress.

Glancing at Brother Thomas, Eleanor was shocked. Rarely had she seen such misery as she noted in his eyes.

Master Gamel turned his face away as if he feared to meet anyone's gaze.

What new tidings of dire import had the two men brought? Eleanor turned to Hugh and saw that he shared her apprehension.

The arrivals looked at each other, their expressions suggesting that each hoped the other would speak first.

"What have you learned?" The prioress could not will her voice to rise above a whisper.

Gamel's eyes shifted back and forth with evident discomfort. Then he bowed awkwardly. "My lady, I would reply but beg your indulgence. I must consult with your sub-infirmarian. May I ask where Sister Anne is?"

"She remains with the Lady Margaret, I believe. She was preparing a weak potion infused with poppy to allow the poor woman some healing sleep. Shall I summon her?"

"I see that she, too, has learned the use of that plant from those who came from Outremer. I am not surprised," he murmured, a smile briefly smoothing the furrows in his brow. In the next instant, he grew somber again and studied his feet.

"I myself shall seek her. If her skills are no longer needed by the baron's wife, I will sit with the lady until she falls asleep and allow Sister Anne to attend you. A woman servant can be found for company," Eleanor said. "Where do you wish to meet?"

"In the Great Hall, if that is acceptable. She and I may have privacy to confer, and we shall be within the clear view of others for propriety."

She wished she might join the pair, yet was wise enough to recognize that her presence would be less help and more of an intrusion. Now her heart began to pound, but she did not know whether that was due to fear or thwarted curiosity. In either case, these men knew something of significance. She was equally convinced the news, when related, would not be cause for joy.

With grace, the physician thanked her and left.

Eleanor also departed to seek Sister Anne, then glanced over her shoulder at the two men remaining.

Hugh and Thomas stood some distance apart, glaring at each other.

The prioress sighed and walked on, wishing she could stay to heal the discord between them. Other matters must take immediate precedence, she decided, and set her mind to the next task. As she entered the stairwell leading to Lady Margaret's chambers, she felt a chill and spun around.

Hugh had turned to look out the window.

Thomas was watching her, his face pale with terror and woe.

Chapter Twenty-Three

The two men watched Prioress Eleanor disappear into the stair-well. The door fell shut behind her with a thud.

Folding his arms, Hugh turned to the monk. "I have the right to know what you learned from Baron Herbert," he snarled. "Any new information might help capture a killer. Your willful delay of this hunt is reprehensible." He rudely gestured at the monk. "A man of your ilk may find the need for principled action difficult to grasp, but surely even you can understand that the rest of us must react swiftly."

There was such contempt in the knight's narrowed eyes that Thomas felt his temper flare like a blacksmith's fire. Only rarely did he want to cast aside the vocation thrust upon him and strike back like any other man whose honor was ridiculed. This was one of those times.

He put his hands behind his back and clenched them. This is my prioress' brother and Richard's father, he said to himself. Whatever Hugh had against him, he ought to simply remind the man that the priesthood was owed courtesy even if he himself was not. The words stuck in his throat and instead he chose to say, "I may not speak of it."

Instantly he knew he had betrayed his fury with his tone.

"Master Gamel has decided otherwise, it seems, and chooses to share his knowledge even with a woman."

Thomas ground his teeth but kept silent.

"Or is the truth of it that you know nothing at all? Perhaps my lord smelled your rank impiety, shut the door in your face, and spoke alone with Master Gamel. Surely you are not claiming the sanctity of confession for the baron?"

Thomas' ears burned from the acidic scorn in the knight's voice. "If you will," he muttered, knowing that any attempt to explain or dispute would be futile.

Those three uttered words were still three too many.

"If *I* will? It is *God's* command if you dare claim that the baron confessed anything to you for His ears." He shrugged. "Yet your soul is so befouled that I doubt you even risk uttering His name. He might strike you with lightning for your blasphemy if you did." Hugh stepped forward to wag a finger in the monk's face. "I see rage burning inside you, Brother. In Outremer, King Edward's gaze often turned earth into fire when he was displeased, but he is God's anointed and that conflagration purifies. You are the Devil's liegeman. Your passions pollute creation."

Thomas grew dizzy as fury mixed with fear. This man did know who he was.

"You mock those of honest vocation when you wear a monk's robe, Thomas of London."

"All men sin, but God forgives those who beg His mercy."

Hugh laughed. "You must have failed to repent and win His pardon. The stench of your true master still emanates from you."

"What offence have I committed against you?" Thomas shouted, his words slicing the air like the sword he did not have. "Since I am a man who serves God, I may not take up a sharp blade and fight for my honor's sake. My only recourse is to beg that you have mercy on me and forgive." But his evident flash of anger contradicted any claim of meekness in his heart.

"What mercy did you grant Giles when you raped him?"

Thomas staggered backward.

Hugh pushed the monk up against the wall. "His father was my friend and told me the story of his only son. Giles screamed, did he not, begging you not to use him like some woman. Nonetheless, you defiled his manhood, an abomination that still festers, leaving him tormented with moments of madness." Hugh grabbed the monk by the robe, twisting it in his hand until the cloth grew tight around Thomas' throat. "His father is now dead, a good and pious man whose life was cut short by the ruination of his son."

The monk gasped for air, and what little he was able to inhale was sharp with the rank sweat of panic.

"I should castrate you. Would that not be proper justice?" The knight laughed, then hit Thomas with the flat of his hand.

Blood splattered as a cut opened in the monk's cheek.

Now outraged and desperate for air, Thomas swung his own fist, an ineffective blow on the ribs, but his knee hit the knight's thigh.

Surprised, Hugh loosened his hold.

The monk shoved him away and struck again.

Ducking, the knight rammed his head into Thomas' chest, forcing breath from the monk's lungs.

Wide-eyed and gasping for air, Thomas summoned will and strength enough to grab Hugh around the neck, immobilize him, and strike again at his groin. This time he succeeded.

Howling with pain, the knight fell to the floor.

The monk collapsed as well. Crouching on all fours, Thomas struggled to pull air back into his lungs.

Hugh cupped his genitals and moaned.

The smell of hate filled the hall like acrid smoke.

It was Hugh who first staggered to his feet.

Thomas sat back on his heels and looked up at his adversary, fully aware that he would lose any further fight. He was weak, his position vulnerable. Should the knight press his advantage, however, the monk swore he would not leave the man unscarred. After the cruel lies Hugh had flung at him, Thomas would not face defeat without making sure that the knight had permanent mementos of the monk he had attacked.

But Hugh stepped away. "Grovel to God, cokenay," he jeered, "and thank Him that I did not cut off your balls. For the good service you have rendered my family, I shall leave you in peace unless you ever fail my sister or address one word to my son.

Should you do either, remember this fair warning: I shall find you, tie you to a tree, and slowly peel your genitals as if they were apples until you beg Satan to take you home to Hell."

Biting his tongue to keep silent, Thomas nodded. His temper cooled. Reason returned. No matter how Hugh treated him, the monk repeated to himself, the knight was still Prioress Eleanor's brother. Owing her fealty, he must also honor her kin, even when the sibling was this man who hated him for a horrible crime Thomas had never committed.

Bowing his head, the monk hoped he could hide his agonized grief. From Hugh's tale, profound anguish had festered in Giles, unbalancing his humors with even greater severity than Thomas endured. Were he to insist on telling the truth of what happened, his boyhood friend would suffer still greater humiliation and far more than his fragile spirit could ever bear.

Thomas had loved Giles too much and too long to cause him further distress. He had little choice but to remain silent and accept full blame. Tears, bitter with loss and outrage, stung his eyes.

Hugh strode down the corridor.

Chapter Twenty-Four

The prioress' offer of solace to Lady Margaret was rejected without a word. Not one utterance, even of polite greeting, had the mother spoken, nor were any tears shed. The woman's grief had passed beyond mortal expression. Lying on her bed, arms limply crossed on her chest, the lady stared without blinking at the ceiling.

Eleanor sat next to her and watched, grateful when the potion Sister Anne administered finally let the bereaved mother fall into deep sleep. As the prioress left the chambers of the baron's wife, she prayed that God would chase away dreams as well.

All I have brought with my stratagem is unconscionable anguish, she thought. Her guilt over keeping Umfrey's survival hidden grew bitter.

She turned around, longing to return and tell Lady Margaret that she still had two sons living. Instead, she dug her nails into her palms and forced herself back to the open windows of the corridor. The mother was sleeping, and the death of so many sons already was hard enough to bear.

The wind screeched through the opening, buffeting Eleanor as if enraged at her despicable abuse of nature. "Whatever imperfections mortals have, we were also made in God's image," she whispered into the grey storm. "A mother's love for her children is part of that more perfect heritage. I know this for the Queen of Heaven exemplified it."

She leaned forward and let the rain whip her. In the distance, she could hear the sea lash the coast and knew that the suffering she had caused Lady Margaret was no less profound that the beating the earth endured with the battering of merciless waves.

"My lady?"

The prioress stepped back and looked over her shoulder. A girl stood behind her, eyes round with terror and hands tucked into her armpits. She trembled.

Cringing at this further proof of her lack of charity, Eleanor swore penance for forgetting that she had required a young servant, in the absence of Sister Anne, to accompany her on this chilly walk through the corridors of the keep.

"You are white with the cold, child. Let us walk on." It was one thing for her to amble along this icy corridor, protected by a long woolen cloak, but this servant, little more than a babe, was not so thankfully dressed.

"Come." Eleanor stretched out her arm and pulled the girl close to her. "We shall leave this place and find a warm fire."

The child tensed, fearing surrender to such ease might suggest disrespect to a religious of such high rank, but then she snuggled into the prioress, sensing that the warmth offered was padded with honest compassion.

As they walked toward the doorway leading to the Great Hall, Eleanor saw Brother Thomas leaning against the wall and staring down into the bailey below. She hesitated, wondering if she should speak with him about his meeting with the baron. Quickly deciding that her curiosity was not idle, she called out to the monk.

He started, then turned to face her. There was a deep cut under his cheekbone, and the skin beneath his left eye was swollen.

"That must hurt," Eleanor said, glad that her evident alarm was appropriate for any prioress to express over an injury suffered by one of her charges. "Have you spoken with Sister Anne?"

"I slipped on the wet floor and fell against the stone wall. The cut is minor and does not pain me, my lady."

His grin was sheepish enough to almost convince her that the tale was true, but she knew he was lying. When she last left them, the tension between her brother and this monk had been too evident. If blows had been exchanged, she would find a way to learn more of it.

She looked down at the burrowed child and decided she took precedence over minor quarrels between honorable men, even if neither had the right to strike the other. "Brother Thomas and I shall follow close by, child, but you must hurry to the Great Hall," she said. "Make sure that the servants have built a fire adequate enough to warm us all. Once you have done that, we shall need some hot cider to chase away the chill. Take a cup for yourself as well."

The girl looked up at her, blinking with uncertainty at the last remark.

"That is my command."

Appreciation flashed across the girl's face, and she raced off to do the bidding.

Sadness stung her heart. No child should be so grateful over such a small kindness, she thought. Eleanor shook her head and gestured for Thomas to follow her. "Can you tell me what is troubling the baron?" Her voice was soft.

He shook his head with evident reluctance.

She nodded. There were some conversations she had no right to hear.

They hurried through the hall in silence. The cold from the outside storm chased after them with fiendish zeal.

"Not all of my conversation with the baron was confided in confession, my lady," he murmured, "but I hesitate to say much else until Master Gamel has spoken with our sub-infirmarian."

"You may speak in confidence, Brother, and perhaps that would be the wisest choice. When you and the physician returned from Baron Herbert, and Master Gamel asked to speak with Sister Anne, I suspected that the baron might suffer an illness so severe that even an eminent medical man required a second opinion. Then and now your eyes express a rare gravity."

"What I might say remains conjecture until Master Gamel and Sister Anne reach their conclusions."

"Lack of knowledge has never stopped mortals from forming opinions. God hopes that some are wise enough to wait until they are taught the truth, but we are impatient creatures." She gave Thomas a brief smile. "I confess I am one. Mindful of my ignorance, I shall treat what you can tell me with caution."

"Baron Herbert believes he has been cursed with leprosy."

Eleanor gasped.

"He has not told his wife nor has he spoken with any of his sons about this. The only one here who knows is Sir Leonel because he observed some of the symptoms in Outremer."

"That explains why he refuses the company of his family and shuns daylight. You and Master Gamel had time to observe him. Is there anything in his appearance that gives reason to hope that he has some other disease?"

"Although not an expert, I have seen a few afflicted with such severity that the nose has collapsed, they have lost fingers and even their eyes. The baron suffers no significant deformity. That fact allowed Master Gamel some hope. What troubles the physician is that Baron Herbert has lost all body hair, his voice is hoarse, and he has no feeling in his hands. To speed diagnosis, Master Gamel bled him and took a sample of his urine."

They entered the Great Hall. As they arrived, the young servant girl rushed forward and led them quickly to seats she had prepared by the fire. Eleanor glanced around but did not see either physician or sub-infirmarian. Had they gone together to see the baron?

Sitting, both prioress and monk were served mulled wine. Eleanor thanked the girl and asked her to sit some distance away, close enough for propriety and far enough to allow private speech. A bit of color had returned to the child's cheeks, and the prioress was pleased to see that she had a slice of cheese to nibble. The girl was little more than skin and bones, she thought, but someone kind had cared enough to slip her a little food.

"Did anyone examine him in Acre or on his journey back to England?" Eleanor kept her voice low as she turned to Thomas. Although no one was near, conversations could carry in the cavernous room.

"Before Baron Herbert set sail for home, a priest was found who agreed to see him in confidence. He confirmed the baron's fears and said that his affliction was God's curse for his terrible wickedness."

"A soldier who sins were forgiven when he took the cross?"

"We have learned to our own grief that men, cleansed of all transgression by that vow, later committed horrible acts."

Eleanor nodded, recalling an event some years back when a madman had threatened Tyndal Priory. She frowned. "I assume he has confessed those offenses to you."

"Although I dare not reveal his words, I will say to you alone that nothing seemed so dreadful that God would likely condemn him to this ghastly fate. Perhaps he withheld something from me, although surely not. Since he has called us here, he no longer has cause if ever he did."

"He remains convinced of God's curse?" She raised an eyebrow.

"He sought a miracle in Rome and consulted with physicians in Solerno and Paris," Thomas said. "The physicians were divided in their opinions. The priest in Rome agreed with the one in Acre. Baron Herbert is confused by earthly medicine and horrified by the sacred. As he said, he might understand being so wicked that God flung this disease upon him. He does not see why his sons must die."

In truth, neither did Eleanor. As for his illness, she quietly prayed that Master Gamel and Sister Anne could give the man a definitive answer. "His desire to avoid spreading the contagion to his family is a wise one, but why did he return home? He endangered all on the ship, any with whom he shared companionship, a meal, or a bed. Even if Sir Leonel is free of contagion, he has been put at risk as well."

"Mortals commit illogical acts when terrified, my lady. He longs to be near his wife, even if he may never look upon her again. As for his sons, he hoped to learn that at least one has become worthy of this patrimony if he must surrender it all."

"And yet they die, one after another." Eleanor grew thoughtful.

"At least he has not succumbed to utter hopelessness and wants to save his remaining son from God's scourge. All others from whom he sought advice were strangers, owing him neither loyalty nor love. That was why he turned to Sir Hugh for aid, a man he calls *brother*."

Eleanor bent to stroke a thick-furred cat that had inched closer to the heat. "Acknowledging that he must be certain, did the physician confide his initial impressions to you?"

"Any diagnosis of the disease is cruel for the person and the family, he said, nor is the decision a simple one. He told me that there are many signs to note before a man is declared cursed with leprosy. Although he is familiar with the disease, he begged to confer with Sister Anne." His lips twitched into a brief smile. "He knows of her reputation as a healer, and their conversations have confirmed the tales told."

"And if Master Gamel concludes that Baron Herbert is afflicted as the priest in Outremer determined?"

"Surely there are places in England he might travel in his quest for a divine reprieve."

"Sister Anne once mentioned Canterbury. Some lepers have been cleansed after bathing in water to which a drop of St. Thomas' blood has been added. Others, who have gone on pilgrimage to great shrines, have been cured or granted a long return of good health. Occasionally, a man has been found clean after a more thorough examination."

Thomas nodded and looked around. The young servant was dozing, the cheese rind still held loosely in her hand. "There is something else I wanted to discuss with you, my lady. It has nothing to do with this matter of leprosy, but it might have relevance to the death of his sons."

"Indeed?"

"The other night, I met a soldier walking on the ramparts. It was he who discovered the old priest's body. When he looked at the corpse, he noticed that the open eyes were streaked with red. His conclusion was that Satan or one of his imps had stolen the priest's soul and branded his eyes with the color of hellfire." He hesitated.

The prioress nodded for him to continue.

"He fears consequences if this information should be traced to him."

"Some means of protection shall be arranged if his testimony is required."

"When he said the eyes were marked with blood, I suspected the priest had been suffocated." He cleared his throat and looked away. "I have seen a man killed in like manner before and remembered that these signs pointed to that method of execution."

Eleanor chose not to ask for any details of this knowledge. "This is frightening news. Did you learn more?"

"Since I am staying in the priest's old chambers, I returned to search but found little. He may have been fond of wine, but he honored his vow of poverty. The very simplicity of his room was so austere that I almost failed to find two strange things. The first appears to be a seal depicting St. Lazarus."

She smiled. "I am sure that you have kept this safe."

He reached into his pouch and gave her the seal.

Gazing at it, she grew pensive. "This belongs to the Order of St. Lazarus."

"The leper knights in Outremer?"

She nodded. "Their main center in England is a monastery called Burton Lazars."

"Might this mean that the baron intended to join them?"

"Either that or he was in communication with them about a proposed gift and they had replied."

"He did not mention this when he spoke with Master Gamel and me."

"Perhaps he thought it of less import than other matters, although I do wonder where the priest found it and why he kept it." She hesitated. Her jaw tightened as she made a difficult decision. "Brother, I have heard that the baron loves none of his sons and much prefers his nephew."

"He spoke little enough of them, except to say that God must have reason to hate him or He would not slaughter his offspring like Job's sons." Thomas raised a hand. "He did mention Raoul, calling the youth an ill-natured cur."

"Other than Sir Leonel, son of his dead brother, I believe that Baron Herbert has no other living nephews. Should all his own offspring die, this nephew would become his heir, a man he loves and honors above any of his own brood."

Thomas looked confused.

"It is possible," she whispered, "that the baron is killing his sons so they will not stand in the way of his beloved nephew's inheritance."

The monk sat back in horror. "Surely not!"

"Since you know that Umfrey is still alive, I shall confide this to you with the understanding that you speak to no one about it. Umfrey believes it was his father who tried to kill him."

Chapter Twenty-Five

Baron Herbert sat in the shadows, the physician by his side. Glancing sideways at the waiting servant, he gestured toward the chamber door.

The man held it open, and a small party filed in.

"Come no closer, I beg you," Master Gamel said, raising his hand in warning. "The air may be rife with contagion."

They dutifully stopped.

The wide-eyed servant edged nearer to the door.

Herbert dismissed him.

Lowering her gaze, Sister Anne modestly tucked her hands into her sleeves. Sir Hugh moved closer to his sister's side, his expression fierce with protective defiance. Brother Thomas stepped aside, as the servant swiftly retreated, and then firmly shut the door.

"You have news for me, healer?" The baron looked up at the window, his unblinking eyes willing the day's light to put an end to all nightmares.

"I do not wish to raise your hopes, my lord, but the symptoms you present are not definitive. This means I cannot say that you absolutely have or do not have leprosy." Gamel looked down at Herbert but kept the focus of his gaze just to the left of the man.

Herbert closed his eyes for a moment, then resumed his intense contemplation of the streaming light from the window.

"As you must surely understand, the decision that a man has contracted leprosy should be made with solemn care. Since some believe the cause of the disease arises from the commission of a dreadful wickedness, it became imperative that Prioress Eleanor and Brother Thomas join us. I can speak only as an imperfect mortal with some poor knowledge of the medical classics."

Herbert snorted. "You have not yet broken the flask containing my urine, Master Gamel. That must mean you do not believe my condition to be incurable."

The physician glanced at Sister Anne.

Catching his look, she nodded her head.

"As I said, my lord, the signs you present do not absolutely prove..."

"What else must you see, or not see, to be sure." The baron's voice was sharp with impatience. "Others of your profession have already blathered to me like witless birds. One insisted on rubbing goat urine, salt, and honey on my head. I stank but gained no relief. I want a firm decision."

"If you will kindly allow me, my lord, I shall explain." Gamel tucked in his chin and cleared his throat. "There are approximately forty signs of leprosy, some strongly indicative of the disease, others of lesser import."

Herbert covered his eyes in despair.

Gamel continued. "Your voice is hoarse, an unequivocal sign, but your breath is not foul nor does your body stink. The absence of those last factors argues against a diagnosis of the disease. You have lost feeling in your hands, some in your feet. This is strongly suggestive of leprosy. Your hair has fallen out, but this is a lesser sign, often found in those, like you, who have suffered a high fever or other ailments. Another hopeful sign is that you do not have leprous nodules; you do not suffer a fixed stare; and your face presents no disfigurement of lips and nose." He took a breath.

"Father Aylmer in Outremer was certain soon after he met with me that I had contracted it. Why was he so confident while you are not?"

"Surely he gave you a reasoned analysis, my lord. Were you to tell me what that was, I would happily respond to each of his observations with full commentary."

"'When the cause is great mortal sin, need men of God provide *reasons?*' That was his answer when I queried him," the baron said. "I bowed my head in shame that I had put a worldly practice above the plain fact of my wickedness."

Sister Anne discreetly gestured to the physician.

"May I ask the cause of this horrible offense to God?" Gamel raised an eyebrow in question as he looked back at the nun.

She nodded approval.

Herbert said nothing for a long moment, then whispered: "Although I tried to remain celibate out of respect for my vows, in Outremer, I began to suffer so greatly from dreams of my wife that I feared for my health and sought relief with a prostitute in the city. Father Aylmer looked into my soul and knew this. He informed me that this whore was even more wicked than Jezebel. She coupled with lepers and then lay with clean men immediately after. For surrendering to the sin of lust, I contracted the disease from her."

Hugh stiffened. "I can no longer remain silent," he said. "I know something of this priest's reputation."

Herbert leapt to his feet and strode to the chamber wall, striking the stones with an open hand. "If you value the friendship between us, do not say a word. Those who spoke against him were known servants of Satan."

"So the priest claimed, but your life is worth far more to me than his self-serving condemnation. If there is still hope that you might be clean, I shall not withhold what I heard." He stretched his hand out in the direction of Prioress Eleanor and Sister Anne. "Included in this present company are those who have dedicated their lives to God's service. Let them decide if my words have merit. I shall abide by their decision." He did not even glance at Brother Thomas.

"You will blaspheme!"

"Then let God curse me. I would never claim purity of heart, but, in this one matter, my motives are as innocent as any mortal's can be."

"You base your opinion on an infidel's word."

"A man who took the name of a sainted physician when he was christened."

"A false conversion, like the assassin who attempted to kill our king. That creature also lied about abjuring his hellish beliefs in order to disguise his wicked intentions."

Eleanor gave Hugh a brief warning touch on his arm, then stepped forward. "If I may speak, my lord?" She waited for the baron's assent. "Let us hear what my brother has to say. He shall tell the tale with simple words, then you may counter with cool reason. As for transgressions, remember that God always forgives the truly repentant. If you have sinned, then confess it with a heart longing for mercy." She turned and gestured toward Brother Thomas.

"There are times when God has even granted the miracle of a cure in such cases," the monk said dutifully.

The baron uttered a soft cry.

"As for what we may hear in this room," she continued, "none of my company shall ever speak of it to another. In the name of the sainted Magdalene, whose own transgressions were forgiven and now gives strength to the penitent sinner, I vow us all to silence."

Baron Herbert nodded, but, unmistakably weary, he rested his forehead against the wall.

"First, if I may, a brief story?" Hugh looked to his sister.

She gave her consent.

"When several of us lay wounded on the battlefield in the burning sun, a passing Muslim soldier paused, not to slit our throats, but to give us water. That act of mercy surely saved our lives. When Father Aylmer heard the tale, he dismissed the man's compassion and condemned us all for choosing life over death because survival came at the hands of an infidel."

The baron said nothing.

"Since Man, despite his frailties, is still made in the image of God, tell me which flawed creature showed the greater understanding of His teaching: the infidel or the priest? Is not mercy one of the great virtues? It is a quality I found most lacking in

Father Aylmer." He hesitated. "Do not forget the parable of the despised Samaritan who proved to be the more godly man."

Eleanor looked up at her brother with amazement, deciding that he would have made a fine abbot had he not been their father's heir. Then sorrow promptly quenched delight. Hugh had never mentioned those wounds he had suffered in Outremer.

The baron shrugged, but the gesture was half-hearted.

"Even before the attack on our king, Father Aylmer doubted the sincerity of all conversions, but he especially hated the physician, Lucas, because he had discovered too many of the priest's own transgressions."

"A priest, however frail himself, may always point out another's errors. That is his duty as God's creature on earth." The baron half-turned to Thomas. "Am I not correct, Brother?"

The monk glanced at the prioress' brother, then nodded with reluctance.

Hugh continued, ignoring both the baron's defense of Aylmer and Thomas' response. "As you often remarked, my lord, you had many enemies in Outremer. Knowing this, Lucas told me that he had overheard Father Aylmer talking to a man who told him of your visits to the prostitute. I questioned the healer further. He could not identify this informant, nor all that was said. The meeting took place in shadows, and much of the conversation was whispered. Yet he was quite certain that a bag exchanged hands, one that jingled with coin." Hugh looked with sorrow on his friend.

"Lucas is akin to the snake in Eden, a creature whose purpose was to cause discord amongst true Christian men. Even if your heathen did not lie to you, this story only proves that he is the spy I always believed him to be. In whose pay was he? Did you ever ask that?" Herbert hissed the last few words.

"If Lucas was a spy, it was on my behalf. Knowing that you had recently become deeply troubled, I asked him to watch you in secret. You did not wish to confide in me, your closest friend, yet I still feared for your safety, wondering if you had been threatened or fallen ill. Lucas happened upon this strange meeting on just such an undertaking. If condemnation is due, it is I who must suffer it."

"I wonder that you dare repeat this preposterous tale."

"Despite your contempt for Lucas, I can vouch for his honesty."

Gamel cleared his throat. "Did this physician observe any symptoms of illness, Sir Hugh?"

The knight shook his head. "He did note some troubling changes such as the loss of hair. As for the numbness, Baron Herbert failed to speak of it, although he sometimes dropped things he held in his right hand. Lucas suspected the baron's severe fever might have caused the hair to fall out but said nothing to me of leprosy." A muscle in his jaw twitched, and he turned to Herbert. "I repeat this tale, my lord, because I now suspect Father Aylmer may have been paid by one of your enemies to give this diagnosis of leprosy, thus causing you to flee Acre. As I recall, you soon set sail for England and before the king left."

Herbert did not reply and kept his back turned to the company. When he finally spoke, his tone was harsh. "Yet despite all your fine theories about plots, I may indeed have the dread disease. Father Aylmer has not been proven wrong, and, if you claim he erred about the severity of my transgressions, then explain why my sons are dying." He spun around, raising his fist. "Are their deaths not a continuation of God's curse?"

Gamel jumped in front of the baron. Keeping his back to Herbert, he raised his arms so that the man's face was hidden. "In God's sacred name," he shouted, "keep your eyes averted, my lord, until we know whether or not you have leprosy!"

Herbert fell to his knees and covered his face. "May God forgive me if I have infected any innocent here with my contagious gaze!" Raising his hidden eyes heavenward, he said, "My sins stink like gangrene, but others do not deserve my curse."

"My lord!" Eleanor cried out. "Your sons may have been killed, not by God, but by a mortal hand. We know that Umfrey was murdered by a man. The killer was seen leaving the chapel."

Herbert's hands slid from his face.

The prioress saw his look of horror and continued. "If one son was murdered by a creature of flesh and blood, then Roger and Gervase may have been dispatched by the same hand."

Herbert recoiled on his heels as if struck, then bowed his head and groaned. Slowly rising, he turned his back. "With due respect, my lady, I must disagree. Roger drowned. No one was seen with him. As for Gervase, he showed many signs of being drunk. I grieve that I had such weak sons, yet my sorrow is greater that they died with all their sins upon them. No man did this. Satan may have or else God in his wrath."

The baron's words were sharply spoken, but Eleanor heard his voice falter at the end. Behind that unbending exterior, did he truly mourn his sons' deaths? Or was the hesitation after the mention of their names a sign of guilt? After all, Gamel said that Umfrey had been quite certain that Herbert had been the one to stab him. Yet Eleanor still hoped this father was not the killer of the sons, no matter how much he might wish that Sir Leonel had been his own eldest son and heir. "Did anyone examine the bodies?" She kept her voice soft to dull the pointed question.

"There was no reason. We buried the first…" He coughed. "Although some claim Roger drowned himself, our old priest let us put my son in sanctified ground. There was no proof of sin, he said. Thanks to Brother Thomas, who granted the hovering soul some peace, we were able to bury Gervase next to his brother. No sheriff or crowner was summoned. The deaths were not suspicious."

Or so you determined, Eleanor concluded, her hopes about the baron's innocence fading. If the king's men can be kept from asking questions, murder may be hidden with ease.

There was a loud pounding on the closed door.

Someone gasped in fright.

"Who dares to come here?" Herbert roared with pent-up anger but lowered his head as he turned around and resumed his seat in the shadows. "Enter," he shouted, then muttered, "But prepare to have cause. Pray for mercy if you have paltry need to speak with me."

Thomas stepped back and swung the door open.

Sir Leonel entered the room. Bowing deeply to his uncle, he said, "Forgive this intrusion, my lord. This is news you must hear."

The baron tilted his head against the back of his chair, clearly relieved that his beloved nephew had arrived. "Your presence brings me a little joy. Speak."

"Raoul cannot be found. He has vanished."

The howl rising from the baron's throat was like that of a wounded wolf. "My last son!" he shouted to the ceiling. "My youngest boy! Is this cur yet another Absalom?"

Eleanor might still be undecided about Baron Herbert's guilt or innocence, but now she trembled with another fear. Might it not be a crueler fate if the baron was blameless, yet his only remaining son was the murderer?

Chapter Twenty-Six

Scowling, Hugh muttered an almost incomprehensible oath as he watched Leonel walk away.

Eleanor approached her brother and stopped in front of him. "You are not joining the search for Raoul?"

"I offered my assistance."

Her frown was sufficient question.

"He refused, arguing that he and his chosen men would know best the secret places where his cousin might be found. If I wanted to serve the family, he said, I should remain here and comfort his uncle."

Glancing at the firmly shut door to the baron's chambers, Eleanor assumed what Herbert's response to such an offer of solace had been.

"I ought to have gone with Leonel," he growled. "I am not a wet nurse, nor is the baron in need of one."

"Do not let anger overcome your usual good judgement, brother."

Looking down at his sword, he fingered the hilt.

"If you allow reason to repossess your spirit, you may find some way to satisfy your desire to contribute to this endeavor without the need to beg leave."

Hugh looked surprised, then grinned. "While I sputter over injured pride, you find answers. I am humbled. Our aunt taught you well, sweet sister, and must have found joy in your kindred spirit."

Laughing, Eleanor waved his compliment away. "Do not be fooled by a calm demeanor. Not only am I determined to discover the truth of what is happening here, I am now resolved that we shall discover it first. Although he surely did not mean to do so, Leonel offended with his easy dismissal of your worth to this undertaking." She looked up and down the hall. No one was nearby. "I have questions."

"Ask them, my lady. I shall bring my few wits to join in your effort." He leaned against the wall and waited.

"We have debated the implications and details of these recent tragic deaths to little avail, so let us start at a different point. What if the source of the current troubles is to be found in the distant past, not during the baron's time in Acre? You have told me what Baron Herbert said on the way to Outremer about his sons, but what do you remember from earlier years? How then did he act with them and what opinions did he hold? You visited here when you were not much older than a boy yourself, and we often note things better when we are young, even when we do not understand the implications."

He folded his arms and stared at the ceiling for a long moment. "The baron has changed little over the years. To his mind, truth is unchanging, including the definition of honor and duty. To doubt this or say otherwise is second only to blasphemy. His concept of how men of rank should behave is narrowly defined, and his sons were expected to concur with his view." Hugh paused. "As boys, they failed to show ardor in ways he thought they should."

"Truth comes from God. As such, it is both perfect and eternal," she replied. "But men are flawed creatures, often confusing their imperfect views with His. The greatest of God's truths is the need for charity. Did he never exercise compassion with his babes?"

Hugh shook his head. "Whether he is right or wrong, the baron believes his way is God's. Yet he is an honorable man, despite a dour and unbending nature. He adores his wife. His loyalty to friends and liege lord is fierce." Touching his chest, he added, "Despite our disagreements in certain matters, he would remain at my side in battle, choosing to die rather than desert me." He briefly smiled. "And he would bemoan my faults with his dying breath."

Eleanor closed her eyes and imagined scales. Did this man's code of honor outbalance his rigid interpretation of virtue? Would such a father go so far as to kill his unsatisfactory sons so that the more acceptable Leonel might inherit? Her mind allowed the premise. Her heart could not. "Would he defend his imperfect sons with equal ferocity or does he condemn them as so unworthy that the very earth must protest their feet upon it?"

"Had he not loved his wife so much, he might have claimed they were bastards for he saw none of himself in any. Yet he struggled to accept the merit owned when one tried to please him. I remember the day the eldest labored in the tilting yard to the amusement of all who watched. His lance usually missed the target by the length of a horse, yet he had a quick eye for catching the smallest error in accounting rolls."

"This was the son who died of fever?"

Hugh nodded. "The baron pulled the lad from the horse, gave the beast to one of his men, and ordered his steward to train the boy in a clerk's skills. When he left for Acre, he praised the young man for how well he had learned land management, although he made it clear he had wished for a warrior heir."

"Gervase was the second."

"As a boy, he cut his finger on a dull knife and never touched a weapon again, clinging instead to a priest's softer robe. A man of faith, Baron Herbert was pleased enough to send one son to the Church. When he received word that this son was now heir, he roared with mockery. I doubt his letters back to the lad were gentle. When Gervase died, I asked myself if he had suffered unendurable melancholy when he traded the vocation he preferred for one in which he had no skill."

"You think he committed self-murder by leaping from the window?"

"He lacked a man's strength and drank too much to soften the world's sharp edges."

Eleanor said nothing for a moment and looked around. Except for the two of them, the corridor was empty of all but the bitter wind from the sea. "Then why wait so long after his eldest brother's death?" she finally said. "He would not have been the first heir to choose a religious vocation, allowing the next-in-line to inherit title and lands. Peter Abelard chose a similar path, although his parents may have valued heavenly objectives more than the baron. They both took vows themselves as well as their son."

Remembering the seal that Brother Thomas had found, she wondered if the baron had planned a similar retreat from the world. If so, he might have been more sympathetic to Gervase than he would have been in years past. In any case, why would Herbert have wanted to kill a son, albeit a weak one, whose religious vocation he did not condemn?

"I doubt Baron Herbert would have permitted it," Hugh said. "Roger, the next-in-line, was neither devout nor clever." Hearing a sound, he looked over his sister's head. A servant scurried past and disappeared through a nearby door. "As I remember him, he was a dull lad but owned broad shoulders and merry enough ways to charm women into his bed. Most went to him eagerly in those early days, but the brightness of his smile often faded with their pains in bearing his children."

"He showed no talent with a sword or lance?"

"He was too lazy. The only weapon he enjoyed wielding was the spear between his legs."

Eleanor put a hand over her mouth to hide her mirth.

"His father abhorred this incontinence. I once overheard the baron shouting that the son had more bastards than the boy knew how to count. The lad next to me whispered that Roger surely had far more than his father knew because the son could not count at all."

"Neither a man of war nor of God." Eleanor frowned.

"Nor truly evil either, rather a middling creature, little inclined to adventure outside his chosen vice."

"Would such a man venture out in a boat on a stormy night? Even to drown himself?"

"He would not have willingly gotten into a boat if Satan had placed a buxom lass with open arms in it. I agree that this death is questionable."

"And what of poor Umfrey?"

"I knew little of him. He was a mere boy when I was last here." Suddenly his face paled, and he turned away from her.

"Hugh?"

He remained silent.

"I am your sister, bound to keep your secrets for the love I bear you. As a prioress, I am obliged to treat all human frailties with compassion and justice. Speak. There is nothing you cannot say to me. We are here to solve foul crimes."

When her brother looked back, his cheeks were red with anger. "I abhor those who mock and belittle others with scornful tales."

"So do I, but I would hear the stories lest there be something in them of value to this situation."

"Baron Herbert never spoke this son's name, and for that reason I fear he had heard the rumors. Umfrey was commonly called *the soldier's wife*. He never was a man. I grieve for the shame his father must have suffered."

After the death of the eldest, the baron was left with a monkish heir, a son of little wit or skill, and one who played the woman with other men. Eleanor took a deep breath. "That leaves Raoul."

"A whining insect."

"Raoul was always the youngest?"

"There were no others. No one liked him, but he especially chose to buzz around me when I least wanted him about."

For a moment, Eleanor saw the annoyed boy her brother must once have been. She almost smiled, despite her grim purpose. "Perhaps he admired you," she said. "He had no elder brother worthy of emulation. He was too young to catch the interest of a distant father, a man who left England before the lad could even lift a wooden sword in play."

Hugh stared at her, then turned sheepish. "I confess I treated Raoul no better than I would a midge, swatting him away. He was stubborn. Looking back, he did show more spirit and determination than his elder siblings." He thought for a moment, then shook his head. "Nonetheless, he was still annoying."

"What did his father say about him?"

"That he was tiresome. Even as a babe, Raoul crawled after Baron Herbert like a slobbering pup. When the baron took the cross, the lad beseeched him to take him too, although he was too young for a man's vows. Raoul would not accept the understandable refusal. Finally, his father lost his temper and…"

"You told me about the public humiliation of his son." Eleanor lowered her gaze, hoping to hide her sadness over the mockery of a child. As she remembered other sons, roughly treated by their fathers, she knew it was possible that Raoul could wish for revenge. "Did he hate his father for this?"

Hugh turned away, went to a window, and looked out at the grey-misted island. He leaned against the thick wall, pressing the side of his head against it as if seeking comfort in the undoubted firmness of stone. "I do not know, for I never saw him again until you and I came here at his father's request."

Eleanor watched her brother and grieved over the change in him since he had left for Acre. Although his face still brightened with enthusiasm, as it did when he was a greener youth, melancholy too often chased all light from his soul. She walked over and clasped his hand, keeping her touch tender with love.

He squeezed her hand affectionately, then pointed toward the uneven surface of the island behind the castle walls. "Raoul might be out there."

She squinted against the force of the wind. "Where on such a storm-blasted island might he hide or find shelter?"

"There are burrows and hillocks big enough to keep a small man safe against the gales. Also ledges of rock with small caves near the sea. Having followed us and watched when we hunted for bird eggs or played at being knights besieging a castle, he should know all the places. Perhaps more than we did. We did not always see him spying on us."

"Especially when you had willing lasses whom you took to some secluded spot?"

Hugh's eyes grew merry with her jest. He looked down at his sister and whispered: "You have put a balm on my hurt pride and chased away my anger. While Leonel searches the castle, I shall seek Raoul on the island and in the cove."

"Take care," she replied, "and may God be with you."

As she watched him walk away, she was filled with doubt and fear. Were Leonel and her brother seeking the wrong man? Was the murderer sitting in his dark chamber, waiting for the capture of his guiltless son who might have little proof of innocence?

And if Raoul had killed his brothers out of jealousy, greed, or revenge, why would he remain nearby? Surely he would leave England entirely to escape hanging.

She grew more confused, unable to see clearly and find the answer that resolved everything. Why would Raoul even commit all these murders? Surely he knew he would be the obvious suspect after so many deaths. He would have to flee and could never become his father's heir. Had he not wanted the inheritance but only revenge against his father for the cruelty he had suffered? She was dissatisfied with that conclusion.

Her thoughts swirled like a flock of birds, unable to find a place to land and settle into a logical form. She found no reasonable motive for the youngest son. If all the siblings died and Raoul was forced to flee as their murderer, Leonel would become the heir, a man his father loved more than any son.

That brought her back to the baron as the strongest suspect. Yet his cries of pain over the disappearance of his last son suggested a man who still cared for his progeny despite his disapproval of them. Could a man so rigid in his thinking be so clever in dissembling?

The many questions were like weeds, catching at her wits and tripping her before she could see the path to the solution. Rubbing her hand over her eyes, she felt as if the sea mist had befuddled her reason. Surely not, yet something had and she had little time left to regain her wits.

The prioress looked down the corridor, hoping to catch a comforting last glimpse of her eldest brother. But he had disappeared, gone to seek Baron Herbert's youngest son, a creature who had never found a place in his father's heart.

That was still a fact she could not easily set aside.

Chapter Twenty-Seven

The sea wind howled, reeking of salt, and honed sharp by northern ice. To keep warm, Eleanor tucked her arms deep into her woolen sleeves and hunched forward as she hurried down the damp, narrow stairs from the chapel. She must take a cup of wine to chase away this chill, she thought, and entered the corridor surrounding the Great Hall.

She had jousted wits with liegemen of the Prince of Darkness often enough, but never had she felt his dark power so strongly. Without Brother Thomas and Sister Anne, she might have been overwhelmed by it, no matter how much she prayed for strength. She did not like this feeling of weakness and confusion.

Although she was not a fanciful woman, and believed that evil wore mortal flesh, she wondered if this fortress was enchanted. Had her brother not visited here in happier times, she might have concluded that their innocent party had stumbled into a mythical castle like knights often did in tales of King Arthur's time. She abhorred and feared this sensation of being powerless, as if a spell had been cast.

Eleanor clenched her jaw. The perpetrator of these crimes was as clever as he was wicked. If this was a test for her, she was resolved to meet it. "Failure is unacceptable," she muttered with new determination, but now a cup of wine and a few minutes in front of the fireplace were required. Her body and spirit had been rendered insensate by the cold.

Entering the hall, her spirit lightened.

Brother Thomas stood by the fireplace, staring into a goblet. His robe was mottled with damp, yet he seemed oblivious to any discomfort.

She slowed, noted his grim expression, and suspected the good monk might share her relief were she to announce that they would return to Tyndal Priory on the morrow. Calling out to him, she was warmed by how quickly his eyes lost their sadness when he recognized his prioress.

He bowed.

Anticipating the comfort his presence always brought her, she smiled.

A voice shattered her pleasure. "My lady!"

Turning, Eleanor saw Sir Leonel rushing toward them. His sodden woolen cloak clung to him. Odors of leather, wet sheep, and sweat grew strong as he came nearer.

She tensed with apprehension. Had Raoul been captured? Was he alive? She hoped that there had not been one more tragedy for this family to endure.

"I was on my way to Baron Herbert until I saw you here." Leonel gasped the words as he caught his breath.

There was a troubled note in his voice. Had something happened to her brother? Despite her will to remain stern, she began to tremble.

Sir Leonel stepped closer. "You are chilled!" He reached out for her arm, as if to steady her, but pulled back before his fingers touched and did not commit the grave offense.

But his warm breath did brush her cheek. Her knees grew weak. Why had she not conquered her susceptibility to this man? She looked up at him and instantly knew that had been a mistake. Her eyes surely betrayed her longing.

The knight gazed back, a curious light dancing in his eyes.

"You have finished searching the castle grounds for Raoul?" Thomas put his goblet aside.

Out of the corner of her eye, she saw that the monk was now at her side. Not only had she sinned with lust for this knight, she feared she had betrayed herself to the one person she did not want to know of it. Anger and humiliation swirled into a lethal mix and burned her face with shame.

"I did fail to find him." Leonel ignored Thomas and smiled at Eleanor, leaning against the wall as he watched her.

She shut her eyes.

"I had hoped to ask your brother some questions. Sadly, I cannot find him." He rubbed at a spot on his chest just over his heart.

Taking a deep breath for control, she forced herself to turn to her monk. "Have you seen Sir Hugh since we all met last?"

Brother Thomas shook his head and scowled at the knight. The red slash on his cheek throbbed in the shimmering firelight.

"He has gone on his own search," she replied, looking down at the stone floor.

"I tried to persuade him otherwise." Sir Leonel's teeth flashed white as he grinned. "But I should not be surprised. He has never been a man to sit idle when there is danger." He paused, and his brow furrowed. "We did not meet in our separate hunts. More's the pity."

Eleanor nodded, not trusting her voice to speak without breaking.

He rubbed at one eye which made him look as if he had winked.

Eleanor felt lightheaded, almost giddy. What was happening to her? She could not concentrate, then caught herself wondering why his eyes were grey in this light. She thought they had been violet.

"Your brother bested us all at the chase in Outremer, my lady. He always knew where the quarry might hide." He turned to look toward the corridor and almost struck Brother Thomas. "I did not see you," he said and offered an apology.

The monk muttered acceptance, but his eyes flashed with displeasure.

"He might well find Raoul." Leonel turned back to face the prioress, his expression worried. "Do you know where he might have gone?"

Brother Thomas cleared his throat.

"He would have been wise to take you with him, Brother." Sir Leonel spun around and slapped him on the shoulder. "A monk's prayers are useful."

Thomas stepped back.

"Do you have reason to fear for Hugh's safety?" Eleanor reached behind her with one hand and felt the edge of a table. Pressing against it, she tried to recover some of her strength from the comforting wood.

The knight looked away.

"If so, please tell me."

"I am not accusing my cousin, my lady. He is surely innocent of all wrong, but, if he is not, I fear him. When cornered, Raoul is like a wounded boar, dangerous and willing to chance anything to escape. Were I to accompany Sir Hugh, we would be stronger together and less likely, either of us, to be injured."

Brother Thomas gestured for permission to speak. "My lady, if I may say…"

"And your prayers to God on our behalf would surely add strength to our cause!" Leonel again tapped the monk on the shoulder, the gesture oddly dismissive although he quickly drew back his hand and gestured with polite appeal. Then he smiled at Eleanor. "Please tell me where your brother has gone so I might join him. I shall take a few soldiers along as well. Methinks that would be wise."

Nodding, she repeated all Hugh had said about hiding places on the island and the cove.

"Ah, yes, the cove." Leonel murmured gratitude. "I humbly beg you both for prayers." He bowed and without waiting for reply, rushed away, leaving behind a scent of musk and leather before he strode through an open door to the corridor and disappeared.

Eleanor felt as if she had just recovered from a virulent fever. Even the table against which she pressed felt as insubstantial as the outside mist. Truly she must be bewitched, she thought, and shook her head, trying to clear her thoughts.

"Are you ill, my lady?" Brother Thomas' brow was creased with concern.

Sick enough with guilt, she thought. Indeed, she would have felt better if she had broken out in spots from some pox. "I have caught a mild chill," she replied. "Perhaps we should request some mulled wine to warm us both."

The monk gestured to a servant who hurried off to obtain the needed drink.

In silence, the two religious stared into the large fire that crackled with fiendish intensity. As Eleanor rubbed her hands to bring feeling back, she swallowed her pride. "I seek your opinion, Brother."

He nodded, his expression lacking all condemnation of what he might have guessed.

How kind he is, she thought. "Although wickedness lives amongst us always, I feel an excess of Satan's influence in this place. The recent events would support that conclusion. But, if he is so all-present, why can we not see him clearly?"

Thomas looked away from her and toward the windows in the corridor just beyond the hearth fire's domain. "I, too, am aware of the Prince of Darkness' presence, my lady." For a long time he was silent, but, when he looked back at her, his eyes were sad. "The Evil One is a creature of unsurpassed beauty. Perhaps the brightness of his countenance has so blinded us that we cannot see him well enough to recognize who he is."

Chapter Twenty-Eight

Hugh rode slowly across the fragile, narrow strip joining island to the mainland. Although he understood the defensive merit, he had never liked this entrance to the castle, even in the summer season when the sea lapped at the land like a gentle hound drinking water. The rock may have been there for longer than any man's life, but he always felt it vibrate when he was on it.

Looking down at his mare, he knew the creature shared his apprehension. She tugged at the reins as if urging a quick trot. With the road slippery with seawater and mud, Hugh refused to comply and demanded a continuation of their cautious pace.

A white wave rose over the side of the rock and broke across the path in front of him. The mare neighed in terror and drew back. Hugh stroked her neck and bent to whisper in her ear as he waited. The water quickly slid back into the sea, taking with it bits of earth as hostage.

The mare snorted with renewed impatience, and he realized without looking that the beast's eyes were white with fear. Keeping a firm grip on the reins, he allowed her to move on with prudent speed.

He might share her dismay, Hugh thought, but knew not to let the mare sense his own uneasiness as they crossed the narrowest part of the road. To keep his thoughts from the jagged rocks on either side, he began to enumerate all the locations he had just searched on the island. Then he listed them all over again.

He was confident that he had not missed any of the secret places he had known as a boy. Over time, some of the covered ledges had collapsed into the sea and the shallow caves made inaccessible. In other places, the winds had gouged deeper hollows, making the caves better shelters for any living creature. Yet Raoul was in none of them, nor had Hugh found any evidence that a man had sought shelter there, however briefly.

Unlike the summers he recalled from his youth, there were no flowers bent with the weight of heavy bees and flashing radiant colors to delight him. The grim winter storms had blackened the island grass with salted mists and frozen shrubs into tortured shapes, bare of life or even a promise of it.

Had he not known that this would change in time, he would have believed that Hell had arrived on earth and bore no resemblance to the fiery furnace of Shadrach, Meshach and Abednego. Instead, it was as barren as the mountains of eternal ice those men, who had come to Outremer from the northern lands, often spoke about. These warriors had claimed that the ice rose so high a mortal could not see the summits, and he had found no cause to doubt them.

His mare stumbled, then quickly recovered. Hugh was startled back into the present, but the shock had chased away his gloomy thoughts. As he looked around, he felt relief. He was now on the mainland and approached the sparse forest that lay between the castle and the main road. Taking in a deep breath of sharp air, he looked over his shoulder.

The castle was almost invisible in the mist. After facing death so often in combat, he did not consider himself a man prone to womanish notions, but he shivered nonetheless. There was something unearthly about the place. "I should never have agreed to this journey," he murmured to the mare.

It was one thing to endanger himself. He had no wife, his son was now well-placed, and his younger brother was a far worthier steward of family lands than he would ever be. To have led his sister, her healer, and Master Gamel into danger was another matter. He would never forgive himself if harm came to them.

As for Brother Thomas, he could not grieve over his fate. If the monk died, Hugh was sure the Devil would rejoice when he took one of his own back to Hell.

"That is as I remember," he whispered when he saw two thin trees with a narrow space between them. The branches of the two were intertwined, the one tree leaning against the other like a wounded soldier helped off the field by his comrade. Surely this was the way to the path that led down into the cove.

He urged his mount to pass through them.

When he found the path, he was surprised that it was still quite distinct. Twisting around in the saddle to look back along the length of the road, he decided that it had been used with some frequency. The earth was sodden, but deep ruts were visible, suggesting that heavy wagons had traveled this way. And quite recently, he thought. Some of the marks were clear despite the mud.

He rode on.

Within a few moments, he reached the crest of the cliff above the beach, and he directed his mare slowly down the treacherous incline. The trail seemed wider than he recalled, then concluded that his memory was in error.

Over time the earth may have slipped from the cliff, but that would have broken up the path, not widened it. And what reason would there have been to improve and maintain it? This track had only been a footpath in his youth, a means for young boys to reach the sandy beach for a swim in the heat of summer or the occasional fisherman who carried a small catch from his boat.

In spite of his cautious descent, Hugh quickly reached the cove. The tide had dragged the water back, forcing the sea to vent the full force of its wrath some distance away. Yet he knew just how close the foaming water came to where he was now standing.

There was good reason to call this cove Lucifer's Cauldron, he thought. When the tides came in higher than usual, the churning sea could pull a man far from shore and roll him under until he drowned. If the tides were that high, and the sea pushed hard by storms, the water swept in with such rapidity that a man could misjudge both power and speed. At those times, men often failed to outrun Death.

He would not remain here for long.

Hugh dismounted and led his mare to a piece of large driftwood. There he secured the creature by her reins.

"Despite that look in your eye," he said, stroking her wet mane, "you will be safe enough until I get back."

Glaring at him, she lifted her tail.

He laughed and walked away, not bothering to check the earth for clues. If Raoul had come here before the last tide, there would be little hope of finding fresh footprints in the sand.

But there should be a large cave just ahead, he thought. As he recalled it, the entry was wide enough for a couple of men to walk through, although the inside was sufficiently vast to give shelter to many. In addition, there were outcroppings of rocks from the cave walls. These were large enough to allow many boys to hide, leap down, and frighten latecomers to the place. The memories might have raised a smile had he not been on such a grim errand.

Looking around, he failed to see that opening. Had he forgotten where the entry was? Then he saw a large boulder resting near the place where he thought the gap should be.

He glanced up at the sheer precipice above and wondered if a rock had tumbled down when the weather eroded the cliff, but the angle of the stone against the cave did not support the conclusion. He could not think of a reason why the boulder might have been dragged here to block the entrance, unless someone had concluded the cave was too dangerous for young boys who might be trapped by the tides. He doubted this. All the lads had known the infernal nature of Lucifer's Cauldron well enough.

As he approached, he saw a small space between rock and cave, still wide enough for a man to walk through. The hair rose on the back of his neck. Had he finally found Raoul's hiding place?

Now he cursed himself for not thinking about the darkness inside. With no dry torch or any means to light one, he might not be able to see without moving the stone. He estimated the weight and knew he could not shift it further without help.

Slowly, he stuck his head inside. A weak beam of light flowed down from a hole on the other side of the cave. That had not been there when he was a boy, but he was grateful for it now. If he shut his eyes and let them adjust to the dark, he might be able to see with the extra light. Closing them now to speed the process, he squeezed himself inside.

After a moment, he blinked and looked around. He could see shadows. Should he call out? He hesitated and fingered the hilt of his sword. If Raoul was a killer, he would have no reason not to add another to a list of those he had already murdered.

He held his breath and listened. Only the sound of the wind outside reached his ears. His back pressed to the cave wall, he crept farther inside.

Looking up, he saw the remembered stony ledges where he and the other boys used to play. If Raoul was anywhere, he would be high up there and away from the incoming tides.

Then something caught his attention, and he moved away from the rock to look more carefully at the higher ledges. If he were not mistaken, there was a chest up there. He squinted. Not just one, several.

He grabbed hold of an outcropping of rock and pulled himself up, inching his way from toehold to toehold toward the objects. Why would anyone store so many chests in such a place?

When he got to the first ledge, he heaved himself over the top and sat, catching his breath. Then he crawled over to one chest and lifted the lid. There was nothing inside. Another was equally empty. In a third, he found part of a gold necklace, caught in a rough corner.

Suddenly he knew why the storage places were here, and he muttered a loud curse on his blindness.

Smuggling.

With care, he descended to the cave floor. Now that his eyes were accustomed to the dim light, he checked the walls of the cave and noted the water marks. These chests were stored high enough to be safe from most tides.

"Cunning," he said. "Bring the goods in by boat. Either there are pulleys stored where I did not see them or the men use ladders to haul the goods up there. And all is hidden and protected until someone can come to take it away for sale," he muttered. "Who is benefiting from all this?"

A sharp object pricked his back. Moisture trickled down his ribs. From the pain, he knew he was bleeding.

"If you came seeking a killer, Sir Hugh, you should have worn chain mail."

A hand slipped the knight's dagger out of its sheath.

"Loosen your sword belt and drop it. If you try to turn around, I shall kill you."

He may have been clever enough to find Raoul, Hugh thought, but he had been a fool to let himself be so easily captured.

Chapter Twenty-Nine

Thomas descended the stairs from the keep and entered the turmoil of the bailey grounds. The muck stank and the air bit at his flesh, but he was too distracted by his conversation with Prioress Eleanor to notice either. She had asked his advice, telling him of the talks she had had with Lady Margaret. Surely there was a significant detail in all they had seen and heard. Nothing came to mind, and he had been of little help to her.

"She likes you, Brother!"

Startled, Thomas spun around and found he was being scrutinized by large brown eyes framed with silken lashes. Their beauty was such that he could almost ignore the narrow face with long nose and big ears, the gangly body and spindly legs. He laughed. No matter that many disagreed with him, he had always been partial to goats.

The female goat sniffed tentatively at the sleeve of his robe.

Gently, he withdrew the temptation. "A fine creature," he replied to the goatherd.

"She may give the best milk, and my wife has made some excellent cheeses from it, yet this one's a brazen thing. Sorry if she's troubled you." The man's expression was polite, but hints of laughter lurked in his words. A symbol of lust, a goat chancing on a celibate religious was an encounter rife with lewd implications.

"May the tale of this meeting between beast and monk bring you pots of warming ale on these cold nights." Thomas winked, then gave his blessing.

Slapping the creature on the rump to send her off, the goat-herd bowed with sincere respect and left to tend his beasts.

The goat cast Thomas a flirtatious look before pushing her way into the midst of her fellows.

The monk stepped back and let the rank and raucous herd pass by. Now that he was pulled out of his musings, Thomas felt the insidious damp and began to shiver with its chill, but his mirth over the goat had chased away much of his melancholy.

Some evil in this place had truly cast spells on them all. He himself had gotten into a fight with Sir Hugh, a violence he regretted. Not once, until now, had he struck another in anger since becoming a monk. A man with other allegiances would have been justified in defending his honor, but Thomas served God. Although his faith was a lesser thing, he had still vowed service to Him. When he returned to the priory, he would beg severe penance from Brother John.

The last goat bounded past him. As he watched the shaggy beasts move toward the gate, Thomas saw a solitary horseman emerge from the nearby stables. It was the baron's nephew, edging his horse through the crowd of milling people and animals. He was alone. That is puzzling, the monk thought.

Hadn't the knight told Prioress Eleanor that he would take a party of soldiers with him to find Sir Hugh? The monk saw no armed men. Where was the promised protection in case Raoul was cornered and turned violent? Or was the nephew going elsewhere?

Uneasy, Thomas pushed his way through the crowd. The press of men's bodies against the horse had slowed the rider, but the monk was able to weave through them and close enough to see that the knight was dressed in chain mail. He also carried a small crossbow along with sword and dagger. The man's purpose must be to find Raoul. He was too well prepared for a fight.

Once more, the monk glanced over his shoulder toward the stables. No other soldiers, mounted or not, were visible. Thomas doubted Leonel had sent them ahead. There had not been enough time to summon a company and also give orders.

Turning around again, he saw that the knight was approaching the gate that led to that rocky finger of land linking castle to coast. The monk decided to follow. Amidst the throng of merchants, servants, and craftsmen, Thomas found an orderly line of people headed to the gate as well, and he joined them.

Sir Leonel was a man of much beauty and great charm, Thomas thought, yet he was curiously unmoved by either. Not entirely, he reminded himself, but his lust had been as brief as a lightning flash. Although he might never be free of his yearning to lie in another man's arms, the incident last summer involving the young man named Simon was too fresh. The memory was like ice on his groin. He sighed with bitterness and relief in equal measure. In truth, he disliked Sir Leonel.

As he continued to follow the knight over the drawbridge, Thomas forced his mind to honesty and asked if his aversion had been formed out of thwarted desire more than reason and experience. As he well knew, men often draped their coarser lusts with the soft cloth of moral rectitude.

Thomas stared at the rider now some distance ahead of him, then shook his head. Other men, since he had come to Tyndal, had tempted him more than this knight, yet their memories brought him the occasional dream of comfort and release. Looking at Sir Leonel, he felt only disgust.

As he thought more on it, he realized that the most likely cause was found in the knight's treatment of Prioress Eleanor just a short while ago. Going over the details of that encounter, he remained convinced that Sir Leonel's speech to her was filled with a mix of sweet honey and the musk of seduction. How dare he treat a woman of her rank and vocation with such dishonor!

Realizing that he had clenched his fists in anger, Thomas stepped out of the moving crowd, shut his eyes, and took a deep breath to calm himself.

The cold air ached in his chest and shocked his wits back into balance. He opened his eyes, fearing he had lost sight of Leonel, but the knight was not far ahead, still riding along the narrow road, his pace slowed by carts coming into the castle. Thomas hurried after him.

Something else about the encounter between his prioress and the knight bothered him. Unlike that meeting with the sheriff at Master Stevyn's manor over a year ago, she did not greet Leonel's shameful behavior with indignation. Instead, she had become timid, an attitude he had never before seen in her. Although she sometimes exhibited feminine humility in the company of powerful men, he had learned that this particular meekness was always accompanied by a tightening of her jaw. Unless the matter was inconsequential to her, she never brooked any obstruction to her will.

Had she actually been tempted by this imp in mortal dress?

From his first meeting with Prioress Eleanor, he had concluded she was a woman fiercely dedicated to God's service. Unlike some who took vows, she neither feared the world nor, despite her youth, was she much tempted by it. He also knew she was a woman of honorable passions, fiercely loyal to family, friends, and her priory. She had shown flashes of anger, directed against those who violated God's law, and often sorrow, when cruelty wounded mortals beyond healing. He had never known her to lust after a man.

Horrified by the thought, he skidded to a stop so abruptly that a merchant ran into him.

The fellow cursed loudly, then realized he had struck a monk. Appalled by his offense, the man stuttered a rambling plea for pardon.

Waving him off with distracted forgiveness, Thomas forced himself to consider the shocking possibility that this woman of masculine mind and iron will might have betrayed the spirit of her vows. Then compassion slowly numbed the sting of his astonishment.

All mortals are weak, he reminded himself, and women deemed the most fragile. Yet he was a man, possessed of reason, and he had committed the same sin—and more than once. What right had he to cast any stone of condemnation against her? Although his vows had been made with no true vocation, he respected them. Since she had come to God with a purer heart, she would surely fight against temptation far more forcefully than he. And if anyone could send the Devil howling back to Hell, clutching his wounded genitals, it would be Prioress Eleanor.

He grinned.

Or, as was also possible, she had not lusted at all but was infected with that strange enchantment that seemed to plague them all in this place. He had lashed out at Sir Hugh. Even Sister Anne, who always retained both a merry heart and sound reason, had grown distracted and moody. With forced charity, Thomas assumed that his prioress' brother was a kinder man by nature. Only Master Gamel seemed untouched, but then the monk did not know him well enough to judge.

Thomas realized he had been standing distracted on the road for too long. Leonel had disappeared into the sea mist that swirled over the narrow ridge.

He walked on as swiftly as he dared in the slippery mud. Ignoring the crashing waves on either side of him and the stinging mist enveloping him, Thomas willed himself to continue across the narrowest part of the land bridge in pursuit of the baron's nephew.

When he told Prioress Eleanor that they might not recognize the face of the Prince of Darkness because they had been blinded by his beauty, he had meant it as a metaphor to explain their inability to find the murderer. Now that he thought more on it, he wondered if he had been more astute than he had realized. Did Leonel own those dazzling features of Satan?

Perhaps the man did not dance naked in the winter storms with fork-tailed creatures owning hooves and hairy buttocks, but that did not mean the knight was uninvolved in worldly wickedness. Not only was there murder to explain, Thomas thought, but that troubling matter of the lights in the cove remained unexplored.

Raoul was the most likely suspect in the murder of his brothers, but Sir Leonel might be guilty of some other plotting, the exact nature of which remained unclear. The two might also be linked in some wrongdoing. Whatever the answers, Thomas was growing more inclined to point at least one cold finger of accusation at the baron's nephew.

"May God keep me charitable," he muttered, "lest I be no wiser than many other men and send curses down upon an innocent man merely because he has angered me."

Wrapping his cloak tighter against his body, he hurried into the icy fog, searching for a pale horse and a well-armed rider.

Chapter Thirty

Eleanor bowed, until her head touched the rough wooden floor of the family chapel, and murmured inaudible pleas into God's ear.

The high howling wind from the single window grew soft as if ordered to respect this penitent's remorse. Even the flickering light from the rushes, brought by a servant and set into wall brackets, exposed only delicate shadows against the walls.

The prioress began to sob.

A woman's hand gently touched her shoulder. "Shall I summon Brother Thomas?" Sister Anne whispered as she knelt. Her breath was soft on the prioress' ear.

Raising her head, Eleanor rubbed her cheeks dry. "Nay," she murmured, banishing all future tears and further evidence of sorrow. She turned to the sub-infirmarian with a weary look.

"I have stood outside the chapel door since you entered," Anne said. "No one has approached to disturb your prayers."

"How long have I been here?"

"Since you spoke with Sir Leonel and our monk."

Eleanor clutched her hands to her chest and groaned.

"What troubles you?"

"How foul my wickedness has been that it has taken so much prayer to heal it!" She seized her friend's hand. "I need your wisest counsel. I fear my soul continues to be blinded."

Anne helped the prioress rise to her feet. Except when a mortal fever had struck her friend, Anne had never seen Eleanor so frail in spirit and body. "I am always ready to offer my poor service," she said and disguised her deep concern.

For a long moment, the two women stared in silence at the altar.

"The smell of death is still strong," Eleanor whispered. "Neither this place nor the common chapel is free of blood." Clearly agitated, the prioress began to pace around the small area of the room. "Is it any wonder that no one comes here to pray? Or does the cause lie in the evil charm enchanting this castle?"

Anne shivered at the question but knew her friend had not finished her thought. She slipped her hands into the woolen sleeves of her robe and waited.

"I have felt evil in this place from the moment of our arrival, yet even knowing the danger, I have fallen victim to it." Eleanor hesitated under the high window that cast a grey shadow down upon her. "After Sir Leonel left us, Brother Thomas reminded me that Satan's exceptional beauty can blind us to his deeds." She turned to face Anne. "I have been dazzled by that splendor, and for the sin I have been begging God's pardon."

Her friend's expression softened with compassion.

"With proper penance, He will forgive, but now that my eyes are opening, I must look again at the events here. Your observations must keep me on the side of angels, lest I am ensnared once more by the glitter of evil."

"May He give me strength," Anne replied.

Eleanor ceased her restless stride and approached her friend. "Baron Herbert loves his nephew more than his own lads. Perhaps with cause. Sir Leonel has demonstrated wit and courage in war, qualities the sons lack. I have heard it said that the nephew should have been the heir, rather than any of the baron's many progeny."

Anne was startled to see the prioress grinding a fist into her palm. Her friend rarely betrayed so much overt anger.

"I find it difficult to ask this question about a father, but I must. Now that he fears he has leprosy, do you think Baron Herbert capable of murdering his own children so Sir Leonel will inherit?"

Anne paled. "If the baron has spoken, either of a preference in heirs or about his sons' failings, he would have done so in private to Master Gamel or Brother Thomas."

"The good doctor confides in you, respecting your opinion and knowledge as do I and all at our priory. He is university trained, yet you bring knowledge of a patient's soul as well as experience in the healing arts. Your words are only for my ears. Be plain-spoken with me."

Nodding, Anne quickly glanced at the chapel door. "Baron Herbert owns no tolerance for weakness." She leaned closer to the prioress' ear and lowered her voice. "This, you have surely observed yourself. A man must be like iron, firm in his faith, unflinching in battle, resolute in loyalty and honor. As he said to Master Gamel, a man who falters is a coward, worthy only of dishonorable death."

"Had he sired daughters, he might have been kinder to them for I believe he loves his wife profoundly."

Anne was relieved to see that Eleanor had unclenched her fist.

"Despite the harshness to his sons, his eyes moistened when he spoke of their deaths. His outrage was scorching when he thought they had been sacrificed as penance for his own sins. Even Raoul, whom the baron called *cur*, was also named *Absalom*, the son loved best by King David despite the boy's rebellion." Her brow creased with thought.

"When the baron confessed he might have leprosy, he asked Master Gamel if fathering weak sons had been an early symptom of the disease. The good physician disabused him of that worry." Anne smiled. "He also told him that he might find the men, who greeted him on his return, different from the boys he left. At first, the baron seemed inclined to dispute this, then fell silent and nodded."

Eleanor contemplated how the pale light bathed the gold altar cross with a sickly glow. "My brother came back from Outremer a much changed man, yet his love for his son has grown stronger with the absence." She turned to Anne. "Why did the baron not feel the same?"

"Sir Hugh did not come home condemned to live while he watched his body rot like a corpse."

Eleanor spoke her agreement while silently asking herself if any man returned without bringing the dead with them to populate dreams.

"You asked my opinion of what I have heard and seen."

The prioress nodded.

"The baron is not one to show his love with open arms. Had he not been terrified of his illness, however, he might have cast a more patient gaze on his sons, willing to gauge their characters as men, not babes. Instead, he fled to a distant part of the castle, unable to bear the thought of infecting his family by looking or breathing on them. Nonetheless, he longed to die as close to them as possible. Baron Herbert may be a hard man, but I think he loves as passionately as he holds to his principles. In my opinion, this is not someone who would murder his sons so that Sir Leonel was left as his heir. He may love his nephew, but the man is his brother's seed, not his own."

A thin smile twitched at Eleanor's lips. "You have confirmed what I have suspected, indeed hoped, would be the character of the man. Umfrey may have thought that the man who struck him was his father, but my belief grows stronger that it was someone else." Then she tilted her head. "Before we speak of that, I know you have more to say but hesitate to utter your thoughts. I hear it in your voice."

"My lady, I do not like the baron's nephew."

Whenever Anne grew formal in private, Eleanor knew she was expressing something she feared the prioress would dislike. "I must hear your reasons," she said softly. For the good of my soul, she added in silence.

"You have said that Brother Thomas spoke of Satan's shining face, a creature that once ranked amongst the highest angels and possessed great beauty while his heart oozed with rank corruption." She stopped and looked with sorrowful countenance at the prioress.

"I beg you to continue." Eleanor dreaded what Anne was about to say, fearing it would echo the voice in her own heart that she had silenced too long. Later, she would condemn herself for not seeing what her friend had recognized far earlier. Her own frailty was of little importance now. The only thing that mattered was catching a killer.

"Sir Leonel is a man possessed of many virtues others rightly praise. He has courage, charm, and stands by his uncle whatever his illness. Despite owning much that is praiseworthy, his manner toward you, a woman vowed to God's service, is too bold. Brother Thomas has thought so as well and fears the man does not have a pure heart."

"I am equal in guilt, if not more blameworthy, for allowing it," Eleanor said, as the weight of her imperfections bore down on her once again with an awful heaviness. She shrugged, determined not to be distracted even by her failings. "You have said what I most needed to hear. My soul is lighter, my reason restored. Now, as always, God has lent His hand to your healing skills."

Anne bowed her head.

"My lady?"

Startled, the two women looked up.

A manservant stood, shifting from foot to foot, just inside the chapel door. He stopped twitching and bowed with mumbled apology. "Baron Herbert seeks Brother Thomas for confession, but I cannot find the good monk anywhere in the keep." He began to wring his hands. "I have gone to his room, the common chapel, and the hall. He was not walking in the passageways." His eyes grew wide with fear. "My master grows impatient."

Eleanor turned to Anne.

"I have not seen him," the nun replied.

"Come!" Eleanor rushed past the astonished servant and into the hall. When she reached a window, she looked into the bailey and gestured to Anne. "Do you see him anywhere?" She stepped aside so her friend could take her place.

The sub-infirmarian peered down and studied the thinning crowd. Suddenly, she pointed. "Is that him?"

Eleanor edged next to her and squinted into the icy mist swirling past the window. "Near the gate?"

"To my knowledge, there is no other monk here and certainly not one with a soldier's height and breadth. It must be Brother Thomas." She stepped back and stared at the prioress. "Where can he be going? He is leaving the castle, and there is no nearby village."

The prioress leaned back from the window and pressed her fingers against her eyes. "Not this!" Blinking and now wide-eyed, she cried out: "As You were merciful to Lot and his family, when you destroyed Sodom and Gomorrah, take pity on two innocent men. Destroy me for my wickedness, but let my brother and that good monk live!"

Anne gasped.

Eleanor spun around and summoned the servant. "Immediately take the two of us to Baron Herbert."

"What has happened?" Anne clasped her hands in confusion.

The servant's ruddy face turned grey, but he gestured for them to follow.

Her own face pale, the prioress spoke to Anne in a low voice. "I told Sir Leonel where Hugh had planned to search for Raoul. Brother Thomas overheard me. As you told me, our monk was not blinded by the nephew's charms. Methinks he may have followed Sir Leonel out of the fortress. I not only fear for my brother's safety now, I also worry that Brother Thomas has left to find my brother. Both men may be in danger from this nephew."

"I did not say I thought Sir Leonel was the murderer." Anne looked at the prioress in horror. "Only that he has fooled many into believing he is a more virtuous man than he…"

Eleanor put a finger to her lips as she pulled her friend along after the servant. "Who gains if Baron Herbert has no heirs?" she whispered. "Suffering symptoms that suggest her womb is no longer fertile, Lady Margaret fears she can no longer bear more sons. Her husband may be cursed with an incurable disease which prohibits him from bedding any wife out of fear of contagion."

"Raoul could still be the killer. Does he not stand to inherit if Umfrey is dead?"

"That he does, but I now see reasons to doubt his guilt. Consider these points. The nephew knows the baron well enough to successfully pretend he is Umfrey's father. Raoul is least likely to remember how his father spoke or gestured. How could he mimic the baron when he was so young when Baron Herbert left? The Lady Margaret has also told me that she sees much of her husband's ways in Raoul. If the father would not kill his sons to make Sir Leonel his heir, would a like-spirited lad think it honorable to kill his brothers in order to raise himself in rank?"

Anne looked doubtful.

"I agree that a mother's soft love would hold little weight in a disputation based in reason. My belief that the knight could dissemble better than the youngest son is also a weak argument. Yet even my brother, who has little love for Raoul and high regard for the nephew, hesitates to call the son a murderer. I grow more convinced that Leonel is the killer. He is a clever man and beguiles others so sweetly that they never ask what motive he has for doing so."

"What is your plan?"

"I must convince Baron Herbert that his nephew is a dangerous man."

"Surely he will defend Sir Leonel, a man who has served him well and like a son for years. Although I dislike him, the knight has proven virtues apart from his charm…" Anne's eyes widened. "Your words ring true. Even though I saw a flaw, when he treated you with disrespect, I never thought to ask if the nephew had a base motive behind his well-played actions within this family."

"The baron has grounds to discount anyone's accusations against his nephew, especially those of a woman, no matter her rank or vocation." Eleanor's eyes narrowed.

The servant stopped at the door to the baron's chamber and glanced back at the two women following.

"Announce us," she said, then quickly turned to whisper in Anne's ear. "But I shall use a woman's power, if I must. I may weep, bend my knee, and plead with him to save Hugh from harm. Whether the murderer is Raoul or Leonel, I have cause, weak woman that I am, to fear for my brother's safety and demand the rights of a guest. Baron Herbert is obliged to offer protection to his friend, a man who came at his behest, even if the danger comes from his family. Indeed, his sense of honor would require it if close kin were involved. At the very least, he will send a company of soldiers out to seek and protect my brother from the killer."

"Have you no way to convince him that his beloved nephew might be the killer?"

"I have one that brings great weight." She winced and pressed the heel of her hand over her left eye.

Recognizing the gesture as a symptom of the prioress' blinding headaches, Anne prayed she would be spared.

"I have just come from the chapel where I begged God for guidance. Did He not bless me with enlightenment and point out my own errors of judgement regarding Sir Leonel? The baron is a man of faith. Without a priest immediately at hand to interrogate me, Baron Herbert would hesitate to conclude that my revelation is false. I may be a woman, but I am still Prioress of Tyndal, a religious office that demands respect."

Emerging from the chamber, the servant bowed and gestured for the women to enter.

"I pray for your success and confess that I also fear for Brother Thomas' safety," Anne murmured.

"I fear most for him," Eleanor replied. "Unlike my brother, he carries neither shield nor weapon. God must provide him with the armor he lacks."

Chapter Thirty-One

Hugh squirmed. The salt-saturated rope, binding his wrists and ankles, cut into exposed flesh. "Untie me."

"Do not confuse the man you see here with the child you once knew. In those days, I was a fool, chasing after you, longing for your approval, and willing to believe anything you deigned to tell me. But after you left with my father to fight the infidel, I learned to act and reason like a man." Raoul laughed. "Were I so stupid as to release you, you would attack me."

"Men also trust."

"Want-wits do as well."

"If I swore not to harm you, what cause have you to believe I would not honor my word?" He stopped. Was he imagining that the roar of the sea was closer? "Surely I was not cruel to you as a boy."

Raoul extended his sword and lightly jabbed Hugh in the chest with the point. "Cruel deeds? The question you ought to ask is whether you ever protected me from them. Remember the time I stepped where your friends swore the ground was firm? I am sure you knew it was not but said nothing. The earth crumbled. As I fell, I watched the sea open its maw to swallow me. Had chance and a rock not caught me, I would have drowned."

"I did not know they had lied, but you should also recall that I was the one who lifted you to safety."

"And laughed because my bowels had loosened with terror."
He stared at the knight, then drew back his sword. "Sir Hugh,
your greatest sin was never cruelty but rather your choice of
boon companions."

"Then why not untie me?"

"Because a man's comrades prove his character."

"You may have been a boy, but I was little older. Boys grow
into men, and men grow in wisdom."

Raoul roared with mocking laughter. "Did some priest teach
you those fine words? Having known enough imprudent men, my
brothers amongst them, I doubt the truth in such judgement."

Again Hugh hesitated and listened carefully. It was not his
imagination. The tide was coming in. "Hear the sea striking the
cliffs?" He gestured with his head. "If this tide is high, we have little
time to escape. Release me, and we shall argue on higher ground."

"And allow you a fair fight? I captured you only because you
had dropped your guard." He waved his sword and chuckled.
"You came here looking for a killer, and, having found my
burrow, long to drag me from it by the ears like a cony. Despite
your poor opinion of me and my wits, I know you are stronger
and more skilled with a sword than I. Do not imagine I will let
you take me prisoner and deliver me to the hangman."

"Listen to reason!"

Raoul wagged a finger at the knight. "I am. There is good
cause to believe that I killed Umfrey, and probably my other
brothers as well. Am I not the only son still alive? That makes
me my father's heir, a fact that must gall him. What proof is
there of my innocence?" He extended the sword again and
playfully waved it over Hugh's bindings. "None, or you would
not have come. Shall anyone praise my virtues, swearing on a
saint's relic that I am incapable of committing fratricide? My
mother, perhaps, a woman who sometimes forgets my name."
He pressed his free hand against his heart. "Or my father who
showed his love by shaming me in front of his friends." Then he
touched the sword point on a spot between Hugh's eyes. "And
you expect me to trust you, a man who would have been relieved

at the removal of an annoyance if I had fallen to my death that summer day?" He drew back his sword.

"Did you kill your brothers?"

"You find it necessary to ask the question." Raoul's eyes narrowed. "That proves I am right not to trust you. Of all those living in this place, only Leonel might defend me. But who would believe a man who never speaks ill of anyone?" He stepped back from Hugh and sheathed his weapon. "If I have confidence in anything, it is my hanging."

Hugh shifted, but there was nothing he could do to find comfort or to keep the ropes from cutting into him. Now raw, his wrists burned with the salt.

Throwing his head back, Raoul murmured something inaudible. The sound was like a sob.

Hugh wished it were, but he doubted it.

"Whether or not you choose to believe me, I am innocent, yet the evidence suggests otherwise in two deaths at least. I did not stay in the castle long enough to learn all details of Umfrey's death, but many surely have no doubt that I killed him."

"Then return and defend yourself. Surely there were witnesses to prove you could not have done these deeds."

"Innocence alone is a fragile shield." Raoul spat. "Roger drowned but was drinking with me earlier that night. Many saw us together. No one saw us part."

"His death was called an accident."

"A man, so fearful of the sea, does not go out in a boat, particularly when the winds are high. Few believe he died by chance. Most conclude he drowned himself, although they choose not to say so aloud out of respect for my father. If men like you suggest murder, many will see the logic of that, look at me, and sagely nod their heads."

Hugh knew he did not have long to probe further. The waves now hit the beach with crashing force. "Gervase fell from the window of the keep. You could not be accused of that."

"Earlier that day, he had sent a servant to me with a message. The accounting rolls showed a questionable loan made to me, one I had never repaid. He required an explanation. Since I had never received such a loan, I was eager to see him, but he fell from the wall before I could. The servant has probably spread this news of my assumed misconduct."

Hugh groaned. "Umfrey. How could you have murdered him?"

"I visited him in the chapel. I shouted that I wished to do horrible things to him and, when a servant appeared, told him who I was, although I had no desire to hurt my brother. My intent was to give Umfrey confidence that I had not come to murder him, but those ill-advised words will be remembered otherwise now. As you see, I am implicated in them all."

"Have you witnesses to your whereabouts at the times of these deaths?"

"My lack of the usual sins condemns me. I whore, but not often. I drink, but rarely to excess. As for companions, I find my own company most pleasurable and claim few friends. Of those, I would safely turn my back on none."

Despite the sting of the ropes, growing numbness in his legs, and the approaching tides, Hugh forced a brief smile. "Adam committed only one transgression in Eden: he ate an apple. A wise man cultivates at least a minor vice, involving potential witnesses, if he ever expects to be accused of murder."

Raoul drew his sword again and pointed the tip at the knight's throat. "And you face death with a merry wit."

"I do not think you will kill me. If I am wrong, God will see my soul soon enough. I also doubt you would kill your brothers, especially in the ways they have died. You remind me of your father, another who stands apart from the crowd and holds to his own counsel. He is no courtier, choosing to use the blunt word and direct act rather than win men's hearts with sweetened phrases. Had you wanted to murder your brothers, you would have finished the bothersome task long before your father came home and greeted him as the unquestioned heir."

"Comparing me to my father was clever, Sir Hugh. The boy I once was would be delighted. The man is not swayed, however, and shall not untie you."

Hugh shifted, trying not to hear the sea, and prayed he had time for another ploy. "Some fear that your father killed Umfrey and would have slain you, had you not escaped. He prefers Leonel as heir."

Raoul lowered his sword but said nothing.

The broken waves hissed as they slipped across the sand outside the cave.

"Surely this tale is untrue," Raoul whispered. The young man's face was softened by the shadows. "You know my father better than any of us."

Raoul is not so far removed from boyhood, Hugh thought with compassion, hearing tears in the youth's whispered voice. The fact of his father's indifference to him as a child was hard enough to bear. That his father might long to slaughter him was a cruelty beyond any son's comprehension. "Your father is a hard man," Hugh said, "but he accepts what God saw fit to give him as sons. He would no more murder the offspring of his loins than he would castrate himself. Aye, he loves his nephew, but he wanted Sir Leonel to earn his own inheritance in Outremer."

Raoul stared for a long time at the hole in the ceiling of the cave. The light from it had grown dim, as if a fast-approaching storm had banished it.

Hugh grew impatient and began to plead again for release.

Raoul looked down at the knight. "There is something I have not mentioned to anyone," he said, ignoring the new appeal. "I have decided to confide in you because someone must consider the implications and report them to my father. As you surely understand, I cannot do this."

Hugh slid backward. The stones at his back were jagged. Were they sharp enough to cut his bonds?

Raoul saw his intent. "You cannot free yourself that way." He lifted the sword.

The knight tensed for the blow.

"I shall not cut your throat. I'll loosen your bonds but not cut them through. I must flee on your horse with enough time to avoid capture. As you noted, the tide will soon be in, but you can find safety on the ledges above if you climb high enough."

Hugh swallowed the lump in his throat. "Quickly, then. What troubles you?"

"I have seen lights in this cove. A soldier noted them as well and told his sergeant. A party of men was sent out and returned without finding anything of note. Later, I heard the soldier claim the lights had been Satan's liegemen, dancing in the storm winds with the souls of drowned sailors."

"You think otherwise?"

"I have confessed my heresy and heard the Church's argument from our dead priest. Despite doing penance, my heart remains certain that the Devil has no cause to lure our souls when he owns the world and all mortals on it." He waited. "You do not gasp in horror?"

Hugh was disinclined to a lengthy theological debate. "Nay," he replied. "But I am a soldier, not a priest."

Raoul squatted close to Hugh and gestured toward the chests on the ledges above their heads. "The lights were not imps. They were torches, brought by smugglers who carried goods from boats and stored the treasure in those chests until the items could be hauled away. Valuable, some of it. I found a large gold cross dropped near one chest. Smuggling's a fine trade, or so I hear."

Hugh frowned. "How long has this been going on?"

"After my father's return. I haven't witnessed this often, but this is not the season for sailing small boats. The gales are fierce."

"You think Baron Herbert might be involved?"

"I believe him to be innocent. He brought back much wealth from his time in Outremer. What need has he for smuggling and the dangers, especially in bad weather? Greed has never been one of his vices, and he will be horrified that such activity is taking place on his lands."

"How did you discover this?" Hugh tossed his head toward the ledges.

"I was curious. Not many apparently know the place where we all once played." His smile was thin. "The soldiers never thought of it, but a large rock now lies against the entry, hiding the entry from any casual observer."

"Why not bring this knowledge to your father?"

"What reason did I have to think he would believe me? He has always greeted me with contempt."

"Tell him now!"

"And hang for taking the chance? As I have already said, I have no good argument in my defense. Perhaps the perpetrator of these murders will be found some day and I can return, cleared of all guilt."

A rattling of stones caught their attention.

Hugh grew numb with fear. Had the sea reached the cave entrance already?

Raoul spun around.

A high-pitched whine split the air.

The son cried out and fell. His sword flew out of his hand, landing far from Hugh.

A man chuckled. "How much better that this lying wretch be killed while attempting to flee."

Sir Leonel emerged into the pale light, stepped over the body of Raoul, and grinned down at the vulnerable Hugh.

Chapter Thirty-Two

Thomas skidded and fell, sliding head first down the remaining path to the beach. Struggling to get on his feet, he felt the damp soaking through his robes. Had he ever been this covered with mud, even as a boy? He shivered.

His teeth chattering with the cold, he looked around. The cutting salt mist twisted like a spiteful imp, driving the chill deeper into his bones. He squinted to see more clearly, but it was a noise that caught his attention. He looked back toward the cliff.

A dark-colored mare was tethered to a piece of driftwood. The sea lapped close to her hooves, and her brown eyes betrayed enough white to suggest she was not pleased with her situation. Another horse of light coat was on higher ground, close to the cliffs. Less concerned with the hissing surf, this beast snuffled at the ground in search of edible grass.

Taking pity on the nervous mare, Thomas approached her with soft words and a gentle touch. Calmer, she let him lead her to the high rocky ground where he loosely wrapped the reins around a dead branch. "If the sea comes too close, you can still escape," he whispered and was rewarded with a nudge of her nose.

From the vantage point of this greater elevation, he could now see two sets of footprints in the sand. The deeper one surely belonged to Leonel, who must have just passed through, but the fainter set could mark anyone's path. Hugh or Raoul might be the most likely guesses, but other tracks, closer to the water, could have been washed away by the incoming tide. Who knows how many men have come here, Thomas thought. If others had, where did they all go?

Returning to the lower beach, he followed the clear footprints as far as he could. When the impressionable sand gave way to gravel, less battered by the sea and nearer the cliff, the tracks disappeared. Protecting his eyes from the salt spray, he gazed ahead and saw that the beach quickly narrowed around the curve that formed the remainder of the cove. He watched the waves exploding against the precipice and knew that no man would have recently traveled that route.

Thomas next scrutinized the nearest cliff. The rock face was wet, and there were no visible toeholds that might help a man climb that steep and dangerous ascent. Even if there had been, only fools or the desperate would try to do so on such a day.

Contrary to legends, he knew that men did not just disappear into the ground and asked himself if there was a cave, hidden from view. Slowly turning, he searched for evidence of one close by.

Stones, hammered loose over time by winds, had tumbled to the beach, shattering as they hit the earth. Although a few of the rock piles were high, Thomas saw no evidence of a hiding place. But nearer the precipice, he did notice an outcropping of crumbling rock that might once have been a bridge to the island. A fractured boulder rested against the spot where the ledge was still joined to the cliff.

The placement was odd, he thought. The rock was broken, but the only other stone large enough to have once been part of it lay some distance away. Considering size and weight, such large fragments should have remained closer together. As he hurried toward the leaning boulder, he saw what appeared to be a well-trodden path through the rubble. Others had been there before him.

Soon he saw a small gap between stone and cliff face. This might be a cave entrance. Cautiously, he edged closer. There was a narrow space, just wide enough for a man.

He slipped through.

Until his eyes grew used to the diminished light, it was unsafe to go farther. He stopped, pressed his back against the rock wall, and shut his eyes. As the pounding of the surf faded, he began to hear other sounds.

Did a man just laugh?

Thomas opened his eyes, extended his hand, and crept along the solid rock until he felt nothing. Hoping he had only reached the end of the narrow entrance and that some deep chasm did not lie at his feet, he cautiously reached out with hand and foot. The ground was solid, and the rock against his back sheered off to the right.

He had had been right. The boulder hid a cave.

But he did not know what lay beyond. Convinced he had heard a man's voice, he decided it was wiser not to alert anyone to his presence just yet. He held his breath and listened.

"You look like a trussed chicken, Sir Hugh!"

Was that Sir Leonel's voice? Thomas thought it was.

"Untie me."

The man replied, but his words were inaudible.

That first voice did belong to Leonel, Thomas decided, and the other man was obviously his prioress' brother. Why was the latter bound, and who had done it?

"You have killed Raoul. He was the one who murdered his brothers. Why not free me?"

"Why should I? Your question was foolish, my lord, but you are arrogant like most men born with rank and wealth." He snorted. "God may usually favor you, but you presume too much on his preference."

"Hard words, Leonel, and ones I do not understand. If I have offended you, reveal my transgression and I shall heal the insult. If you resent my birth, you have no cause. As Baron Herbert's nephew, you hold rank enough and have gained the esteem of men, honor, and a king's praise in Outremer for your courage."

"Yet when you spoke, the Lord Edward listened and once dropped a jeweled ring into your hand. Aye, he knighted me but never otherwise showed me favor. I was only a landless knight, not a baron's heir."

"Your uncle's regard…"

"Meaningless. He smiled on me but never gave any gift of coin or plate. He took all my service to him as his due."

"He gave you the means to earn your own renown and wealth: weapons, armor and horse. As for the king's regard, the Lord Edward has always honored loyalty and courage. He would find you a place in his court."

"And I would spend my life in servitude, never standing above other men as my talents warrant. I do not lack for wit, my lord."

"Neither Baron Herbert nor I believed otherwise."

"But if I were to unbind you, I would be a foolish man. As it is, your predicament serves my purpose well."

Hugh mumbled something in reply.

Now fully able to see in the gloom, Thomas quickly looked around him. The cave, carved out by the sea, had ledges protruding from the high rock walls. From overhead, a weak beam of light filtered down but slanted away from him. Concluding that he was safely in shadow, he chanced a peek around the corner.

Hugh sat on the sand, bound hand and foot. A body sprawled to the knight's left, and Leonel stood with his back to the cave entrance. There was a small crossbow at his feet.

Leonel gestured at the ledges above them. "All this is mine, you see," he said. "There is wealth to be had in smuggling, but my uncle, suffering as he does from a brittle righteousness, would never have approved of the opportunity I saw. Had he known what I was doing here, he would have sent both me and my men to the gallows, rather than praise me for cleverness."

"Smuggling? You?"

"Who else? Surely you would not expect this effort from my limp-cocked cousins! Like my uncle, they are men with imagination no better than that of worms."

"Did you not gain wealth enough in Outremer?"

"Compared to my uncle, I acquired nothing. He is miserly, willing enough to feed me scraps from his table and toss the odd bauble picked up from looting an infidel village. He owed me far more for my long and devoted service to him. I saved his life once. He grasped my shoulder and thought the gesture adequate."

"He paid your father's debts to his own detriment, leaving you free of the burden, and he treated you like a son."

"And did I not prove to be a worthy one? I deserved to be his heir."

"He had sons of his own body."

Leonel roared with merriment. "He'd have been better served if he had spilt his seed in the earth rather than his wife. That monk you brought from Tyndal is more of a man than any of my cousins. I swear that at least two of them were gelded at birth."

Hugh growled. "Then it is you, not Raoul, who killed them all."

"A snail might have been swifter than you to discover the truth. But with due humility, God has the honor for the eldest. When I learned of that death, I began to reason thus: if my uncle had died before his marriage, leaving my father as heir, I would have title and this castle. Wasn't I worthier than my uncle's womanish sons?" He waved his hand around. "As master here, I could grow so rich with smuggling that I might buy the loyalty of prominent men. Who knows how high I could rise amongst those upon whom King Edward smiles? Nor would I have to pay smugglers as much if they could bring the goods here in milder seasons. Men demand too much gold when they fear their boats will sink in a winter gale."

Hugh's next question was lost as a huge wave shattered against the shore near the cave entrance. Shuddering, Thomas understood that the tide was coming in faster than he had realized. Then he remembered the high water marks on the cliffs he had seen from the castle wall. If this tide was high enough, they were in danger of drowning here.

Almost as loud as the incoming tide, Leonel's laugh echoed in the cavern. "Why should I enlighten you about my methods? But I shall give you one hint and leave you until the Day of Judgement to discover my meaning. Unlike my uncle, who disdained the Infidel, and, you, who were blinded by them, I studied their methods of killing with a critical eye. Do you not remember hearing tales about the Old Man of the Mountain? His men leapt to their deaths from the citadel walls at his whim and exposed their hearts to daggers, after killing the man they were sent to murder. They all faced death with joy."

"They were promised rewards in paradise."

"But death must be suffered first, and men are often unreliable when the scythe sweeps toward them. Have you not seen men flee battle? Nay, Sir Hugh, their master found a method of giving courage and, at the same time, blinding them to actual consequences."

As the roaring sea grew louder, the monk grew more anxious. Surely the baron's nephew knew the dangers best, he told himself, and Leonel had yet to flee.

Thomas mouthed a silent curse. Although he knew he might delay the knight at the cave entrance, he could never stop a man with a sword. He had no weapon or any way to save his prioress' brother. Hugh would die. He probably would as well, and Leonel could escape unscathed.

Franticly, he looked around.

"If men are fearful, Sir Hugh, there is a way they may face their terrors, and I learned it in Acre. Encouraging words and promises for the life after death are well enough but rarely suffice. Consider the tales of the assassins and see if you can discover my secret, but I rather doubt you shall on this side of Hell."

When Hugh replied, the monk could not hear him.

"Surely you do not expect me to remain here, spewing the many details of each exploit like a murderer who hopes for mercy. The waves come closer. I have little time, you even less, so I shall humor you only briefly.

"Drunken priests, who pry when they should be praying, die with few to mourn them. I caught him in my chambers where he discovered evidence of my uncle's illness. When he swore to tell the family, I tried to dissuade him. I needed more time for my purpose. He was strangely obstinate. A pillow was sufficient to my task and took but a little while.

"With Umfrey, I was forced to act with ill-considered speed, but my plan was to suggest his death had been self-murder. As the soldier's whore, how could he continue bearing the shame and taunting over his loss of manhood?" He roared with merriment. "If your monk had not seen me leave the chapel, the ploy would have been another success."

"And now you have killed Raoul…"

"No more questions, my lord. It's a pity I arrived just after my cousin drove his sword through your heart. When he refused to surrender and tried to run away, I shot him with my crossbow. I grieve he could not be brought to the king's justice, but I dared not allow such a heinous murderer to flee. Indeed, the truth of the matter is that I barely escaped death in Lucifer's Cauldron myself."

Thomas almost wept with despair. Although forbidden to wield a sword, he cared little now for the prohibition and wished he had a sharp blade in hand.

Suddenly, he saw a possible solution: a large stone lay on the ground. He picked it up and weighed it in his hand. His spirit brightened with hope.

"I'll allow you to ask God to forgive your sins first, Sir Hugh, but pray quickly. The tide comes in." Leonel raised his sword.

Chapter Thirty-Three

Thomas threw the rock.

As if propelled from David's sling toward Goliath, it flew straight, striking the baron's nephew in the back of the head.

Leonel crumbled. His weapon dropped from his hand and clattered on the rocks.

Thomas raced to the three men. Bending down, he confirmed that the baron's nephew was alive but unconscious. Then he grabbed the fallen sword and slashed the ropes binding Hugh.

The knight staggered to his feet, briskly rubbing feeling back into his feet and hands. "Why did you do that, Brother? I am no friend to you."

Thomas fell to his knees by Raoul's side. "You are my prioress' brother and Richard's father."

Frowning, Hugh picked up one sword, dropped it into his scabbard, and knelt by the baron's son. "Surely he does not live."

"He breathes but has lost much blood. The bolt hit him high enough he may survive if we can get him to Sister Anne for care." He grunted as he began to lift Raoul. "I need help, Sir Hugh. We must get him out of here before the tide comes in and drowns us all."

A sudden noise startled them, and the knight leapt to his feet, spun around, and drew his weapon.

Leonel was running to the cave entrance.

Hugh started after him.

"Let him escape!" Thomas shouted. "Either you capture him or we save Raoul."

Hugh hesitated, then turned back.

Hoisting the unconscious man between them, the two struggled to edge Raoul through the narrow entrance to the cave.

Outside, the sea lashed the shore with increasing fury and had almost reached the hidden cave. As they stumbled across the pile of loose rocks and onto the small remaining strip of beach, long fingers of water stretched out to them like claws of a ravenous beast. Once Hugh slipped, caught himself, and the men staggered on.

Panting, they reached the mare Thomas had taken to higher ground.

The other horse and Leonel had vanished.

With the last of their strength, they raised Raoul and draped him across the mare. Hugh mounted, then turned to Thomas, reaching out a hand to pull him up behind.

"Go!" Thomas shouted. "I can run fast enough to reach the path, but my weight will overburden the horse and slow you down."

Hugh paused as if to argue.

"Go!" Thomas screamed.

The knight turned the dark mare toward the rising path. She leapt forward without further urging.

Thomas held his breath and watched mare and rider climb steadily to the top of the cliff. When they were well out of the way of the incoming sea, he exhaled.

Now he looked down at his feet. Water swirled around his ankles and sucked at the sand underneath him.

He had lingered too long.

Thomas stumbled forward, his feet finding little purchase in the liquefied earth. Willing himself not to panic, he knew he still had a chance to flee to the path and safety once the water receded. The opportunity was also brief. If a high wave caught him, he would drown.

He fell, sliding to his knees in the wet sand. Staggering upright, he murmured a plea to God for the strength needed to save himself.

A wave struck the shore. From the hissing sound, he knew it was weak and resisted the temptation to look back. The sea howled behind him, and he dared not slow. The next wave would surely have greater force, and he would not survive it.

Suddenly, his feet went out from under him and he splashed into a shallow muddy pool.

Desperate, he reached out, grabbed a piece of driftwood, and clawed his way forward, not caring that his fingers bled with the effort.

Then he found rougher ground and pulled himself upright. With a roar of defiance, Thomas stumbled and ran until he was halfway up the road. Only then did he turn and shake a bloody fist at the sea.

Gasping for breath, he watched the waves strike the base of the precipice below like a maddened viper. Exhaustion swiftly claimed him, and he began to shake with previously denied terror. Sweat stung his eyes, but he had nothing dry to wipe it away. Instead, he raised his face to the sky and let the heavy mist cleanse him.

Now he turned his back to the cove and began the final ascent to the top. It was not far, but he felt as if it were as distant as London. Determined not to give in to weariness, he concentrated on not slipping in the mud.

When he reached the crest, he stopped and peered into the thin woods. He could hear nothing over the roar of the incoming tide below, and the mist swirled too thickly to see any shape more than a short distance away.

There was no sign of Hugh, Raoul, and the mare.

At least the three had gained the crest of the cliff, he thought, and sighed with hope. It was likely that the they were riding through the forest and back to the castle.

But where was Leonel?

If the baron's nephew were wise, the monk thought, he would be on his way to some port where he could seek a boat to take him to the continent. A man with his experience could sell his sword. Many mercenary leaders cared little what innocent blood might have been shed with the weapon as long as it was sharp.

Had Thomas been less weary, he would have grown hot with anger at the failure to exact justice for Baron Herbert's dead sons. Instead, he looked down at his wounded hands as if they had failed him and walked back to the edge of the cliff. Perhaps all he should ask of God was that Raoul survive. He waited to see Sir Hugh cross the narrow isthmus to the castle.

The fog was too dense, and he could see little except the precipice edge when he approached it. Then the mist parted like a curtain moved by an unseen hand. Looking across at the fortress, Thomas froze at the sight.

A lone rider galloped toward the castle gate.

Thomas squinted to see more clearly. Was that his prioress' brother? What had happened to Raoul?

But the horse was light in color, and Thomas realized it could not be Sir Hugh. The knight was riding a dark horse, and, with the weight of two men, the beast could not move quickly. Surely they were still traveling through the forest, but Leonel had left the cove before them. The rider must be the baron's nephew.

Thomas stared in disbelief. "Why return to the castle? The man should have fled."

Just as the rider reached the narrowest part of the road, a company of mounted soldiers clattered across the drawbridge toward him. There was no room for the man to pass through them, and the troop did not slow their swift pace.

The pale horse reared, slipped and fell backwards, rolling over onto its side in the middle of the road.

Throwing himself free, the rider landed on the sloping edge of the sheer cliff.

With the roar of the surf, Thomas could hear nothing but knew Leonel must have screamed.

Clutching at air, the baron's nephew slid off the edge, flailing and twisting as he plunged toward the sea. Then his back struck a rock. Chiseled sharp by wind and tides, it pierced Leonel's body through like a well-aimed lance.

Chapter Thirty-Four

Umfrey sat up in bed and bent his head. Pressing his folded hands tight against his brow, he mumbled a torrent of words.

Brother Thomas bent forward and gently touched his shoulder.

On the other side of the room, braced against the wall, Raoul sat on a stool, one arm immobilized in a wrapping of linen. He tried to cut a fingernail on that hand with a small knife. Difficult though the task was, he stubbornly persisted. "I would never have left you to drown." He glanced up at Hugh and flashed a roguish grin.

"So you claimed then and now." The knight's reply was sharp-edged.

"I needed time to escape, but, once I loosened the ropes, you could have freed yourself and climbed to safety on the higher ledges. Surely you were familiar with the tides and how far you must climb to escape them." The baron's son tilted his head and studied the effect of his words on the older man.

"And you believe I would have been able to do so before the sea flooded the cave?" Hugh snorted.

Raoul set the knife on the floor with a exasperated grunt.

The knight ignored him and watched Thomas whisper into Umfrey's ear, the monk's face a study in compassion. Hugh frowned as he considered this. "Perhaps wicked men can change," he murmured with reluctant charity.

"So Christ taught." Despite his often expressed contempt for faith, Raoul's words were heavy with hope.

Hearing the longing, the knight knew this son sought forgiveness, but it was a gift he could not grant. He did not, and never could, trust him. Instead, Hugh shrugged and said, "You are healing faster than I expected from such a wound."

Raoul gazed at him with disappointment but disguised it with a wave of his good hand. "I shall not die easily. Were Satan to battle too little for my soul, he would not value it highly enough. I want a place of honor when I arrive in Hell."

This time, Hugh responded with sincere agreement, and then added, "Sister Anne and Master Gamel are due much credit for saving your life. They did not draw the bolt out until pus formed, then washed the wound with wine. It has not grown foul."

The baron's son sighed. "Yet I think the vintage was wasted in the treatment. I would have preferred to drink it instead." His tone was playful, but his eyes narrowed with memory of the pain.

"You did know about the smuggling."

Raoul started at the abruptness. "You accuse me of being part of the scheme?"

Hugh's lips twisted into a mirthless smile.

With the gesture of a defeated man, Raoul leaned his head back against the wall. "I am no more skilled at word play than I am with swords. If I speak plainly, will you swear to listen with the ears of a fair judge?"

"I shall." At least, the knight promised himself, he would try to do so.

"After lights in the cove were reported, I watched from the ramparts until I witnessed them as well. They were no fantasy. The soldiers sent to investigate returned too quickly to have done their task properly. I was surprised that they were not sent back for a more extensive search. Whatever faults my father owns, his reputation speaks of a man who would never tolerate the failure to discover the cause for the lights." He gnawed at his rough fingernail.

"Why did you not join the search to guarantee it was a careful one?"

"I have rarely found joy in raising questions, begging to be heard, or asking to be included," Raoul snapped. "I learned caution in boyhood." He raised his head and looked up at the knight, his face grey with weariness. "Whatever your opinion of me, remember that I am still my father's son, and you did give your word to justly hear me out."

Hugh agreed and rubbed a hand over his mouth as a reminder to keep it shut.

"Soon after, I went alone to the beach, thinking it odd that no one had mentioned the cave. Many of the soldiers might not know about it, I thought. Few grew up here or now have sons who play in the cove as you and my brothers did. I suspected that the entrance had been concealed and did discover that a large rock covered it." Raoul looked nervously at the prioress' brother.

Asking him to continue, Hugh stole a quick look at Thomas.

The monk was holding Umfrey's hands, the wounded man's expression soft with tranquility.

"I discovered those chests high on the ledges. They were empty, but I found broken pieces of gold and silver scattered about, some large enough to reveal fine crafting. When I discovered a large cross, fallen into a crevice, I concluded that the cave might be used to hide unlawful goods smuggled in by sea. The gold cross I kept, since I could sell the object as well as any other man." Raoul gestured awkwardly toward his elder brother. "Later, I gave it to him as a comfort while he hid in the chapel." He grimaced. "If confession is due, I am a thief, albeit one who robs from others who steal. There were more baubles, but I left them. My greed is easily satisfied, and too much glitter hurts my eyes."

This time Hugh's look was kind. "Master Gamel says the cross saved Umfrey's life."

"That pleases me. My stolen object served a higher purpose than the mere reflection of a fat priest's eyes when he looked upon the smuggled goods for purchase." Raoul turned his face away.

The knight inclined his head toward the monk. "Some would call that remark blasphemous."

Nodding in the same direction, Raoul replied, "The one who might has suggested that God used me to assist in the miracle of my brother's survival."

The knight stared at Thomas.

"From the beginning I doubted the smugglers had come here accidentally," Raoul said. "The closeness to the castle and the dangers of the cove in winter argued against that. As I told you, I discounted my father's leadership and began to think one or all of my brothers were to blame. When they began to die, I also lost suspects. Although I doubted Umfrey had anything to do with the smuggling, I did ask him if he knew of any crime he or our dead brothers had committed. He didn't, and I believed him. My brother owns a womanish nature and was never clever enough to scheme." Raoul looked up at Hugh and was surprised.

The prioress' brother was looking at him with an expression bordering on respect.

"When only Umfrey and I were left alive, my suspicions turned reluctantly to my cousin. Since all communications went through Leonel, I realized that he might never have spoken to my father about the lights. The hasty nature of the investigation may have been his decision, or else he jested that the soldier must have imagined the sighting. If the last, the search party would have learned his desired conclusion from his light manner. Had there been questions later about this, he could have claimed that he did not want to trouble my father with a matter than seemed so insignificant."

"There were times in Outremer when I suspected your cousin of deciding problems on behalf of your father without consultation. The instances were minor, and I never questioned the baron."

Raoul exhaled with evident relief.

Thomas rose from the bedside and made the sign of the cross over Umfrey. The baron's son wore a smile radiant with joy.

Hugh shook his head, then turned his attention back to Raoul. "Yet you never spoke of your findings to anyone at all?" He hoped he had kept his tone devoid of accusation.

"Whom could I trust? I had no proof of guilt and little reason to believe my words would be greeted with anything except blows or insults." He carefully shrugged the uninjured shoulder, then grinned to disguise his evident pain. "Although I did not suppose my cousin was the head of the smugglers, I suspected he knew and might have been getting a fee for his silence. So I delayed until I had irrefutable proof to name the leader of this band, and, had I done so, I could have demanded an audience alone with my father. He'd not mock facts. How better to prove myself a worthy son?" His grin vanished. "Or not. The wisest choice would have been to join the outlaws for a share in the wealth."

With those words, Hugh's lesser opinion of Raoul returned. "In the cave, your cousin confessed he had organized the smuggling." He waited for a response, then sneered. "So you claim never to have approached Leonel?"

The son's eyes flashed with guarded anger. "Why would I? If I'd found proof, I would have gone to my father!"

"I wonder that you did not suggest to your cousin that he could pay for your own silence about his involvement."

"Despite your poor opinion of me, I own some sense of honor. I looked for more answers in the cave and found nothing. Some night I thought to spy on the men unloading the boats." He glared at the knight. "If I had discovered the leader, I would have omitted any mention of my suspicions about my cousin."

"You didn't slip into his chambers and search his possessions for proof of his involvement?"

"Like some common thief?"

Hugh nodded.

"I have never met you before this visit," a man said, "yet I believe you did go through his room for evidence."

Startled, Sir Hugh instinctively gripped his dagger as he turned to face the speaker.

Brother Thomas smiled, then gestured at the baron's son. "You argued well for the innocence of your father, took good measure of your brothers, and described your cousin as a master of semblance. Why not conclude that he was the chief smuggler, a task that requires just such careful stealth? Having pondered the question, I believe that you did think him guilty and most probably searched his room for proof. Greed may not be your favorite vice, but protecting yourself is your main strength. Roger had died unexpectedly and under questionable circumstances. Gervase soon followed him. You would have grown wary."

Turning pale, Raoul stared at the monk.

"Had I been you, I would have waited for a chance to look through Leonel's possessions." Thomas folded his arms and waited.

"Why? I thought my cousin was a good man who served my father well. Now you suggest that I believed him guilty of murder as well as smuggling?"

"Only a fool would not have feared it to be so, and you are possessed of a clever mind. Even if the smuggling and deaths were unrelated, a wise man would not dismiss the connection too quickly until he was convinced otherwise."

Raoul began to deny the accusation again but chose not to dispute further. "Although I did not conclude he was guilty of more than gaining coin from the smuggling, I did search his room."

Hugh looked at both monk and Raoul with amazement.

"What did you find?" Thomas spoke gently.

"Naught that pointed to my cousin's involvement in either transgression. I was both relieved and disappointed."

The monk considered that response. "I hear hesitation in your reply. You found something."

"An oddity, nothing more."

Thomas reached into his pouch. "Something like this?" He pulled out a roughly rounded and flaky lump, cupped the dark object in his palm, and extended it so Raoul could see.

The baron's son touched it and nodded. "I did not know what that was and thought little more about it."

Hugh asked to see the thing, then sniffed and studied it for a moment. "I recognize it," he said. "This explains what he meant by his reference to the Old Man of the Mountain and those who so willingly died after killing others."

"Hashish." Thomas took the lump back.

Hugh's eyes widened. "You have knowledge of it?"

The monk shook his head. "A soldier from Outremer told me that the substance intoxicates and expels all fear of death. Before I found this in the dead priest's belongings, I had never seen it. Events kept me from revealing my discovery before Leonel's death, but Master Gamel has since identified it."

"Leonel must have brought the hashish back with him from Acre," Hugh said. "Perhaps he took it himself to gain the battle courage he did not otherwise own. And then he used it to slaughter the innocent in order to inherit his uncle's lands and title."

Raoul frowned. "I do not understand how."

"If he slipped hashish into a spiced wine," Hugh said, "the peppery taste would be disguised and all reason would not flee until some time later. By that time, Leonel would be elsewhere with witnesses to confirm his innocence. I suspect he persuaded Roger that the infusion would cure his fear of the sea and urged him to stand on a cliff edge to prove it. Unsteady and incautious, he fell to his death."

Raoul shifted uncomfortably.

"You know still more than you have told?" The monk gently urged Raoul to explain.

"Roger visited me the night before he died and confided he would soon prove his manhood to our father. As I did his tales of swyving women, I took this boasting lightly. He was drunk. I was impatient to reclaim my solitude and refused to hear more of it. Blame rests on me for my selfishness. I might have saved him, Brother." The young man looked like he was about to weep. "He brought a wineskin with him. A gift, he said, but refused to share it when I was rude. I drank a small cup with him, but the wine was my own."

Thomas took pity. "Do not put the burden of this death on your soul and be grateful you were so bad-tempered. Had you drunk from this wineskin, the gift might have been the undoing of two sons instead of one."

Raoul was little comforted. "What of Gervase? What caused him to leap from the window in front of both our mother and cousin?"

"You said that he was to meet with you over a questionable debt." Hugh remained unsympathetic.

"I neither met with my brother nor did I understand the accusation. I was innocent."

Blunt skepticism was evident in Hugh's eyes.

"I believe you are," Thomas said. Leonel must have tried to implicate Raoul in each death. Perhaps the nephew knew that the youngest son was least likely to fall into his devious traps, the monk thought. Leonel's purpose would have been well-served if Raoul became the primary suspect in the deaths.

"You are pensive, Brother." Raoul looked worried.

Dispelling the young man's unease, Thomas finally remembered a discrepancy between the two stories told about Gervase's death. There was a detail from Lady Margaret that was missing from Leonel's version of the son's fall.

According to Prioress Eleanor, the lady had mentioned the nephew's remark about angels being angry if Gervase did not show manliness. From the description of his actions, this son was probably drunk, and Leonel must have laced the wine with hashish. Had Leonel suggested that he might prove the strength of his faith by leaping into the arms of angels? Was this the oath Grevase swore?

Thomas could establish nothing and chose not to speak his thoughts. "I fear that no one will ever know exactly what happened to Gervase," he said.

"As he promised, Leonel took many of his secrets with him." Hugh's expression betrayed acute frustration.

"And returned them to his true liege lord, the Prince of Darkness, along with his soul," Thomas replied.

Chapter Thirty-Five

Master Gamel directed those entering the baron's chambers to the places where they might safely stand.

Baron Herbert sat in a chair against the far wall, his head covered by a hood and his face in shadow.

Waiting near the open door, Eleanor leaned close to her brother. "Did you visit Raoul and Umfrey earlier today? I have not gotten word on their health," she whispered. "Sister Anne and Brother Thomas were still with the patients when I was summoned here."

"Both continue to thrive. Master Gamel said the danger of festering is now slight, and they will surely live."

Acknowledging the physician's gesture, Hugh led his sister to their assigned places. The fortress commander bowed as the couple passed.

"You had little cause to fear," her brother continued. "Your priory healer has used so many foul-smelling concoctions that even the Devil would flee the stench. Master Gamel, on the other hand, looks upon her work with such a pleasant expression that I imagined him in a sweet-scented meadow. What odd creatures these healers are to find pleasure in so many strange potions." He chuckled but quickly turned solemn. "Sister Anne and Master Lucas should meet one day."

Eleanor had feared this request. Although her brother's physician from Acre had accepted baptism, few of his ancestry came to England. Since his arrival, many whispered their distrust and apprehension of the man. She herself was uncertain. Looking up at her brother, she decided that God would give her direction in this matter when the time came to deal with it. For now, all she need give him was a noncommittal nod.

Slipping into the chambers at the last minute, Sister Anne and Brother Thomas found places near Lady Margaret. Two stewards stepped back to give them precedence.

Master Gamel's expression brightened, then he gestured to the servant who left, closing the door behind him.

With evident hesitation, Baron Herbert rose. Keeping his head bowed, he cleared his throat. "Since returning home, I have distanced myself from all who greeted me. They celebrated my safe arrival from Outremer with joy. I answered their smiles with harsh words and turned my back on their shouts of *hosanna*." His voice was hoarse. "To all, my actions were cruel. Some wondered aloud if I had lost my reason." Coughing, he took time to glare at the rushes around his feet as if something there had offended. "I have even heard it murmured that my wife caused me grave displeasure. For her offenses, I rejected her."

Lady Margaret bowed her head but not quickly enough to hide her pallor and moist eyes.

"Then my sons, one after the other, suffered strange, violent deaths." He fell silent. Turning to stare out the window, his mouth twitched. "I soon heard tales that God was punishing me for a dark and secret sin." He looked back at the assembled, carefully looking over their heads. "I undoubtedly sinned, yet my greatest wickedness lay in trusting one of Satan's spawn, a viper I held to my breast as if he were my son." Tears began to flow without restraint down his cheeks. "Had God not revealed the serpent's true nature to Prioress Eleanor, I might have remained blind to the evil by my side."

"Such love may have been misguided, my lord, but not sinful," Brother Thomas said.

The baron nodded with a bitter smile. "So you have said to console me, Brother, but snakes bite. I was blinded to Leonel's nature by my own sinful pride, seeing in him an image of myself.

I thought him perfect in his manhood, fighting in Outremer as I did for God's honor. In comparison, my sons were weak things, little better than daughters." He clenched his fist. "Because of my arrogance, God ripped my boys from my arms, one after another until, in His mercy, he left me two. For a short while, I thought one of those was dead and the other a murderer…"

"I seek pardon for misleading you, my lord," Eleanor said.

"God guided you in that decision," he replied, "for my soul had to suffer utter despair. Only then could I learn compassion. When I grieved that I had discovered it too late, God saw repentance in my heart and gave me back two sons."

Lady Margaret began to sob.

"Raoul was a child when I left," the baron said, "a boy whom I humiliated without true cause. When I returned, he had grown to manhood, but I never looked at him, casting my loving gaze only on my nephew. Leonel was Satan's creature, feigning the son I longed to have, blinding me to the son who had become all I wished." He rubbed at his eyes, angry with the tears they bled. "How my boy must curse me!"

"Take comfort, my lord. Both your sons speak passionately of their love for you. Indeed, their only sorrow was hearing the news of your…" Sister Anne stopped, her face flushing, and bowed her head.

Baron Herbert turned to Master Gamel. "You have told them?"

"I did, my lord. Was it not best that they hear the news from me rather than rumor-whispering servants? Your sons begged permission to stand by your side today, but I forbade it in your name, fearing the visit would endanger their still fragile health."

"Then I shall no longer hesitate to reveal the horror of my state to those assembled here. When you leave, you shall convey the truth to those of lower rank under your authority. It is my wife, however, who must bear the greatest burden."

Lady Margaret raised her head and stared at her husband.

He did not meet her eyes. "My strange actions since returning home were not due to any fault in you, my beloved wife. I stand back from your embrace only because I am now the vilest of creatures. My desire to remain separated from my beloved family lies in a contagion I brought back with me from Acre." He gestured around the chambers. "I do not look at you because the noxious disease may be transmitted through my poisonous gaze. In order to protect you from my deadly breath, Master Gamel has asked that you come no closer to me than you have been bidden." He stopped, his mouth opening and closing with the effort to speak, but no words came forth.

The physician gasped, fearing apoplexy had struck his patient.

"I am a leper!" Baron Herbert howled, covering his face with his hands.

Lady Margaret shrieked, stretched forth her arms, and collapsed to her knees.

Kneeling beside the lady, Sister Anne hugged the trembling woman close and murmured comfort.

Herbert turned his back and tried to swallow his pain. "Lady, our union came about because our families found profit in it. On our marriage day, I prayed only that you might prove fruitful and obedient. In return, I vowed to grant you the respect due a mother of sons. Then God blessed me beyond all hope, and I grew to love you beyond all measure. The birth of our five sons further proved He smiled on our union." His voice coarsened with tears. "Now I must flee from you, a corpse without a coffin, and make a widow of you while I still live."

With the help of Sister Anne, Lady Margaret rose to her feet, her face bereft of all color. Her lips quivered.

"I may deserve this curse as punishment for my sins," Herbert said, "but you do not. Can you ever forgive me for the affliction I have laid upon you?" No hope softened the question.

The lady stiffened, then gently pushed aside the nun's arm. She stepped forward, hesitated, then took another step.

Even the wind outside grew hushed, waiting for what she might say.

"My lord."

Herbert turned, drew his hood closely over his face, and stared at the floor.

Lady Margaret walked up to her husband and knelt at his feet.

Master Gamel reached out to restrain her, then drew back when she glared at him with determined fury.

"Look upon me, my lord. I beg it of you."

Herbert obeyed with eyes shut.

Margaret reached up and grasped his hand. "A wife must ever obey her lord husband, for so the Church commands. Yet is it not also our duty to serve as needed?" She glanced back at Brother Thomas.

He nodded, his eyes sad with understanding.

For a moment, she caressed her husband's hand, then realized he did not feel her touch. Gently, she tugged at him.

He opened his eyes and gazed at his wife. Horrified, he tried to draw his hand away, but his will lacked strength.

Clinging to her husband, Margaret smiled. "I obediently vowed myself to you at the church door, but my heart soon learned to rejoice in its duty. Now I renew that vow given in our first marriage hour. From this day until our spirits go to God, I shall never leave your side. If God wills that I remain free of this contagion, I shall tend you until He demands your soul. If I join you in this affliction, we shall endure it together and do so with joy, not sorrow. Godly men proclaim that a leper's earthly travail shortens the time his soul must spend in Purgatory. If that is true, I shall rejoice in whatever misery we must endure together."

The baron began to protest, trying again to loosen her hold.

She gripped harder. "Forgive me, my lord, for my unwomanly rebellion against your will. Although your wish to abandon me is meant kindly, I have suffered too many years alone after you took the cross. I am a woman, frail and lacking a man's stomach in the face of troubles. I truly need your strength to continue in this world. Does God condemn women who perform their duties with love? I think not and beg you to allow me the right to carry out this service."

He may not have felt her tender touch on his hands, yet Herbert's face revealed that he felt the gentleness in his heart. He raised her to her feet, then looked in the general direction of the physician, his eyes pleading once more for a reprieve from the torment of his deadly illness.

Gamel wiped the tears from his cheeks and chose to address the wife instead. "My lady, I will offer you one hope. Your husband does not exhibit enough signs of the affliction to be certain he has the disease."

"There must be some cure…"

"There are as many treatments as there are physicians. A few claim success with castration which cools the body. Others praise potions of honey mixed with rosemary or cumin and drunk with wine. More use cupping or bleeding." Gamel looked over at Sister Anne. "I have found nothing of man's creation that heals leprosy, my lady. Instead, I advise your husband to seek a cure at the shrine of St. Thomas at Canterbury, well-known for many miracles. Lepers bathed in water blessed with a drop of the martyr's blood have been spontaneously cleansed."

"Hope," the lady murmured.

"Until such time as the true nature of his condition is revealed, I have promised your husband that I will remain by his side." He turned his head away from the sub-infirmarian. "I shall inform my son of my continued absence from London. My own need for pilgrimage is great, suffering as I do from so many sins. St. Thomas shows much kindness to the penitent."

Margaret's eyes brightened as she looked up at the baron. "In that case, my lord, we must swiftly arrange a marriage for Umfrey, your heir. While we undertake this healing pilgrimage in search of God's mercy, he shall act in your stead here. A good helpmeet will give him the comfort he needs in that endeavor."

Herbert winced as if the thought of Umfrey as heir struck him like a dagger blow. "He is not capable…" Looking down at his wife, he fell silent.

Margaret continued gazing upon her husband with unblinking joy.

Thomas stepped forward. "May I have leave to speak on behalf of your two sons, my lord?"

The baron nodded permission, his eyes never leaving his wife's face.

"Although bound to honor your will with filial obedience, Umfrey begs to be released from worldly duty. In penance for his sins, he longs to serve God for the remainder of his life and to renounce his right of inheritance in favor of Raoul. Were he able, he would come before you and swear that the miracle of his survival is proof that God demands his service, a command he would obey. He asked me to kneel on his behalf and beg you to grant his plea." The monk got down on his knees.

Herbert blinked in surprise. "What does Raoul say of this?"

"Your youngest son humbly adds his supplication to that of his brother, saying that he dare not ignore God's clear intent, although he will honor your decision in this matter." Thomas gestured toward the physician. "I must add one detail in support of Umfrey's belief that God saved him for His service. Master Gamel concludes that the cross Raoul brought to comfort his elder brother diverted the knife blow."

Gamel swiftly concurred.

"Should you grant your heir's entreaty, Raoul vows to build a hermitage on this island where Umfrey may live out his life in solitary prayer. In this way, the brothers shall not be parted. Each man swears to perform his new responsibilities with honor and courage." Thomas rose and stepped back.

"Grant Umfrey's plea, my lord!" Lady Margaret placed one hand on her heart.

For the first time since his return from Acre, Baron Herbert smiled with happiness. Then he gave his consent.

Chapter Thirty-Six

There was a hint of sweetness in the wind, although it was chill against the skin like the touch of a fall apple picked on a frosty morning. The sea below murmured softly, a sound sailors called mermaid lullabies.

As Sir Hugh of Wynethorpe's company rode over the narrow isthmus between castle and mainland, Prioress Eleanor took advantage of the cautious pace and glanced down at the jagged rocks which had slain Sir Leonel ahead of the king's hangman. She felt an ache of sadness, wished that she had not, and then wondered if God had also grieved when His most beautiful angel tumbled into Hell's pit.

Perhaps my fault lies not in mourning the loss, she thought, but rather in succumbing to the sorcery of a fair demeanor. And that the baron's nephew had most certainly possessed, in measure equal to what he lacked in honorable intent. She was not often fooled by fine words and a pleasing face, but Eleanor knew lust had blinded her. Forcing herself to look away from the precipice, she prayed that her sorrow over his death would prove as shallow as the nature of the man.

Near the cliff at the edge of the forest, the travelers paused until all had crossed and gathered closely together for safety. Looking up at the trees, Eleanor watched the damp, crooked branches shimmer in the rays of winter light that burst through gaps in the broken clouds. "Have I dreamt all that happened?"

the prioress said aloud, delighting at the sight of this more tranquil land.

Sister Anne looked around and edged her mount closer to her prioress' side. "If only that were true." Her murmured words splintered into white mist.

Together, the women turned to gaze back at Baron Herbert's stronghold.

A morning haze wafted around the towers of *Doux et Dur* as if it were a light veil swirled by a woman's hand. Nearer the ground, thick fog hid the dark foundation stones with a magic cloak. Like an image in a dream or vision, the fortress appeared to float above the island.

The friends looked back at each other in wonder. Had they not just left the gates, they might have concluded that the place was home to a mocking and devious spirit. Most others would surely think the place ill-omened. Shivering, they turned away from the sight and sought comfort in fellow mortals.

Seeing her brother at the head of the armed guard, Eleanor raised her hand in greeting.

He waved back, then ordered the party forward along the road through the forest.

The company was eager to travel on.

This segment of the journey would be the most dangerous. Outlaws hid in the dense woodlands and fed on the purses of travelers who were not so well-protected by armed men as this prioress and her high-born brother. Nonetheless, those who assumed that numbers and good swordsmanship were adequate protection often fell prey to the onslaught of desperate men. Sir Hugh made sure that his soldiers remained as alert as dogs in the hunt.

For Eleanor, however, the most perilous part was over. She was going home. As the company entered the dense forest, she found comfort in the heavy evergreen boughs overhead and thick greenery encroaching on the road. All this was God's creation. Compared to the evil she had striven against in the baron's castle, this otherwise forbidding woodland was reassuring.

She sighed, then turned to seek her friend who was riding nearby.

A rare flush of color rose to Anne's cheeks, and she quickly bent down to touch something on the neck of her mount.

"Shall you confess to Brother Thomas?" Eleanor softened her words with understanding, knowing well where her friend's thoughts had drifted. "His heart is as gentle as his eyes are sharp. He will not be troubled by your admission regarding Master Gamel," she said. "I think he saw what was growing between you and the good physician early in the journey here."

"I sinned, my lady."

"Not in the flesh."

"Is the heart not flesh? Do the eyes not offend? Our bodies may not have committed any transgression, yet our thoughts did." Anne's cheeks began to glisten in the sunlight. "Does a woman ever forget a man's loving touch once she has been pleasured in bed?" She covered her eyes with one hand.

"Soft, my friend, soft." Eleanor could only sooth with words, although she longed to take the woman into her arms and let her weep. "Had your husband died and you not sworn yourself to God's service, Master Gamel would have found a loving wife in you and rejoiced in the happiness you gave him. There is no sin in knowing that, only in seizing what cannot be."

"I may have entered the religious life with little longing for it, but I have tried to honor my vows and serve God well. Indeed, I found comfort and purpose at Tyndal. Had I stayed in the world, I would have remained alone, banned from remarriage after my husband took his own vows."

"And you have served Him with honor," Eleanor replied.

For a long while, they rode in a silence broken only by the clop of hooves and the nickering of horses.

"Brother John and I never see each other now," Anne said. "He grew too fearful of committing a grave sin because we spoke together."

The prioress nodded, wondering what solace she could offer her friend. As she had learned soon after arriving at Tyndal, the pair met on occasion, their encounters as chaste as expected between a couple converted from husband and wife to brother and sister on taking monastic vows. For the innocent comfort it gave them, the prioress had never forbidden the brief meetings, although she knew many would condemn her leniency.

Now Brother John had finally severed this last tie to the secular world he had eagerly fled. She should not be surprised, considering his increasing asceticism. Were he to beg permission to become an anchorite, she would understand.

But this decision to utterly abandon his wife, who had taken vows at Tyndal only because she could not bear to lose him completely, had robbed Anne of the last comfort to which she had clung for strength. Since she had never cast the world aside in her heart, Eleanor knew its joys still beckoned to her.

Fortunately, Master Gamel was a good man who would never have lured the nun to sin, even if he had wished he could wake up by Anne's side for the rest of their lives. Nonetheless, the situation could have ended with a tragic difference. How much of Anne's suffering was her fault, Eleanor asked herself. Lust had tainted her own reason for too long and most significantly on this journey. She cringed at how much she had let this friend down, a woman who had never failed her.

She looked up. The first person she saw was Brother Thomas, riding by himself a short distance ahead of her.

The sight of the monk brought her both warmth and comfort. For once her longing to hold him had nothing to do with desire but all to do with gratitude. He had saved her brother's life, brought peace to a dying man, and pulled her out of her soul's darkness.

She had never told Sister Anne of her desire for the monk, but her own feelings informed her compassion for the subinfirmarian. They both loved men who had rejected the joys of the marriage bed, and, if she suffered lust-filled dreams despite her chosen vocation, Anne must suffer greater agony having taken vows in sorrow, not joy. Was there a way to peace for them both?

Suddenly a thought struck her, the needed gift of insight. Surely God had been teaching all of them lessons during this visit. As she pondered this, she grew both hopeful and relieved.

Recalling all that had happened during the time with Baron Herbert and his family, however, she shuddered. Now that she had escaped, the feeling that they had each been put under a spell grew stronger. Lessons there might have been for them all, but what a price every one had paid.

Her brother and Lady Margaret had almost committed an adultery neither of them wished for. Brother Thomas had fought with Sir Hugh, then saved his life with another act of violence when he cast a stone at Sir Leonel. Neither act was acceptable for a monk; neither was even likely for one as gentle as he. What, she wondered, had been the lesson for her monk and brother? Perhaps she understood best what Lady Margaret had learned, for she had seen her walk to her husband's side and swear to remain there until death.

In her case, her feelings for Leonel were just blinding lust. Her heart did not grieve over his death, only her body. Were Brother Thomas to die, she would mourn until God deigned to take her soul as well. Her longing to couple with the monk might be wicked, but there was a grain of purity in her love as well. How else explain why they worked so effectively together in rendering God's justice? Somehow she must cling to the virtue of that love while rejecting the forbidden.

And what was her sub-infirmarian's lesson? Perhaps it was the knowledge that she must seek strength in a different kind of love.

When Brother John cut the last bond to his earthly wife, Anne was forced to let go her hold on him. Like Master Gamel, the nun had long clung to a dead spouse. In Anne's case, the spouse was dead only to the secular world. When she and the physician met, they each discovered that they could find another love in this life.

Eleanor was sure that Master Gamel would remarry one day. As for Sister Anne, she must finally make peace with her husband's choice to leave her for God, but what path she would take was unknown. There were dangers.

Perhaps I did err in letting Brother John and Sister Anne continue to meet, the prioress thought. Had I forbidden it, she might have stepped away earlier with less pain than she suffers now. In any case, I must take very tender care of her. Not only is she my friend, she is still vowed to God's service.

Sister Anne said something.

Eleanor asked her to repeat it.

"I shall ponder much that happened here, but there is one incident I do not understand. Why did Sir Leonel ride back to the castle after leaving the cove? He would have found safety on the continent."

"There are two conclusions I might make. The man had left Brother Thomas and my brother with the wounded Raoul. The tide was rising swiftly. There was only one horse. Raoul would surely drown. If Hugh and our monk fought over the horse, or had hesitated too long over saving the baron's son, both might have been caught by the sea as well. From Sir Leonel's reasoning, that was likely, and he would be the only witness to what had happened in the cave. Rest assured, he would have told the tale to his benefit."

"And the baron would have believed him instead of you?"

Eleanor smiled. "His nephew had manipulated the truth for many years. He surely thought his skill would be a match for anything I might claim."

"Then he misjudged your persuasive arguments, as proven by the baron's swift action in sending the soldiers after you spoke with him," Anne replied. "There was a second possibility?"

"Men are wicked, but they are still made in God's image. Although Sir Leonel plotted against his cousins, his uncle was the only father he had truly known. I would not discount the possibility that he returned to the castle, in part, because he wanted to hear Baron Herbert proclaim him his son as well as heir. Call it a tainted love, but I suspect the nephew did love the man who had taken him into his heart."

"So much wickedness occurred in that place. I am grateful to escape it."

"In that I join you, for I sinned enough there myself."

"Will you also seek Brother Thomas for confession? He knows the circumstances so well."

"I shall speak with Brother John," the prioress said.

"I may not." The words were sharp-edged. Anne flushed, then continued more gently. "He has always had a wise heart. You will be guided well by him."

"Yet you would be right to seek counsel from Brother Thomas. God understands we are weak creatures but gives courage when the right path is chosen. Had you and Master Gamel been less virtuous, Satan would have triumphed. That he most certainly did not. When you speak with Brother Thomas, he will bring you even more comfort in this matter than I."

Sister Anne stretched out her hand, and Eleanor briefly squeezed it. Smiling at each other, they wordlessly conveyed the understanding born of friendship.

As the company emerged from the forest and joined the better traveled highway leading back to Tyndal, the sun cast aside the veil of clouds and shone down with all the warmth possible in that dark season.

Someone in the company began to sing an old ballad.

Another joined him.

The journey home promised to be a joyful one.

Author's Notes

Leprosy, now properly called Hansen's Disease, terrified our ancestors for thousands of years. Although frequently mentioned in the Bible, not every suspect case may actually have been the illness, but dread of this disfiguring, maiming, and fatal ailment made it the default diagnosis.

Since the mid-twentieth century, Hansen's Disease has been curable, although the exact method of transmission remains unclear. Like the bubonic plague, AIDS, or tuberculosis, lack of knowledge about the method of contagion, joined with the failure to develop a reliable cure, fueled reactions based in atavistic fear. As one who remembers the early days of AIDS and has lost many friends, I can understand those feelings, but there is no excuse in the modern era to turn to superstition when medical science has the ability, given adequate backing, to discover the process of infection, treatments, and eventual cures. Medical knowledge was not so advanced in Prioress Eleanor's thirteenth century. Hysteria existed, although compassion and love trumped fear far more often than we have been led to believe.

Because sins of the flesh are inevitably blamed for any incurable illness (a practice akin to the gathering of the usual suspects in *Casablanca*), unapproved sex was considered a likely cause for contracting leprosy in medieval times. As one example, some thought a man would catch it by having sex with a woman who had just slept with an infected person. Another assumed method of transmission was looking directly into a sick individual's eyes or breathing the same air as the afflicted. (A direct touch, oddly enough, was less feared.) With this in mind, we can see that Herbert's avoidance of his family actually shows his love and concern for them. As for Leonel's easy access to his uncle, both would have concluded that the former was already exposed, but the precautions mentioned here would have been taken. In fact, Hansen's Disease is very difficult to contract.

Despite the fear of contagion, not all lepers were segregated nor did they lose their rights. There is an early thirteenth century stained glass panel at Canterbury showing a mother tending her severely ill son. King Baldwin IV of Jerusalem not only ascended the throne after his illness was diagnosed but led in battle and ruled for eleven years until his death. Leper hospitals were built near cities and on busy roads so that the sick could directly seek alms from travelers. The reaction to the disease was as complex as its diagnosis.

Although medieval physicians did not know the origin or transmission method, archaeological digs at leprosarium cemeteries suggest an impressive diagnostic accuracy. In part because the responsible physician was very cautious about making a firm judgment with such a serious and terrifying illness, they tried to be quite precise. Doctors had some forty symptoms to consider before a final decision could be made. This list dates to the second century (Aretaeus) and was refined over the centuries by such medical men as Bernard de Gordon, Bartholomeus Anglicus, and Gilbertus Anglicus. Unfortunately, priests were also allowed to determine whether or not a person was infected. Their accuracy rate was not high.

Cures were sought, but in the Middle Ages, the best that might be expected was an easing of symptoms. Borderline Hansen's Disease may take a long time to fully develop, for example, and baths in water with mineral or sulphur content (Harbledown Hospital near Canterbury was well-regarded), ointment massage, or an improved diet could make the sufferer feel better. This relief was sometimes confused with a cure. In other cases, the disease might be misdiagnosed (psoriasis, eczema, scabies) or temporarily improve. One form of the disease (*tuberculoid*) can spontaneously disappear.

The Order of St. Lazarus of Jerusalem (also called the Leper Knights) has a fascinating history, and I recommend the very readable Marcombe book listed in the bibliography following these notes. The Order was founded in early twelfth century Jerusalem and included infected brothers who were assisted by healthy ones. It was run, however, by a brother chosen from the lepers. The monks included Templars, who were allowed to switch Orders upon infection, and this provided a unique band of soldiers. Although their actual performance in combat was unsuccessful (and they probably served mostly as scouts or foragers), their presence was welcomed, albeit at a distance. Because the suffering of lepers was linked to that of Jesus and Job, soldiers felt the inclusion of the armed band in combat was like carrying a living relic into battle.

Although crusaders came to the Holy Land believing the illness was caused by sin, many were influenced by the eastern view that contagion was not a moral issue. As a consequence, they moderated their harsher views which resulted in greater acceptance and kinder treatment. The care given at the Order's hospital was geared toward making the sick comfortable and included frequent baths in part because of the palliative effect but also to replicate the healing of Naaman in the Jordan River.

In England, Burton Lazars (Leicestershire) was the Order's administrative center although it was a small one. In the late 1270s, it had a master and eight monks. The brothers wore a grey habit, with the couped cross of St. Lazarus, and were bearded, perhaps to hide facial disfiguring. Someone of Baron Herbert's rank might well have communicated with them, intending to join the Order. His administrative talent alone would have been welcomed at a time when the Order owned considerable land. After the fall of Acre in 1291, the center suffered a decline but struggled on until dissolved by Henry VIII.

Debates over legend and fact continue about the original *assassins*. The word may have come from *hashishiyyun*, or *hashish user,* a derogatory term applied to the *Nizaris* by their Muslim detractors and intended to suggest moral degeneracy rather than a person who actually took hashish. Historically, they were a splinter faction of the Ismailis, who had previously split from the Shiites, and exist today as a very peaceful group, ruled by the Aga Khan.

In any case, the crusaders feared them, believed all the superstitions they heard, and even embellished the tales, especially about the era of Rashid al-Din Sinan, the original "Old Man of the Mountain" and most legendary twelfth-century leader of the Nizaris. Hugh and Leonel would not have been alone in their assumptions.

In fact, the Nizaris probably didn't use the drug to commit their relatively few assassinations or joyfully leap to their deaths at their leader's whimsical command. They certainly did not become phantoms to evade heavily guarded targets. As for the stubborn persistence of the legends, we owe much to that consummate storyteller, Marco Polo.

That noted, medieval Nizaris did include some members willing to undertake suicide missions against the enemies of their faith, both Christian and Muslim, although most preferred missionary work which is usually less violent. These *assassins* were highly successful primarily because they gained the target's confidence before stabbing him to death. The man who tried to kill Edward I was a convert to Christianity and a trusted servant to the crusader cause. As for the medieval use of hashish, the drug was available in the Holy Land, and some soldiers of all types may have used it to gain courage in battle.

On a lighter note, the drink called *Ypocras,* offered Eleanor by Margaret, was named after Hippocrates and considered very healthy. The base was red wine, just turning sour, which was spiced with cinnamon, ginger, cloves, and honey. For those interested, there is a translated recipe easily found on the Internet from the *Gode Cookery.* One ingredient that may sound strange is still available today: grains of paradise. I've tasted it. Although it was a pepper substitute, merchants called it *grains of paradise* because they claimed the spice came directly from the Garden of Eden. Spurious marketing hasn't changed much in eight hundred years...

Bibliography

The history of Hansen's Disease is grim, but the excellent books on the subject are enlightening. They prove that brave and curious people have always been willing to push beyond ignorance to discover the facts hidden by superstitious prejudice. This may be called *science*, but the compassion involved is also one of the finer human virtues. For this reason, I did not find the books depressing and list some for readers who wish to learn more about treatments and attitudes in the medieval era. Not all was the way we often assume.

As always, I do not pretend to be an authority on any subject. The experts may guide but cannot be blamed when I stray off the path.

The Assassins: The Story of Medieval Islam's Secret Sect, by W.B. Bartlett, Sutton Publishing, 2001

By Sword and Fire, by Sean McGlynn, Weidenfeld &Nicolson, 2008

English Castles 1200-1300, by Christopher Gravett, Osprey Publishing, 2009

Handbook of Leprosy, by W.H. Jopling & A.C. McDoughall, CBS Publishers (fifth edition), 1996

Leper Knights: The Order of St. Lazarus of Jerusalem in England, 1150-1544, by David Marcombe, Boydell Press, 2003

Leprosy in Medieval England, by Carole Rawcliffe, Boydell Press, 2006

Leprosy in Premodern Medicine: a Malady of the Whole Body, by Luke Demaitre, Johns Hopkins University Press, 2007

Medicine & Society in Later Medieval England, by Carole Rawcliffe, Alan Sutton Publishing, 1995

Medieval English Medicine, by Stanley Rubin, Harper & Row Publishing, 1974

To receive a free catalog of Poisoned Pen Press titles, please contact us in one of the following ways:

Phone: 1-800-421-3976
Facsimile: 1-480-949-1707
Email: info@poisonedpenpress.com
Website: www.poisonedpenpress.com

Poisoned Pen Press
6962 E. First Ave. Ste. 103
Scottsdale, AZ 85251